Dead & Breakfast
and
Other Stories

Marilyn Todd

White City

Press

Claudia Seferius has successfully flattered her way into marriage with a wealthy Roman wine merchant. But when her secret gambling debts spiral, she hits on another resourceful way to make money—offering her "personal services" to high-ranking Roman Citizens.

Unfortunately her clients are now turning up dead—the victims of a sadistic serial killer.

When Marcus Cornelius Orbilio, the handsome investigating officer, starts digging deep for clues, Claudia realizes she must track down the murderer herself—before her husband discovers what she's been up to.

Paperback ISBN: 9781963479324 — eBook ISBN: 9781963479294

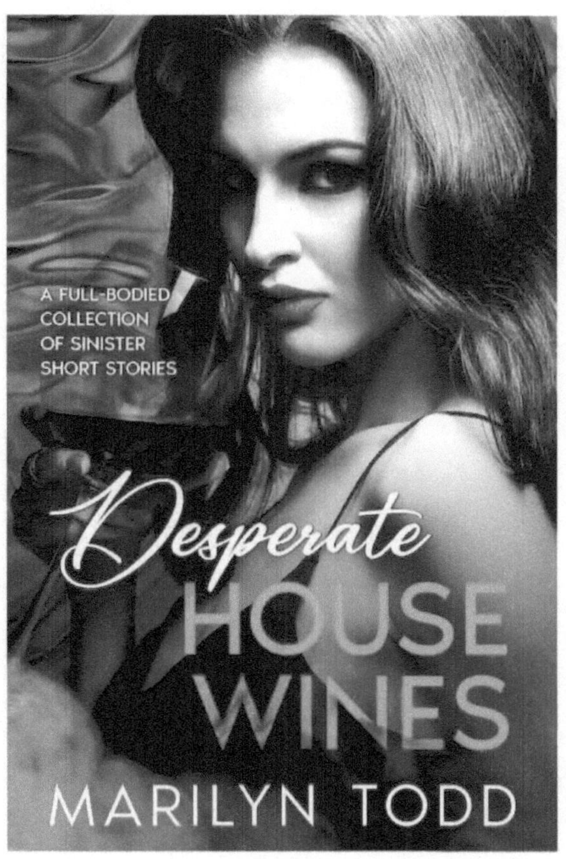

You can hide the evidence and bury the body
But you can't bury the truth or hide from retribution.

From theft to murder via double cross, they all think they're smarter than justice. Like when two people walk out to a rocky promontory and only one comes back… Or faking your own death… Even smuggling on Britain's wild coast can prove dangerous….

Whether they choose poison, arson, bullets or rope, will they get away with their crime?

Paperback ISBN: 9781963479683
eBook ISBN: 9781963479669

Dead & Breakfast
and
Other Stories
Marilyn Todd

The following works have appeared previously in print:
Dead & Breakfast, 2009

Distilling the Truth, 2008

Something Rather Fishy, 2013

667, Evil and Then Some, 2009

Petrified, 2015

The Longboat Cove Murders, 2015

The Way It Is, 2013

A Taste for Ducking, 2006

The Great Rivorsky, 2001

Heaven Knows, 2014

Bad Taste, 2014

Stakes & Adders, 2006

CONTENTS

To Margot & Arthur.
Some friends are more than friends.
They're family

Dead & Breakfast

'Georges, have you put those pillows in No. 22 yet?'

Pillows. Pillows. Georges dragged his eyes away from the grebes out on the lake as he remembered the pile of goosedown in his arms.

'Doing it now, Mother.'

But it was so comical, the way they dived for fish. You watch them go down, follow the ripples on the surface, then pick a spot where you think they'll come up. Except you're wrong. Every time, it's that much farther from where you expect them to, and this time one of the grebes had caught a fish. A big one. Georges watched, fascinated by the contest between predator and prey. One false move and the fish was gone forever. Both sides fighting for survival.

'And don't forget to unblock that drain in the second floor bath while you're up there, love.'

Drain? He looked at the spanner in his hand. Oh. Drain. 'No, no,' he called down. 'I won't forget.'

Georges loved this lake. He loved the way the boats bobbed on smooth days as well as rough weather, their yards clanking gentle lullabies, their hulls gleaming in the sun. He loved the way that spring dawns glimmered hazy and yellow on the surface, like melted camembert. How fiery sunsets multiplied out and flickered on the water. How autumn mists swirled round the islands and then disappeared, as if by magic, and how the moon reflected double on the lake. And none of this would be possible, were it not for the pines that surrounded it, repelling the winds that drove in from the west, fending off the snows that swept up from the Pyrenees, thwarting the desiccating frosts that gripped the rest of France. In fact, he thought, if it wasn't for the gulls, flapping round the perimeter in search of tiddlers in the shallows, you'd think the coast was a lot farther than eight kilometers away.

Except not everyone enjoyed neat promenades that served up ice creams and carousels, or took pleasure in roasting themselves on broad, white sandy beaches that stretched to infinity in both directions. The people who holidayed at Georges' lake were more discriminating. Not for them long treks through woods, laden with parasols and picnic hampers, just to then do battle with the highest dunes in Europe. Let others wrestle with deckchairs and drink lukewarm lemonade—

'Oh, Georgie!' His mother jerked the pillows from his arms with a good-natured, but nonetheless exasperated sigh. 'Will you ever stop your silly daydreaming?' She gave his cheek an affectionate squeeze, before setting off down the corridor to give 22 their extra pillows. 'But if you don't mind, love. The drain?'

The what? Oh, that. Second floor. Blocked. At last, the grebe managed to turn the wriggling fish and gulp it down. Almost at once, it was diving back down for more.

'Now, if you wouldn't mind.' She didn't seem entirely surprised to find her son still staring out of the window when she returned. 'Breakfast'll be over any minute, and the guests are bound to need the bathroom.'

'Right-oh.'

He mightn't have won any prizes for spelling, maths or grammar, but Georges was handy with his hands. In no time at all, he'd unscrewed the waste and was flushing out the pipe, though he didn't see what all the fuss was for. A few hairs, a bit of gunge, and *bien sûr*, it would reduce the drainage to a trickle, but that was no reason to go grumbling to his mother. She went to a lot of trouble to make the guests feel welcome. She set vases of flowers in their rooms, left them boiled sweets on the dressing table and placed moth balls in the drawers. The sheets always smelled crisp and clean and fresh.

But then some folk were never satisfied, he thought, his big, strong hands spannering the pipes back into place. If they weren't griping about lumpy mattresses, they were moaning because there wasn't an ashtray, or could someone change their bedside lamp, it wasn't bright enough to read by. Still. He mopped up the puddle of dirty water with a towel. Surrounded by such stunning scenery, people probably expected the same level of perfection from *Les Pins*. Most of the time, they blooming got it, too.

'I don't believe it!' An hour must have passed before his mother came storming into the dining room, where he was cramming the last of the unwanted croissants in his mouth. 'Look what you've done to Madame Fouquet's towels!'

Eh?

She held up the filthy, sopping linen. 'She's absolutely livid, and quite frankly so am I.'

Oh. *Those* towels. 'Then she should have taken them back to her room,' he said, spraying crumbs over the table. 'Instead of leaving them in the bathroom for anyone to use.'

'That's still no excuse for you to use them as rags. And to just leave them lying there, as well, you lazy toad!'

'Sorry.'

It wasn't often that he saw his mother angry, and it wasn't simply because she had endless patience with him. She simply could not afford to lose control. Georges' father, Marcel, was the chef, and since food was his passion as well as the foundation for his business, he was either shopping for it at the market or else creating magnificent works of art with it in the kitchen. The hotel management was Irène's responsibility, something she accomplished with a combination of politeness, style and military crispness, being just strict enough to keep the chambermaids on their toes, but not so tough that they looked for work elsewhere. Welcoming enough towards the guests, but not so sociable that they might be tempted to take advantage.

'Oh, Georgie, it's not you,' she said, instantly calm again. 'It's that wretched bloody bathroom that's got me so worked up.' She swiped her hair out of her eyes with the back of her hand. 'I'm going to have to call a plumber out, and god knows how long that'll take in August.'

'Why?' He might be big and slow and clumsy, but Georges took great pride in his work.

'Why?' Her voice rose. 'Because that stupid, bloody washbasin's blocked up again already.'

Washbasin. Not bath…

'I'll take another look.'

'Not sure there's any point, you've only just been up there.'

'Yes, but I'll check farther down the pipes.' He turned away, so she wouldn't see how red his cheeks had gone.

'Will you? Oh, you are an angel. And while you're up there, would you put clean towels in 34 for Madame Fouquet? I can hardly leave the poor woman with just a hand towel for her bath.'

'Right-oh.'

Washbasin. He wrote it on the back of his hand with a biro, so as not to forget. Second floor, he scribbled underneath. And towels.

Which was just as well, because by the time he'd brushed Minou the cat, topped up the bird bath and then fed the ducks out on the lake, it was fast approaching midday. Four o'clock before he actually got round to fixing it.

Madame Fouquet never saw her towels.

* * *

For all its pine-scented air and picture-postcard views, it wasn't always easy here for Georges. Life was comfortable enough. Marcel and Irène were the first to think of shipping in sand, to create a private lake-front beach. They revamped the gardens with Mediterranean palms and oleanders, tacked on a veranda, then a terrace, and built moorings for the hotel clients' boats. This was good. With every improvement, the hotel grew and prospered.

The trouble was, in order to capitalize on a silence broken only by the croaking of frogs and the splash of fish—the very qualities their middle-aged, middle-class guests looked for in a holiday—his parents also banned transistor radios and banished TV to the public lounge. Their intention was that busy Parisians should come down, plug into two weeks of time-warp bliss, then go home refreshed and free of stress. But for Georges, this was his home. And, rather like the resort itself, which had grown up to create its own identity but in doing so had paradoxically isolated itself from the outside world, so he, too, became disconnected.

While other teenagers were rebelling, flower power passed him by, and whatever the Summer of Love might be, it never came his way, but not being "groovy" didn't trouble him. To be honest, he didn't know what groovy was, so it didn't matter that Jesus might be loving Mrs. Robinson more than she would ever know, much less that Mick Jagger was having his mind and other things blown by honky tonk girls. But then he turned sixteen and things began to change. Not being clever enough to stay on at school, the few friends that he'd had quickly drifted away, and though he took over as the hotel handyman from doddery old René, the staff were invariably too busy to stop for idle chit-chat. Naturally, Georges picked up the broad outline of events from the national news, but what he wasn't getting was life's rich tapestry of trivia, and this became a problem. All he wanted was to do what the Parisians did, only in reverse. Plug into normal life. But how?

The more time passed, the more his desire—his need—to tap into normality intensified. It wasn't that he was lonely, exactly. He'd always enjoyed his own company, but there was a hole somewhere, a big black hole that needed to be filled, and whoever said it was the little things that mattered was absolutely right. And it was the little things that were missing from his life.

At least that was the case until one warm and sunny April morning when his mother asked him to oil the sticky lock on No. 17. And would you believe it, there was the answer. Staring him right in the face. He oiled, he turned, he oiled, he turned. No sticking. No rubbing. No catching.

No noise...

At long last, Georges had found a way to connect to the world beyond *Les Pins*.

* * *

The idea of being called a peeping tom would have cut him to the quick. There was nothing mucky about what he was doing. Nothing sinister about his motives. He was simply using his master key to slip into the rooms, and there, just being among the guests while they slept, he was able to note other people's eccentricities and foibles. The big, black void was filled.

While Irène was just delighted that her son had at last showed some initiative by oiling all the bedroom locks, not just the one.

* * *

'Madame Garnier's eldest daughter's getting married,' Georges told Parmesan, the heavy horse who used to pull a plough but had long since been put out to pasture. 'I saw the telegram on her dressing table.'

MAMAN PAPA GUESS WHAT STOP HENRI PROPOSED AT LAST STOP ISN'T THIS JUST WONDERFUL STOP

'Both Monsieur *and* Madame Garnier were smiling in their sleep,' he added. 'So they must be pleased about it.'

Although he still spent the same amount of time fishing, bird watching and watching squirrels in the woods, Georges and Parmesan tended to see a lot more of each other these days. Blissfully unaware, of course, that Marcel was having to drop his *bœuf bordelaise* to drive at breakneck speed, so the Gérards / the LeBlancs / the St. Brices or whoever didn't miss their trains. Or that the Duponts, the Brossards, the new people in 38 had to lug their cases up several flights of stairs, because the handyman had forgotten to reconnect the lift after re-greasing the cogs and chains.

'Mother doesn't like that Madame Dupont with the blue rinse hair who rustles when she walks. She thinks she's hard and crusty, but she's not.' Georges passed the horse an apple. 'She's soft as dough inside.'

He knew this because of the soppy romances Madame Dupont read, and more than once he'd had to pick up a paperback that had fallen from her hand, replacing the bookmark and laying it gently on the cover next to her.

'You wouldn't think it, but 27 wears a toupee.' It gave Georges quite a fright, seeing it draped over the foot stool. He thought it was a rat. 'Someone should tell him he looks a lot younger without it, though.' Unlike Madame 27, whose teeth snarled at him from the glass beside her bed. 'She snores, as well,' he said.

In fact, it was quite a revelation, seeing what the guests were really like, as opposed to what they wanted you to think. For instance, Georges could tell who was putting on a front, pretending to read highbrow literature when they were sneaking tabloid news inside their daily papers. He knew who was sloppy and who was not from the way they folded their clothes or tossed them on a chair, and, even more importantly, by squeezing the towels, he knew who took a bath every day and who only took one once a week and disguised their lack of personal hygiene with cologne.

Darker secrets came out, too. Major Chabou, for instance, swapped dirty pictures with the banker in the room upstairs. Suzette the chambermaid was having an affair with No. 14, even sleeping in his bed after his poor wife had to rush back home to see to her sick mother. Mind you, Suzette didn't sleep in curlers, like the other female guests. Or wear a hairnet, either, for that matter.

* * *

So summers came and summers went, and even though Georges assumed the Year of the Cat was just one more Chinese holiday, who cared? The same people booked the same rooms for the same two weeks in the season, and simply by taking stock of their toothbrushes, their writing pads, their cosmetics and their clothes, he was able to follow the changes in their lives and circumstances.

Some guests never changed, of course. Monsieur Prince still put his dirty shoes on Irène's clean white linen sheets. The Bernards still stashed the hotel's face flannels at the bottom of their suitcase. Madame

Morreau still treated Georges the same way she did when he was seven, only now instead of ruffling his hair and giving him a bag of aniseed, she had to reach up on tippy-toes just to pat his shoulder. But she still brought him aniseed, which Georges had never liked but which he could at least feed to Parmesan, even though it made him kick and swish his tail. And Georges still very much looked forward to her visits.

Which made it doubly hard when Madame Morreau died.

'Take a look at these architect's plans, love, and tell me what you think.'

From the outset, his parents had involved him in their projects, but to be honest, the squares and boxes on the page confused him. What did it mean, "drawn to scale", he wondered? Fish had scales. Kitchens had scales. But gardens? And this 250:1 stuff. Georges didn't understand where bookmakers fitted into plans for new extensions, and whenever he saw things like this, he was glad he hadn't been forced to stay on at school.

'Ten new bedrooms to be built during the winter shut down, and what about this?' The excitement in his mother's voice was catching. 'No more trotting down the corridor in the middle of the night for *our* guests. As of next spring, they'll have their own individual, private bathroom!'

'And now the world's opening up to foreign travel, son, what do you think about including couscous on the menu?'

Would that be meat, or some exotic vegetable, he wondered?

'Every room'll have its own mini shampoo and soap.'

'Osso buco, perhaps?'

'Hairdryers in the bathrooms.'

'Definitely paella—are you all right, son?'

'Yeah.'

But there was no fooling his mother. 'Oh, Georges.' She laid down her fountain pen. 'You're not still upset about Madame Morreau, are you?'

Marcel had brought him up that it was wrong to tell a lie, but for some reason he felt ashamed of saying yes out loud. Madame Morreau had been different from the other guests, somehow. Special. For a start, she was one of the few who weren't wary of this big, shambling young man, who was constantly wandering round the hotel with a distant expression on his face and a toolbox in his hand. And she didn't talk down to him, either. In fact, quite often she had to rebuke that weasel-faced nephew of hers for poking fun at him.

Georges is a wee bit slow, Jean-Paul. You need to make allowances.

Jean-Paul. That was Weasel's name. Jean-Paul. And it was a funny thing, but until Madame Morreau said that, Georges had never thought of himself as slow. And yet, now he came to think of it, he *had* always been in the tail of any school race. How she knew all that was a mystery to him, but even so, Georges always made a point of quickening his pace when he saw her coming. Especially once Jean-Paul began to mouth *Slowpoke* at him behind her back.

'A bit,' Georges admitted.

'Don't be, love.' His mother squeezed his hand. 'The old dear had a long and happy life, and you should be pleased she died peacefully, snuggled in her pillows.' She turned to Marcel and pulled a face. 'Even if it was in our hotel.'

'The undertakers were very discreet, I thought.'

'Only because you slipped them lorry loads of *francs*, but it's the chambermaids I'm proudest of. None of them so much as screamed.'

'They wouldn't bloody dare,' Marcel muttered under his breath, but Irène wasn't listening.

'The guests had no idea that anything was amiss, and even Madame Morreau's nephew carried himself well, I thought. Considering.'

When Georges closed his eyes, he could see Jean-Paul in conversation with the doctor that the hotel had been obliged to call. Saw him showing him the pills Madame Morreau took for her bad heart. Heard him telling how she'd had two seizures this year already.

'Nice boy,' Irène added, with a sigh. 'Always so conscientious when he stayed here with his aunt.'

'No, he wasn't.'

If anyone was an expert on the subject of being chivvied up, it was Georges. But never on account of being lazy.

It's very good of you to do this for me, Georges.

I like doing it, Madame Morreau. Honest.

Unlike some, who wouldn't be seen dead supporting an old lady's arm while she took a walk along the lake.

I don't know where Jean-Paul's got to, I really don't.

Georges did. As soon as she said she wouldn't mind a stroll, Weasel had been off. Greyhounds on a track don't run that fast.

It's so nice to be able to take a walk, while I'm still able. He remembered the sad little smile she'd shot him, as she patted his arm. *I'll be in a wheelchair next year, Georges.*

That'll be good, though, won't it? I'll be able to push you round the lake. In fact, I'll run.

Will you? Will you, Georges? Her laugh suddenly became happy and girlish, and for a moment he saw how she must have looked sixty years ago. *You've no idea how exciting it'd be for an old woman, to feel the wind in her hair again.*

You bet, he'd promised, and he meant it.

'Jean-Paul thought fetching things and looking after her beneath him,' he told Marcel and Irène.

It wasn't because he sneered at him, or called him names behind her back, that made Georges despise the nephew. More the way he scowled at having to trek upstairs to fetch her cardigan because her legs weren't up to it, or screwing up his face when she forgot things. Georges scuffed his foot. He knew all about forgetting things, and saw how much it embarrassed Madame Morreau, being dependent on someone else to put it right. Especially someone who resented doing it…

'I don't think he was even sorry that she died.'

Georges had never encountered sudden death before, so he couldn't be certain. But that look on Weasel's face when the doctor signed that piece of paper—

'I wish I could put a name to that expression,' he said, but his parents were back poring over their plans, discussing power points and colour charts, and debating whether the floor tiles in the bathrooms would be better white or cream. To them, the incident was closed. But for Georges, the misgivings wouldn't go away, and though the winter gales came lashing in from the Atlantic, bending the pines around the lake and causing them to hiss like angry snakes, his mind remained on aniseed and ruffled hair. Of cardigans that smelled of lavender, and happy, girlish giggles.

People imagined Madame Morreau was as well-heeled as the other guests, but Georges knew otherwise. Her suits were quality, but seconds; he'd seen the crossed-out labels. Also, her petticoats had worn thin, her stockings were darned and her shoes, although good quality and polished to a shine, were almost through to holes. And even he, who didn't understand figures very much, knew that red ink on a bank statement was bad news. Which is why he thanked her so politely for the candy every year, and refused a tip for carrying her bags. She'd had to really scrimp and save for her fortnight at *Les Pins*, and go without a lot of things to pay for her nephew to come with her. He knew all this, because he'd read it in her diary.

And her diary said nothing about heart attacks and seizures—

'Oh, Georgie. You've let the paste go hard.'

Paste? Then he remembered why he was up this blooming ladder. Sticking fresh wallpaper on No. 21. 'It's not right, Mum.'

'Not now it isn't, love. It's set like concrete in this wretched bucket.'

'I don't mean the glue. Madame Morreau.'

But by the time he'd trundled down the ladder, both his mother and the tub of paste were gone, and he'd painted the whole of the first floor corridor and was half-way through undercoating the ceiling in Reception before it dawned on him.

'You said pillows,' he said, laying down his brush.

'No, I didn't, love. I said windows. Can you wash the windows when you're done? Only Suzette's gone and got herself pregnant, and god only knows who the father is. But the point is, I don't want her up a stepladder, not in her condition.'

'You said she died snuggled into her pillows,' Georges said, except she couldn't have. Madame Morreau never used a pillow, stacking all four neatly in a pile beside the bed, and that's where she used to rest her diary when she'd finished writing up her day. On the pile of pillows, with her specs. 'She liked to sleep flat,' he added. For her neck.

'Suzette?' Irène looked confused. 'Anyway, the thing is, the hotel inspector's coming down to view the new extension, and I would really like the whole place looking its best for when he comes. Sparkling from roof down to the cellar!'

Georges tried to imagine the roof sparkling, but couldn't. 'Madame Morreau had a good heart.'

'Indeed she did, love. She was kind and patient, just like you, and I know you were fond of her, Georgie, but you have to accept that her poor old heart was simply worn out with age.'

Was it? All night he couldn't sleep for worrying, because who could he tell? Who'd listen to the ramblings of a daydreaming handyman who couldn't spell and couldn't add up, either?

Who would believe a man who crept in people's rooms at night?

* * *

'Hey, Carrot Top!'

The season was in full swing again.

'Fetch me a cold beer, will you? I'm absolutely gasping.'

Georges paused from emptying the hedge clippings on the compost. That voice— He peered round the corner and could hardly believe his eyes. Madame Morreau's nephew!

'Yes, you. Gingernut.' Jean-Paul was addressing a girl, whose bare feet were half-buried in the sand. 'You wouldn't allow a man to die of thirst, would you?'

'She's not staff,' Georges said. 'She's—' For the first time he took a good, hard look at her. 'She's—'

'Recently moved in across the lake.' Her little snub nose wrinkled in apology. 'Sorry. Am I trespassing? Only I was curious to see what our village looked like from this side.'

'No. I mean, yes, but—'

He could see how Jean-Paul mistook her for a waitress. Black skirt, white blouse. Red hair tied back from her face.

'What he means is, can't you read?' Weasel pointed to the big, bold sign that proclaimed *Private Property*. 'It specifically says "No Carrot Tops Allowed".'

'Don't call her that.' Georges felt something stir inside. 'It's mean.'

'True.' The nephew winked, then turned and walked off whistling. 'I'll stick with Gingernut instead.'

Over in the car park, Georges saw Madame Morreau's ancient Peugeot straddling two bays. The mirror shine had gone, the number plate was black with flies, and rust had begun to creep along the sills. A pair of fluffy dice, one pink, one blue, dangled above the grimy walnut console.

'Thanks for sticking up for me,' the girl said, scuffing her toe deeper into the sand. 'But I'm used to being ribbed about my hair.'

The teasing still hurt, though. He could tell by the way her skin had turned bright pink, right down to her neck. 'Is that why you tie it back? To hide it?'

'Wouldn't you?' The greenest eyes he'd ever seen misted over. 'I tried dyeing it, but that made it ten times worse.' This time the nose wrinkled in disgust. 'It's horrible hair. I hate it.'

'You shouldn't.' For some reason, he had an urge to reach out and feel how its curls would spring about between his fingers. 'It's beautiful.'

'It's bright red!'

'Like maple leaves in autumn,' Georges said, nodding. 'The colour of a robin's breast and squirrel's fur and sunsets on the lake, and you know what else? Your face. It reminds me of a wren's egg.'

'Because of the mass of brown freckles on a very white background?'

'Because it's small and smooth and fragile,' he corrected.

Across the lake? He glanced at the dots that were the village in the distance. She did. She definitely said, across the lake.

'Is it true you know where every swan and heron has its nest?'

Her name was Sandrine and she worked in the boat hire office that her father had just opened and which, according to her, was doing exceptionally well. Despite her leaving customers lined up outside because she forgot to open up, or else stranded on the open water, having not filled up their gas tanks.

'Are there otters in the lake?' she asked, peering through her binoculars.

'No, but there's a family in the river that feeds into it.' Her legs were long and slim, and covered in the same pretty freckles that covered her face and arms. 'I built a hide to watch them.'

He could have talked for hours, and the odd thing was, he had the feeling Sandrine would have listened, too. But round the door of Reception, he could see a finger being crooked, beckoning him. An arrogant, bony finger, with a weaselly sneer on the end of it.

'Going to carry my cases for me, Slowpoke?'

Through the office, Georges could see Irène had had to take an urgent phone call, and remembered that although he'd serviced the lift earlier this morning, this was yet another occasion when he'd gone off to cut the hedge without reconnecting the blasted electricity.

'Number 45,' Jean-Paul said, grinning. 'Top floor.'

In many ways, Georges had inherited his mother's temperament. In many way, he had not. He chewed his lip. Almost smelled the aniseed.

'Certainly, sir.' A phrase he'd never used before, but one which he'd heard Irène trot out a thousand times each season. 'This way, please.'

He glanced at the *Out of Order* sign. Would that have made things worse, or better? Four flights of stairs made for a long, slow climb, but at least they went up separately. In the lift, they'd have been locked in, face to face.

'Here we are, sir. Your aunt's old room.'

'Nice view.' Jean-Paul let his breath out in an admiring whistle as he stepped out onto the balcony. 'Better than that crummy cupboard she used to put me in. I mean, who wants to overlook a bloody car park?'

Georges wanted to tell him that the single rooms weren't crummy, and they weren't much smaller, either. It was because they had ordinary windows, rather than French doors, that made them appear darker.

'The view will be better once the new swimming pool's installed.'

'I can't swim, so who cares, and in any case.' Jean-Paul sniffed. 'Wild horses wouldn't bring me back to this dump.'

Georges had the same urge he'd had when he was eight years old and Jacques Dubois kicked down the matchstick train that Georges had spent all winter building. He wanted to punch him on the nose.

'This is the best room in the house,' he said instead.

Madame Morreau used to stay here with her husband before he died; he'd read that in her diary, too. The reason why she scrimped and saved to come back again each year. To relive the happy memories they'd shared.

'Two weeks of R and R in the best room in the house, all paid for in advance? Not bad, eh?' Weasel threw himself down on the bed. 'Not quite the Cote d'Azur I'd had in mind, of course. But since the old girl coughed without a penny, it's better than bloody nothing, I suppose.'

No money, poor health, and a nephew who couldn't give a damn.

'Y'know, Slowpoke, I'm betting the beds in this place could tell a tale or two.' He chuckled as he bounced up and down on the mattress.

Georges swore his heart stood still. 'That one could.'

The bouncing stopped. 'Oh?' Jean-Paul's eyes narrowed as he advanced across the room. 'And just what might you mean by that?'

Never tell a lie if you can help it, son. Marcel's voice echoed in his head. *It'll only come back to trip you up.*

'Honeymooners,' he said. 'The last guests were honeymooners.'

Weasel's shoulders went slack again, but for a second Georges saw the same expression cross his face as when the doctor signed the death certificate. At last, he could put a name to it. Relief.

'Will there be anything else?' he asked in the same neutral tone he'd heard the chambermaids use.

'Just that beer—and Slowpoke?' Jean-Paul dipped his hand in his pocket. 'A tip for carrying my cases.'

His generosity took Georges by surprise. 'Thank you,' he said warmly.

'Look both ways before you cross the road.'

Weasel seemed to think this was the funniest joke he'd ever heard, while Georges was so ashamed that he'd actually held his hand out to this man that he forgot to switch the lift back on, and once again Marcel had to abandon his *canard à l'orange* and dash the Brandons to the station, while Irène couldn't understand what a cold beer should be doing on her desk, but was so glad to see it that she downed it in one go.

'He killed her,' Georges told Parmesan, feeding him the carrots that Marcel had earmarked for his *julienne* vegetables in garlic. 'Jean-Paul murdered Madame Morreau, and it isn't right.'

It wasn't right that she should die, simply so he could get his hands on her money. It wasn't right that he should run around in her beloved Peugeot, letting it go rusty and not even washing it, or that he should profit from a holiday she'd had to make huge sacrifices for.

'Then to come back to the hotel where he killed her, throwing his weight around, bouncing on the bed where she died and making tasteless jokes. It's not right, Parmesan. It's not right at all.'

And so another night passed in which Georges didn't get a wink of sleep, but this time it was different. Lying on his back, with his hands folded behind his head, he watched the Milky Way swirling across a cloudless sky with only one thought in his head.

She knows what wrens' eggs look like…

* * *

The following week Georges took Sandrine to watch the otters from the seclusion of his hide, showed her all the secret places where rare warblers could be found, pointed out the heronry and the favourite perches of the kingfishers, and introduced her to Parmesan at her request.

'I used to slip him aniseed balls.'

Sandrine dug around in her handbag and eventually came out with half a roll of extra-strong mints. 'Do you think he'd like these?'

Like was a moot point. With the aniseed, he used to kick and swish his tail. The effect of the extra-strong mints made him snicker, buck and, considering his age and size, practically gallop round the field, his nostrils snorting out peppermint strong enough to fell an oak. But since he kept coming back for more, they made a point of packing them with the carrots, oats and apples every time they paid a visit.

'I think he's addicted,' she giggled.

'Guess that makes us pushers,' Georges quipped back, because her laugh was as magical as rainbows, hoar frost and snow melt waterfalls, and he was as hooked on its sound as this old plough horse on mints. Sometimes he feared he would drown in those freckles.

And in return for otters, squirrel drays and badger setts, Sandrine introduced Georges to the Bee Gees, *Star Wars* and the thrills of racing power boats, courtesy of her father's hire business.

'Night fever, night fever,' they'd sing together, Sandrine clicking her fingers, while Georges sped the sleek blue and white "Hire Me for 30F An Hour" advertisement past the new resorts that were springing up around the lake.

He'd never known anything like it.

It's just your jive talkin', you're telling me lies…

Music that stirred his feet and his blood.

Tragedy.

A girl with hair the colour of the rich, red, Gascony soil and eyes greener than pastures in spring.

When the feeling's gone and you can't go on, it's tragedy…

And now this. Scenery whizzing past in a blur, shirt billowing wide and the wind in his hair. Georges cut the motor. The power boat went dead.

'What's wrong?'

'Madame Morreau,' he said sombrely. 'All she wanted was to feel the wind in her hair.'

Instead, Jean-Paul was feeling it in his for thirty *francs* an hour. Using Madame Morreau's money.

* * *

'That's the first I've heard of any fishing competition.' Irène looked up from her accounts. 'Funny time of year, isn't it?'

Never tell a lie if you can help it.

'This is something new they're trying out for tourists.' Georges crossed his fingers behind his back. 'You're not allowed to keep the fish, you have to throw them back, but there's a prize of—' He'd been going to say a hundred *francs*. 'Three hundred *francs*.'

'Goodness me, I think I'll dash out and buy a fishing rod myself,' Irène laughed. 'Who's putting up the money, do you know?'

Georges was prepared for this. 'The man who runs that new boat hire company.' He sneaked a peek at the notes scribbled in the palm of his hand. 'He says the prize money is nothing compared to what he'll fetch, renting out his boats to the competitors.'

'Sharp,' Irène said admiringly. 'Maybe I should try to find something that'll attract more visitors to *Les Pins*. Afternoon tea? *Apéritifs* on the terrace?'

'You will tell Jean-Paul Morreau, won't you, Mother?'

This was how the conversation had started. With him asking her to pass the message on.

'I don't really see him as the fishing type,' she said doubtfully.

'None of the other guests is interested, I've asked,' he cut in quickly, because the last thing he wanted was for her to broadcast it round the hotel, only to discover it was a better work of fiction than the Harold Robbins he was reading. Also… 'It would be good publicity for us, too, if he won.'

'Good heavens, Georges, you do surprise me sometimes!' Every mother is proud of her children, but at that moment Irène thought her heart would burst out of her chest. 'But you're right, and what young man could possibly resist the lure of such a competition, given the right motivation by his hotelier!' Irène cocked her head. 'Pity you're not a tourist. I'll bet you know exactly where the big fish live.'

Bingo! The moment he'd been waiting for.

'Oh, yes,' he said, unable to hide the big, broad beam that cut his face in half. 'I know where to find the winner.'

As the door closed behind him, Irène became aware of hot tears coursing down her cheeks. She couldn't pinpoint the precise moment when her son had grown into a man. But was fiercely proud of what he had become.

* * *

Fishing is as much about patience as anything else. Having baited his hook, Georges sat back, ready to reel in Jean-Paul, but even he was surprised at the speed with which he bit.

'Got a proposition for you,' he said, less than one hour later. 'You help me catch the winner and I'll go fifty-fifty with you.'

Georges swallowed. 'The best time's dusk. That's when they rise to the surface.'

Weasel looked suspicious. 'I thought they sank to the bottom.'

Never tell a lie if you can help it. Suddenly, they were trotting out like ants. 'Not the big ones.'

'Dusk it is, then.' Jean-Paul rubbed his hands together. 'Tonight?'

Georges studied the sky, confident the weather would hold. 'Perfect.' The only thing that could have spoiled his plans was a storm that whipped up the water. But on a calm, moonless night, there'd be no tourists on the lake, and with his parents busy serving dinner, there'd be no one around to notice that two men went out, but only one came back.

* * *

'What was that about?' Sandrine asked Jean-Paul, seeing him swagger out of Georges' shed. She was about to get on her scooter to ride home. He was off to the coast for livelier entertainment than what was on offer at *Les Pins*.

'That, my little Gingernut, is about winning a competition, and you know the best thing?' He chuckled as he unlocked the car. 'We're going fifty-fifty.'

'What's fifty-fifty?' Sandrine wasn't good with math.

Jean-Paul slung his jacket on the passenger seat and winked. 'It means he catches me a fish and I give him fifty *francs*.'

'I wish someone would give me fifty *francs*,' she sighed. 'I'd buy myself a haircut just like Farrah Fawcett's.'

* * *

'Bloody dark out here. Sure you can see to row?'

'I've fished loads of times at night,' Georges said truthfully, but all the same his hands were clammy. 'I know this lake like the back of my hand.'

'Not surprised, considering they're the same size,' Jean-Paul sniggered. 'Where'd you say the big boy lives?'

Georges couldn't meet his eye. 'Far side of the island.'

Jean-Paul squinted towards a dark lump in the distance. 'Wake me up when we get there.' He leaned back and pulled his cap down over his eyes.

Georges listened to the slapping of the oars and the pounding of his heart. It wasn't too late. He could turn round. Tell Jean-Paul he had a headache or stomach pains, even admit he'd made the whole thing up…

It's so nice to be able to take a walk, while I'm still able.

Madame Morreau's sad smile hung in the air like the Cheshire cat.

Will you run? Will you, Georges?

And that was the problem, wasn't it? Madame Morreau was never going to feel the wind in her hair. He looked at the shoreline, growing thinner with each stroke. Glanced over his shoulder, at the island looming closer. She'd never see the sun set from the room where she'd shared so many good times with her husband. Never smell the leather of the seats of her old Peugeot, or run her hands across its walnut dash. She wouldn't even have the chance to chide her nephew, or wonder where he'd got to when she needed him.

'We're here.' He nudged Jean-Paul with his foot.

'It's the middle of bloody nowhere!' Lights from the villages twinkled like miniature fireflies around a lake as black as soot. 'Still, for three hundred smackers, it's worth getting spooked, eh, Slowpoke?'

'Stop calling me that, my name's Georges.'

His tone made him look up. 'Right.' Both smile and voice were unusually tight. 'Georges.' Jean-Paul shifted in his seat. 'So how long do you reckon it'll take to track down our little winner?'

'Depends.' Georges pulled out a flashlight and leaned over the water. 'Could be minutes, could be hours—whoa! Look! It's—'

'Give me that.' Jean-Paul's unease vanished as he grabbed the torch from Georges' hand. 'Where? I can't see any—'

The rest was drowned by the splash of two giant hands tipping him over the side.

'Hey! Hey, I can't swim!'

'I know,' Georges said, rowing out of range with a speed that would have surprised Madame Morreau's nephew, had he not been gulping so much water. 'You told me.'

'All right, all right, you've had your fun. You've humiliated me, shown me who's boss, and fair do's. I called you names, bullied you a bit, and now you've got your revenge—but for Chrissakes, man, I'm drowning.'

'No, you're not. Not if you kick your feet about a bit.'

Jean-Paul had nothing to lose. He kicked his feet about a bit, but the fear of being sucked in wouldn't leave. 'Enough's enough, you stupid bloody halfwit.'

'You killed her,' Georges said, pulling out a piece of paper and reading it by flashlight.

'What?' Jean-Paul's arms flailed and flapped in the water. 'Is that what this is about? My stupid bloody aunt, you stupid moron?'

'My mother thinks she had a long and happy life, but Mother's wrong.'

For one thing, Madame Morreau was only sixty-eight. Georges saw her identity papers lying on the table once, and sixty-eight was no age at all these days. Also, reading her diary, he saw that she'd never got over the devastation of not having children, sinking all her love in her husband instead.

'When he fell ill with cancer, she had no qualms about spending every last *centime* on finding him a cure.' He didn't know what a qualm was, but it sounded so good that he'd quoted it anyway. 'She even mortgaged her house.'

'I know that, you stupid idiot.'

'Not when you killed her, you didn't.'

'I don't know what you're talking about. Now listen to me, Georges. You've had your laugh, you've made a fool of me, so come back and pull me out before I drown, you bloody retard.'

'She was too proud to let people know she hadn't got two *francs* to rub together—' Or, more accurately, too ashamed to admit she'd blown their entire fortune on charlatans and quack cures. '—and like everybody else, you assumed she was well off. You were her only heir, and so you killed her. For her money.'

'Yeah, well, prove it, dumb-ass.' But the fight had gone out of Jean-Paul as the struggle of trying to keep afloat began to tell.

'You smothered her with her own pillows, then tried to make it look like natural causes, and because she was old and because you convinced the doctor that she had a bad heart, you thought you'd got away with it.'

'All right, all right, I killed the old bitch, so what? She was like a bloody succubus, *can you fetch this, I forgot that, would you mind giving me a hand to the table.* I lost my temper that night and rammed the pillow over her face, all right? She was sick and old. I was doing her a favour—oh, God, help—'

The water glugged and gurgled as it covered his head. Georges felt his stomach turning somersaults.

'Please,' Jean-Paul said, bobbing up at last, and Georges could tell that he was crying. 'Help me—'

'You didn't lose your temper. You planned to kill her long before you left Paris.'

'I swear to God, it was the heat of the moment. For god's sake, don't let me die! I'll give you anything. The car. Take the car...'

'You brought the medication with you. That's premeditated murder.'

'Whatever you want, name it, it's yours.'

'A confession,' Georges said. 'I just want to hear you admit it.'

'All right, all right.' Jean-Paul was spluttering words and water in equal amounts now. 'I thought she was rolling, I bought heart pills from a chemist's in Paris, I held the pillow over her face and—'

'Did she struggle?'

'Yes, of course she bloody struggled! I had to wake her up to get her to unlock the door, spinning some cock-and-bull story about needing to talk, put her back to bed, and guess what? No pillows.'

'She used to pile them on the floor.'

'I know that now, but at the time I had to search for them, so yes, the old bitch put up a fight—oh, Christ.'

His head went underwater, and once more, it took forever before it surfaced. Even Jean-Paul, who couldn't swim, knew the third time was his last.

'You don't know what it's like,' he screamed. 'Do this, do that—'

'You wanted her money, you just didn't want to earn it.'

'I'm young! I'm not cut out for fishing false teeth out of glasses, just because the stupid bitch forgot to put them in before going down to dinner! I killed her, and the only thing I'm sorry about is that she didn't have the money. Satisfied?'

'We certainly are,' boomed a voice from nowhere, and suddenly the night was filled with blinding sunshine. It took Jean-Paul a few seconds to realise they were searchlights from other boats.

'Help,' he spluttered, and it didn't matter the water was swarming with police uniforms. He was saved. 'Help me, I'm drowning!'

'No, you're not,' Georges said. 'If you put your feet down, you could walk to the island.'

* * *

Autumn came, and the leaves on the trees turned to the colour of her hair, fluttering across the ground like the freckles on her skin. Out on the lake, grebes dived, the last of the swallows fattened up on flies, and in a rowing boat a young couple talked of wedding rings and babies.

Irène was already converting the old barn into a cottage.

'I'm so proud of you,' Sandrine said, dabbling her fingers in the water. 'The way you went to the police, told them the only way to prove Madame Morreau had been murdered was by a confession by her killer, and then offering them a way that they could get it.'

She hadn't cut her hair like Farrah Fawcett, why would she? Not when a big man with a broad smile loved to run his fingers through it, telling her it shone like fire and smelled of lollipops and roses.

'I may have thought up the competition, but you gave it substance by saying your father was sponsoring it.' He'd had to lie, telling Sandrine that Madame Morreau confided in him on their walks. But this would be the last lie he ever told, he promised. 'Without you to hold my hand, I'd never have plucked up the courage to walk into the *commissariat*.'

'In that case, come over here and show your appreciation properly,' she giggled.

'I'd rather do it improperly,' he grinned back, 'but first.'

He prised the master key from his ring and, with great solemnity, consigned it to the lake. As it sank, a breeze sprang up, rippling across the open water and ruffling his hair. Georges swore it smelled of aniseed.

Distilling the Truth

The instant Marie-Claude's husband told her that he'd compiled a dossier detailing the Chief Inspector's corruption, complete with dates, names and times, then placed the file personally in the hands of the Commissioner, she knew it was all over. No wonder he waited until he'd finished his *tartiflette* to tell her what he'd done. She'd have thrown the damned dish on the floor and to hell with dinner, and he could have whistled for his *île flottante* as well. As it was, she didn't hear him out. What on earth was the point of lengthy explanations?

'You're a fool, Luc. No one likes a whistle-blower.'

'I didn't join the police to be popular.'

'It's the end of your career, you know that? They won't keep you on in Paris after this!'

'Blackmail, extortion, what was I supposed to do, Marie-Claude?' He laid down *Le Figaro* and turned his gaze to her. 'For years, Picard has been preying on the very people he was meant to protect. I couldn't simply turn aside.'

'And I'm sure the Commissioner shook your hand and thanked you warmly for your efforts.'

One side of Luc's face twisted uncomfortably. 'Not exactly, no.'

'You see? No one likes a whistle-blower. They'd rather close ranks and have a bastard in their midst than admit to one bad apple, and you already know my feelings about the Commissioner.'

Like when they were invited over to dinner and she overheard him talking to her husband in his study when she went to find the bathroom.

'Your wife is truculent, selfish and a pain in the *cul*, Luc—'

The rest was drowned by children's laughter upstairs, but who cared? That's the last time she'd eat at that pig's house, she told Luc, and if her husband felt bad about making excuses when future invitations arrived, then so much the better. She wanted nothing to do with a man who insulted her, and it wouldn't have hurt Luc to have stuck up for her, either.

'—couldn't agree more, sir—'

Truculent and selfish, her *cul*. She pushed her thick curls back from her face. She had married too young, that was the trouble, and to a man ten years older than herself at that. Admittedly, after six years Luc was no less handsome and his back was as strong, but that type of love can't sustain a marriage indefinitely. And when he wasn't working all the hours *le bon Dieu* sent, he had his head stuck in a file or wanted to talk politics, and not even French politics either. Honestly! Who cared whether rich diamond deposits had been found in Siberia or how many communists this Senator Mc-Whatever-His-Name accused in the American State Department? What was going to actually change people's lives were things like the new television transmissions that were now coming out in colour, not some piece of paper signed by Egypt and Britain over a canal in Suez that Luc insisted was going to have far-reaching consequences. But however exasperated Marie-Claude got with her husband, she'd never once known him to lose his temper.

Not even when, a mere fortnight after delivering his sanctimonious dossier, the Commissioner transferred him to Cognac.

'You'll like the South,' Luc said confidently, as their train pulled away. 'Twice as much sunshine, warmer summers, better winters—'

'Better theatres, Luc? Will they have better street cafés and shops? Will they get subtitled versions of *On the Waterfront*, do you think?' By all accounts, it was set to scoop an Oscar. 'Will they have better parks? Better gardens? Women in *peignoirs* leaning over the balconies, calling obscenities to men in the street?'

He looked at her beneath lowered lids as the train chugged through the forests of Rambouillet. 'You never liked Montmartre.'

'It had life,' she retorted. 'It had character and substance, it was always noisy, colourful, constantly changing—'

Marie-Claude broke off. Why was she referring to these things in the past tense? For heaven's sake, it wasn't as though she wasn't going back! No, no, once she'd seen Luc settled in (she owed him that) she would start a new life. A new life with a man who appreciated art, the cinema, fashion and fun. Someone who liked dancing, for sure!

'I'll bet they've never heard of Perry Como in Cognac.'

'You can probably count yourself lucky if they've heard of Bing Crosby,' he murmured behind his guide book. 'But this is promotion, Marie-Claude. We're lucky to get it. Do you want to look through this, by the way?'

Marie-Claude shook her head. She'd seen enough of those military vines and flat-bottomed boats from upside down, thank you.

'We'll be able to afford a house of our own, instead of a poky apartment on the fifth floor where you can hear everything that happens next door. We're close to the seaside, and I'll bet the air's better, too.'

There was nothing wrong with the air in the *Rue de Roc*, she wanted to say, but his nose was back in the pamphlet and, as Orleans rumbled past, she stroked the hat in her lap. Such a jaunty little number, as well. *Très* Audrey Hepburn with just a dash of Ava Gardner. She sighed and closed her eyes. By the time she got chance to wear it again, it would either have too many feathers or too few, and who would be seen dead wearing green for next season? At Tours, the only other couple in the carriage got off and an old woman with a runny nose got in.

'Amazing,' Luc said, turning the page of his paper to avoid creasing. 'It says here construction's underway on the St. Lawrence Seaway that'll allow deep-draught ships direct access to the rich industrials of the Great Lakes. Direct access. Can you imagine?'

Marie-Claude switched off. Her husband was clever, conscientious, honourable, but dull. Handsome, rugged, muscular and tall, yet he lacked passion where it really counted. And now, it seemed, he was a failure into the bargain.

At Angoulême they changed trains.

She blamed herself for marrying him.

* * *

A week later, the vineyards around Cognac sprang into leaf and an Englishman called Bannister ran a mile in under four minutes. Less than two months down the line, once the vines had been pruned and tied back, an Australian beat the Englishman's record, but by the time the summer sun was swelling the grapes on the hillsides, the Englishman had once again reclaimed his crown in Vancouver. Little Mo's tennis career was cut short by a riding accident, and a pair of Italians were the first climbers to reach the peak of K2. These things seemed to excite everyone except Marie-Claude, but it didn't matter, because she kept herself busy making the house nice for Luc.

It was pleasantly located in the old quarter, halfway between the chateau and the covered market, where the streets were narrow, hilly, twisting and cobbled, and the houses built of thick stone to keep them cool in summer, retain heat in the winter, and with fireplaces large enough to hide a small army. But an old man had lived alone here for the past twenty years and she was damned if she'd be accused of leaving her husband to a place which looked (and smelled) like a pig-sty.

A week's scrub with carbolic transformed it no end, but the shutters could use a coat or three of paint, and although she'd considered returning to Paris in August, the weather was perfect for strolls along the tow path, and whilst Marie-Claude knew of lots of people who didn't bother with curtains and just used the shutters, Luc worked so hard that the very least he deserved, if he wasn't to have a decent dinner waiting on the table, was to be able to pore over his paperwork in a house that was cosy. One or two rooms, that was all. Bedroom. *Salon.* Enough to lend a bit of warmth and character where it mattered the most.

By the time workers had been drafted in for the harvest and Pope

Pius X had been canonised, the Algerians had started a guerrilla war against their French protectors. *This Ole House* was on everyone's lips and Marie-Claude had run up another pair of drapes, this time for the kitchen, and accepted the offer of part-time work in an upmarket dress shop.

'I'll be late tonight,' Luc announced one lunchtime, as he washed his hands in the sink. Close by, the bells of St. Leger pealed merrily. 'The proprietor of one of the smaller cognac houses has been murdered.'

Marie-Claude laid the *cassoulet* on the table and lifted the lid. 'Good.'

'Good?' He chuckled as he sniffed appreciatively through the steam. 'Some poor woman has been battered over the head and all you can say is *good*?'

'Not good that she's dead.' She heaped his plate. 'Good that you've got some proper detective work to do at last.'

All he'd been called upon to investigate over the past five months had been robbery, the inevitable smuggling and once, right at the beginning, an art theft that turned out to be a simple insurance fraud. Luc was a first-rate detective and at last this would give him something to sink his teeth into. In fact, with such a high-profile case demanding his attention, Marie-Claude doubted he'd notice she'd left, although she might as well wait until the warm weather ended. Paris was desperately wet in October.

'Marie-Claude, this duck is delicious.'

It was the market, she explained, scraping out the dish for him. So close it made shopping each day easy, and you could buy the freshest produce without it having been hanging around in a van for several days as it made its way slowly up-country. Luc shot a covetous glance at the second pot on the stove.

'Tomorrow?'

'Certainly not!' Tomorrow she was planning *coq au vin*. 'I made that for Suzette next door. Her husband died last year from an accident in the boiler room in one of the distilleries down on the quay, so with three small children and no work, I thought it might help.'

'That's very generous.'

'Nonsense. We can easily afford one extra duck. My job, your pay rise—'

'No hat bills, no theatre tickets.' He wiped both *cassoulet* and smile from his mouth with a serviette. 'Do you miss them, Marie-Claude? Honestly?'

'If you've finished, I need to get back to the shop,' she said briskly. 'Madame Garreau's visiting her mother and I'm all on my own this afternoon.' She scraped the bones into the bin while he brewed the coffee. 'So who died, then?'

'A woman by the name of Martine Montaud—'

'Madame Montaud?' She wiped her hands on the dishcloth and set out a plate of *palmiers* still warm from the oven. 'Handsome, late forties, with dark hair?'

'You know her?'

'As one would expect of the owner of a cognac house, she was one of Madame Garreau's best customers.' Marie-Claude sat on the table and began swinging her legs. 'Very elegant lady,' she said. 'Exquisitely made up, hands neatly manicured and I wouldn't like *her* hairdresser's bill, I can tell you.' She sighed. 'I shall miss her coming in, though,' she added. 'She never took offence when I told her what didn't suit her—'

'Marie-Claude, that's the reason Madame Garreau adores you. You give her clientele an honest appraisal and you don't hold back. People respect that.'

She wondered how he could possibly know her employer's opinion. As far as she knew, Luc had never met Madame Garreau, but that was beside the point. No woman wants to be told lilac suits her when it makes her look bland, any more than being sold the concept that wide stripes will flatter her hips. Especially Madame Montaud, who invariably left the shop hundreds of francs lighter, but every inch looking the successful businesswoman she was.

'She never struck me the type to get herself murdered,' Marie-Claude said, sipping her coffee. 'Well, not bashed on the head, anyway. It seems so…vulgar.'

'You'd have preferred she was strangled?'

She shot him a look to say that wasn't funny. 'Who killed her, do you have any idea?'

'Everything points to the cellar master,' he said sadly. 'Like that art theft back in May, there's very little detective work involved in this case. Oh and talking of art, I suppose you know Matisse is dead?'

'Cellar master? Luc, the cellar master of a cognac house is just one step below God. He's not just responsible for the blend, he oversees the whole process of distillation from beginning to end, he even chooses the oak trees from which the barrels are made that will store his precious cognac, for heaven's sake!'

'And you know this because…?'

'Suzette. I told you. Her husband died in a boiler room fire.' She brushed a curl out of her eyes with the back of her hand. 'We spend a lot of time talking when she picks up the kids.'

'You *babysit*?'

'Don't sound so surprised. It gives her chance to do a typing course and—*hein*. The point is, you're looking at the wrong person, Luc. The cellar master couldn't possibly have clonked Madame Montaud on the head. That wouldn't have been *his* style, either.'

'Ah. You'd have preferred he strangled her?'

'That wasn't funny the first time, and besides, what motive would he have for killing his employer?'

'Something sexual probably, it usually is.' Luc shrugged as he reached for the last pastry. 'Money or sex lies at the root of most murders, plus his were the only fingerprints that we lifted and I found one of her earrings in his bed—'

'It was so obvious, you searched his house?'

'Not exactly.' He leaned his weight against the back of the chair and folded his arms over his chest. 'But because her body was found in the cellars, I conducted a thorough search of the entire factory, including the distillery, which happens to have a small room sectioned off that serves as the cellar master's bedroom.'

'Only from November until March, when distillation takes place around the clock and he needs to be on hand night and day.'

'Suzette?'

'Suzette.'

'Hmm.' He scratched his chin. 'Well, if you know so much about the cognac process and you don't believe my suspect is the killer, why don't you go up there and tell me who is?'

Marie-Claude jumped down from the table. 'I'll need a cardigan.'

'What about the shop?' he called up the stairs, and look, it proved the acoustics in this house were rubbish. It sounded for all the world as though he was laughing.

'What about the shop?' she called back, reaching for her green hat with the feathers. 'They're rich, these women. They can afford to wait a while longer.'

Poor Madame Montaud could not.

* * *

The Domaine de Montaud lay on the north side of Cognac, protected by woodlands and snug inside a bend in the river. For almost two thousand years, its sun-kissed slopes had gazed over the valley of the Charente and the hills that unfolded beyond, but the acidic soil and low alcohol content played havoc with the wine's conservation and so, in the seventeenth century, foreign merchants hit upon the idea of importing it in spirit form and diluting it on arrival. Because of the double distillation process involved, the Dutch named this spirit *brandwijn*—burnt wine—which had the added advantage of being cheaper to ship. But no matter how economical the costs of transport, when recession hits, luxury goods are the first to suffer. Huge stocks of brandy piled up in the cellars. Things were not looking good.

Until local producers noticed that their spirit not only improved with age, it tasted even better drunk neat...

But as cognac was born, so evolved a world of secrets and magic. In each dark saturated cellar, the cellar master became sorcerer, blending smooth with mellow, amber with gold, elegance with subtlety, to produce a unique and individual range of cognacs, from the youngest, at under five years, to prestigious *reserves* that had been maturing in oak casks for decades.

Marie-Claude had imagined such sorcerers to be sober, unsmiling, aloof and dull. Undertakers in different suits. If they were, Alexandre Baret broke the mould.

'*Enchanté, madame.*'

Any other time and the eyes behind the spectacles would be twinkling flirtatiously. The crows' feet either side said so. But today they only viewed the inspector's assistant with mistrust, and were clouded with something else, too. Guilt? Grief? Fear? Marie-Claude couldn't say, but following him through the shadowy barrel-lined chambers, their walls black from evaporation, she felt prickles rise on her scalp. With its rigorously controlled temperature, light rationed to brief and rare visits, the oaky tang to the air, it was like walking through a cathedral. That same air of reverence. Humility. Silence. Tranquillity. The taking of life here seemed sacrilegious.

'I have informed the workforce that this area is out of bounds until further notice,' Monsieur Baret said, studiously avoiding the outline of a body chalked on the flagstone floor. 'But in any case, only a handful of employees have access, and I assure you it is quite impossible to enter without the necessary keys. Indeed,' he added dryly, 'one would stand a better chance breaking into the *Banque de France.*'

'You don't think this could be a robbery turned sour, then?' Marie-Claude's voice echoed softly. 'After all, there are hundreds of migrants in the vineyards right now, breaking their backs to bring in the harvest.'

Alexandre Baret watched dust motes dance in the air over the spot where every trace of his employer's blood had been scrubbed clean. 'No, *madame*, I do not think that.'

'You're not exactly helping your case,' she said, and behind her heard Luc grind his teeth.

'Why?' The cellar master swung round sharply to face him. 'Am I under suspicion, inspector?'

Marie-Claude was acutely conscious that her husband didn't look at her when he replied. 'Madame Montaud was found with just one emerald cluster in her left ear,' he said mildly. 'An identical cluster was found in your bed next to the still.'

Monsieur Baret said nothing, but his eyes flickered, she noticed, as he opened the door from the cellars. Perhaps it was nothing more than passing from darkness into the light.

'I cannot explain that,' he said at length. 'But if you are suggesting—' he indicated the cramped sleeping quarters partitioned off with nothing more than wood and glass '—I'm sorry, inspector, you are mistaken.'

Marie-Claude opened the door and peered in. There was just about enough room for the bed and a small chest of drawers. The blankets did not look very clean.

'The night watchman confirms that you have been leaving very late. Past midnight on several occasions.'

'I did not conduct an affair down here with Madame Montaud,' Baret insisted, 'that's simply too sordid to contemplate. I am a married man. And the notion that I killed her—pff! What possible motive would I have?'

Luc drew a carbon copy from his breast pocket. Reading upside down, Marie-Claude saw that the letter bore yesterday's date, was addressed to the cellar master and had been typewritten.

'This was on top of the paperwork in Madame Montaud's desk,' Luc said. 'The desk, incidentally, that we were only able to open with the key that was found in her pocket.'

Baret took the proffered letter and, as he read, the colour drained from his face. His jaw tightened. 'I—I have never seen this before.'

Marie-Claude didn't get chance to read every last word before it disappeared back inside Luc's pocket, but the gist was enough. In the most civil of terms, Martine Montaud was dismissing her cellar master.

* * *

'Is it, do you think, too sordid to contemplate?' Luc asked, once they were alone in the distillery. 'Tall, fifty, and with that thick thatch of dark hair, it seems perfectly reasonable to me that the earring of the widowed and lonely Martine would end up in his bed.'

'Not this bed,' Marie-Claude said, sending clouds of dust into the air as she tried to pull the curtains and found the hooks had rusted solid.

'Wouldn't the risk of discovery have been the spice, though? Two educated, articulate, respected people fired by the danger of being caught in the act?'

'If there's any danger, it comes from fleas, not ruined reputations,' she said, prodding the unsheeted mattress. 'And anyway, who said she was lonely?'

When Madame Montaud tried on clothes in the shop, those were not sensible foundations garments she'd been wearing underneath!

'Who else has a key to the distillery and cellars?' she asked.

'No one who doesn't have a cast iron alibi.'

'While Monsieur Baret…?'

'Claims he went for a walk, and if you believe that, you believe anything.' Luc ran his hand over the ticking on the bolster. 'You know, Marie-Claude, just because they're both polite, refined individuals, it doesn't mean they don't enjoy the occasional foray into degeneracy.'

She considered the new baby doll pyjamas that were all the rage at the moment. Both she and Luc agreed that these were the most depraved and decadent garments that had ever been invented, and indeed they'd considered them so depraved and decadent that they ripped them off no less than three times last Saturday night.

'So you're saying Alexandre met with Martine last night, as usual. They came down here, as usual, made love in his seedy little camp bed, as usual, where she lost an earring in the heat of their passion…then fired him?'

'No,' he said, leaning his hip against the chest of drawers. 'That's what the evidence is saying. Not me.'

Marie-Claude threw her hands in the air. 'Luc Brosset, you are the most impossible man on God's earth! If you suspected all along that this was a setup, for heaven's sake why didn't you just come straight out with it and tell me you wanted my help?'

'That's funny,' he said. 'I thought that was exactly what I had done.'

* * *

Centuries had come and gone, but the method of distilling cognac hadn't changed. The still itself, the *alambic*, was made of gleaming red copper and, with its swan neck, long pipes and balloon shape resembled more a giant oriental hookah than a boiler. For nearly four months of the year, once the grapes had been pressed and their precious juice extracted, these three pieces of apparatus would be working night and day to produce the first distillation, the *brouillis*, before undergoing its distinctive second boiling. Only after that could the "heads" and "tails" be separated from the clear "heart" of the spirit that would eventually mature into cognac.

During these four months, though, the cellar master would virtually live next to his *alambic* while, outside, the town would grow warm from so many boilers pumping round the clock, the air would become impregnated with the sweet smell of brandy, and the characteristic black on the buildings would deepen, a symbol of status and pride. Incredibly, a tenth of the cognac was lost to evaporation, a contribution known as the angels' share. Marie-Claude wondered whether Madame Montaud would be able to distinguish her own cognac from where she sat on her cloud. And how silly to get misty-eyed over someone she hardly knew!

'The way she was killed,' Luc said, 'hit on the back of the head with a marble bust of the founder that took pride of place next to the *alambic*, that suggests the crime wasn't premeditated.'

Marie-Claude thought about the key in her pocket. The fact that Alexandre's were the only fingerprints. The way nobody else here had access.

'It suggests an earring coming off when she fell,' he continued, 'and the killer taking the opportunity to implicate someone else.'

She wondered what the gem-smith who made Madame Montaud's jewellery would have to say about such odds.

'Or,' she said, 'it's a double-bluff designed to look that way.'

Luc spiked his hands through his hair. 'You mean Baret planned it from the outset, then left clumsy clues that pointed directly to him, leading us to think they had been planted?'

'If it was a spur-of-the-moment act, why didn't he plead *crime passionel* straight away? Cellar masters are respected all over France, Luc, and think about it. Sex, rejection, dismissal? Any one of these things is enough to make a man feel emasculated and strike out in the heat of anger, yet here we have three stacked on top of each other. Alexandre Baret could have thrown up his hands and admitted his crime, and even the worst advocate in the country would have had him walking away a free man.'

She stared up at the shining copper works and saw Madame Montaud holding up two evening dresses, the navy blue and the green. *What discount will you give me, Madame Garreau, if I take both? I see. Well, thank you for your time, but I think I'll drive into Angoulême and see—Why, yes, Madame Garreau. Ten percent would be perfectly acceptable. But shall we say twelve?*

'Madame Montaud was elegant, successful, she drove a hard bargain, but by all accounts, she was fair. While a man who blends cognac that not only his successor won't see sold but *his* successor either, is a man who is patient, clever and selfless.'

Luc scratched his head. 'Are you saying he did or he didn't?'

Marie-Claude straightened her hat in the boiler's reflection. 'It's late,' she said. 'I have to get back to the shop.'

* * *

'Some joint,' she murmured as they snubbed the workforce's entrance in favour of the broad sweep of the drive.

'Twelve bedrooms, five wings, and ceilings so high you can house a giraffe in each room, should you so desire,' Luc said. 'And to prove how handsomely this business pays, the house is surrounded by seventeen hectares of beautiful but totally unproductive parkland.'

'If you think I'd live there, you're mistaken,' Marie-Claude said. 'Look at the number of windows for a start. And the height of them! I'd spend all my day washing them.'

'You'd have people to do that for you.'

'I would not,' she protested.

What? Strangers trooping all over her house, snooping all over her business?

'Some people might envy the rich for their lifestyle,' she said firmly. 'Not me. Madame Montaud may have been successful, but the poor woman was a martyr to the business, she barely took a day off, and look at that sister of hers. Dresses like Grace Kelly, but never gets a chance to breathe, much less be her own person. No privacy, not even a house to call her own, and when her husband leaves the shop, it stinks of stale wine and cigars for simply hours.'

'Oh? And what do I stink of?'

'Nutmeg and citron and cool, mountain forests,' she said, and his eyes weren't just green, they crinkled at the corners and were flecked with red, grey and brown, and his mouth twisted sideways when he smiled. With his thick mop of dark hair and square practical hands, she was glad Luc would have no trouble finding a new wife once she'd gone.

'Hmm.'

He stuffed his square practical hands in his pockets and whistled *Mambo Italiano* under his breath as they sauntered past the bustling vineyards down the hill towards the river. Since the Domaine was only a fifteen-minute walk from the house, they hadn't bothered with the car, and Marie-Claude was wrong about the cardigan. She hadn't needed it at all.

'I don't suppose this sudden obligation to duty has anything to do with the sister?' he asked after working his way through *Three Coins in the Fountain, Smile* and *Hernando's Hideaway*.

'Madame Montaud wasn't having an affair with her cellar master,'

Marie-Claude said, wondering at what point her arm had become linked with his. 'She ordered far too many evening gowns for an illicit liaison.'

More likely she was being courted discreetly, preferring to wait and see how things developed before going public with the relationship.

'Loose women aren't taken seriously in business,' she pronounced. 'But the sister, Madame Delaville, now that's a different story.'

Husband reeking of stale booze and smoke, choosing all her clothes? She'd lost count of the number of times she'd seen him sitting in Madame Garreau's plush armchair, squat and pot-bellied like a cocky little toad, while his wife paraded in unflattering suits with slow and mechanical precision.

'Natalie Delaville is a woman of loose moral standards?'

'Exactly the opposite,' Marie-Claude said, turning the key in the shop. 'Her husband has the word *bully* all but etched on his forehead, but the more I think about it, the more I remember that her chin hasn't drooped quite so much lately, there's been colour in her pale cheeks, and miracle of miracles, Madame Delaville actually called in half a dozen times on her own over the past month. I want to look up what she—*voilà!*'

'Well?' Luc held out his hands in exasperation. 'Are you going to tell me what the little mouse bought?'

'Certainly not.' Such matters were private! 'But I can tell you that the dresses were feminine and flattering, and I can tell you whose account they were charged to, as well.' She shot her husband a sideways glance. 'Alexandre Baret.'

'All right…' Luc rubbed his jaw in thought. 'But is this actually getting us anywhere?'

'It explains his unease and reluctance to provide an alibi.'

'Because he was protecting Natalie Delaville.'

'Absolutely.' She locked the door and tested the catch. 'Now all we have to do is prove how that bitch killed Martine.'

'Metamorphosis is a wonderful thing,' Luc observed, stretching his pace to match hers. 'One minute she's a mouse, the next she's a bitch—what? What have I said?'

'Honestly!' Marie-Claude stopped outside the baker's and shook her head in disbelief. 'I don't know where you get your ideas, sometimes! Not Madame Delaville, Luc. She didn't kill Madame Montaud.'

It was Madame Baret, of course. Alexandre's wife.

'*And* she killed the wrong woman.'

* * *

As the hills slowly turned to russet and gold and the French populace finally came to terms with defeat in Indochina, the Empire State Building had been eclipsed as the world's tallest structure, civilization was facing extinction from something called Rock and Roll, and Luc had been proved right about Suez, especially in light of that botched attempt earlier on the Egyptian president's life.

'By the way, Marie-Claude, I received a letter from the Commissioner this morning.'

More and more these days Luc had taken to joining her on walks along the tow path, although sometimes their route took them through the town hall park or onto the islands, where they would take a picnic providing they wrapped up warm.

'He writes that he has finally rounded up everyone involved in the blackmail and extortion ring. Some seven police officers are awaiting trial, he says, and commends me for a job well done.'

'That the letter?' Marie-Claude tossed it into the Charente, where a squadron of ducks came steaming in, mistaking it for a bread roll. 'You know my opinion of the Commissioner.'

'For the life of me, I can't imagine why.'

'He said I was truculent, selfish and a pain in the *cul*.'

Luc laughed. 'Well, if you overheard that much, you'd have also heard him qualify his statement by adding that you were spirited, funny, and I was lucky to have you.'

Couldn't agree more, sir, Luc had replied, and damn those horrid children upstairs for drowning out the Commissioner's words.

'He congratulated me on the Montaud murder, as well.' Luc stuffed his hands in his pockets. 'Being a high-profile case, I suppose word found its way back to his desk, but what I'm getting to is that he ended by saying that, now the corruption ring's been wrapped up and my life is no longer in danger, there's a job for me in Paris, should we want it.'

'You never told me your life was threatened!'

'Hell hath no fury like a Chief Inspector jailed. So then. Do we? Want that job, I mean.'

'It might have been high-profile, but it wasn't exactly brain surgery, Luc.'

All those late nights in the distillery, indeed! *I did not conduct an affair down here with Madame Montaud,* the cellar master had insisted, *that's simply too sordid to contemplate.* Quite right. It may have been his employer's sister he'd been carrying on with, not his employer, but he wouldn't have dreamt of taking the delicate, browbeaten Natalie to the distillery had it not been the only place where they could meet and not be either seen or overheard. His office was too close to the main works. They dared not be seen in public. So they either sat down there, talking long into the night, or they sneaked off in his car to plan their new life together, and what a lot of planning there was. For all that cellar masters are handsomely paid and live in grand houses, they still don't live like the Montauds! There would be no majestic mansion for Natalie once she left Delaville. No parklands, no servants, no prestigious balls. Alexandre had wanted her to be one hundred percent sure before making the leap. He knew there would be no going back.

For her part, of course, Madame Baret hadn't believed for a second that her husband had been required to work late.

In the way of deceived wives everywhere, she followed him, saw the lights in the distillery, knew about the bed, heard him whispering on the telephone in the hall. She'd had no trouble tracing the number to the Domaine and knew immediately who he was carrying on with. (Who else was there, for goodness sake? Hardly that pale, downtrodden sister!) So, again in the way of deceived wives everywhere, she hoped and then prayed the affair would blow over. Until the day she overheard him talking about their new life together…

From that moment on, revenge was all that consumed her. Revenge on the woman who had destroyed her life. Revenge on the man who discarded her.

'The marble bust might look like the instrument of a crime of passion, a spur-of-the-moment decision, grabbing the first object to hand,' Marie-Claude said, as they paused to watch the churning waters of the millrush merge with the stately river. 'But equally it smacked of a squeamish reluctance to be facing the victim.'

A uniquely feminine approach to murder. As was the cold-blooded planning.

'It was easy enough to get a set of her husband's keys cut.'

'One of the locksmiths confirmed it straight away, but as evidence it was still far from conclusive.'

'No, but it all mounted up.' She kicked the fallen leaves as she walked. Alder, willow and poplar. 'Madame Baret's mistake was planting the desk key in Martine's pocket.'

Good heavens, women as elegant as Madame Montaud don't use pockets! They tuck items away tidily in their *Chanel* handbags, which meant someone had used that key to get into her desk and replaced it in a hurry. And if it wasn't to take something out, then it must be to put something in.

A quick check of the keys proved that the letter had been typed on the Barets' private typewriter, not in the office at the Domaine, but it had been a clever move on Madame Baret's part. If the head of a cognac house wanted rid of their cellar master, this would not be made public knowledge. A gentleman's agreement between the two parties, however bitter underneath, would not show on the surface. Both had too much invested in the business to jeopardise their reputations.

'She was smart about fingerprints, too.'

Taking care the only ones lifted were her husband's, and who would think anything odd about seeing a lady of quality going round in evening gloves? Exactly. And whatever excuse she'd used to lure Madame Montaud down to the cellars, she must have thought it was her lucky day when Martine agreed so easily. But then, of course, she didn't know she was setting a trap for the wrong woman.

'Too smart about the fingerprints,' Luc said. They had stopped to watch one of the wooden, flat-bottomed *gabarres* pass through the lock, laden with casks lashed with ropes. 'That was one of the things that bothered me from the outset. That if Martine Montaud was exerting so much passion in the cellar master's quarters, why weren't hers there, too?'

'She misjudged the calibre of Madame Montaud's jewellery, as well.'

How cold must her heart have been, as she stood over the corpse, unscrewing the emerald cluster? Extracting the key from Martine's handbag, placing the letter of dismissal in her desk, then walking out as if nothing had happened and secure in the knowledge that her husband would not plead *crime passionel*. Why should he, after all? The man was innocent.

'Never mind Madame Baret,' Luc said. 'Just tell me whether we want that job in Paris.'

Marie-Claude watched the *gabarre* sail round the bend and disappear from sight. Above, the sun shone through the falling leaves and blackbirds foraged in the litter. Next week *Dial M for Murder* would be running back to back with *Rear Window* and in subtitles, plus she still hadn't finished those curtains for the bathroom, the cellar really needed a new blind, the old one was a disgrace, the bedroom could use fresh wallpaper, ditto the *salon* now she came to think about it, and she'd promised Madame Garreau two more days a week with the winter collection.

'Maybe when the rains come,' Marie-Claude said slowly.

Besides. She wasn't sure Luc was quite ready to live alone yet.

Something Rather Fishy

As scams went, this was a winner every time.

Patti and I would drive through the leafy suburbs of whichever town took our fancy for that week. Canterbury, Oxford, St. Albans, York. Cambridge, Chester and Harrogate. All of them stylish towns, you note, with fine, upmarket restaurants to suit its genteel clientele.

The van itself was a bog-standard 6cwt Ford, white, but beautifully polished, with the sign on the side in gold lettering.

H.H. Willoughby & Sons.

Purveyors of fine fish and shellfish to the restaurant trade.

Unfortunately, as we'd be driving through around four in the afternoon, we'd reach a T-junction, I'd be at the white line, just about to turn, when the van would splutter to a stop and refuse to start. Well, really! Dolly birds can't be expected to deliver fish and know what goes on underneath a bonnet. This was the summer of Woodstock, after all. 1969, not 1989, when it was considered endearing that women didn't know about such things. Out we'd get, though, pulling at our miniskirts to preserve our modesty, wearing our crisp, white fishmonger uniforms, with H.H. Willoughby embroidered on the collar. We'd open up the bonnet, peer inside and shrug our pretty shoulders. Patti would fiddle with a lead or two. I'd try the engine. Nothing, zilch and nada.

Luckily for us, we were close to a telephone box. Patti would run off to ring the AA rescue team, then phone Mr. Willoughby and tell him what had happened. When she returned, she'd be in floods of tears, and after she'd told me what he said, I'd be crying, too. We were very good at bubbling up in those days.

Most of the time, this little drama would be enough to bring the housewives out of doors. Of course, there were the odd occasions when no one noticed and we'd have to knock on doors, but the whole point is that T-junctions are not exactly obscure locations. Often, we'd have the van skewed on the half-turn, attracting other drivers, too.

'Is anything the matter?' the helpful housewives would enquire.

'It's the fish,' we'd wail. 'The AA can't get here for another three hours.'

Long waits were standard back then.

'Willoughby's sacked us. Said we should have taken the other van, so he's docking us for the fish it has cost him.'

Refrigerated vans weren't common in the Sixties. No one doubted it would have gone off by the time we finally got underway.

'That's terrible,' the housewives would say.

'How dare he!'

'It's not your fault.'

'No, it wasn't,' we'd sniff, launching into a joint demolition of Mr. Willoughby's character. Oh, the things that man had done!

'The pig.'

'The scoundrel.'

'There should be a law against exploiting the workforce!'

That came later, in the Seventies. In the meantime, two young girls were stranded in the middle of nowhere, out of a job, out of pocket, when all they'd been trying to do was earn enough money to buy books for college.

OK, scene set. Marks primed. Time to get down to business.

'What a waste,' one of us would moan.

Top quality seafood. It said so on the side of the van. And to prove it, Patti would open one of the rear doors, lift the lid on the front half-dozen boxes and we'd stare miserably at what diners at the top restaurants wouldn't be eating tonight. Prime crabs and prawns. Succulent cod. Lemon sole.

'I wouldn't mind buying a box,' someone would say.

'Me, neither.'

Patti and I would look at each other, and you could see what we were thinking. Marvin Gaye was hearing it on the grapevine. The Rolling Stones were having their minds blown by honky tonk women. Us? We were cutting deals for rotting fish.

But we were young and resilient. Hope shone through the tears.

'At least we wouldn't lose *everything*, Stevie.'

"S'pose not,' I'd blub, accidentally flashing the price on the lid. £5 for a stone of best haddock—and that was trade.

'I'll give you £1 for it,' someone would offer.

'£3,' Patti would shoot back, while me, I was more concerned with when they'd be eating all this fish. At five in the afternoon, they'd already have dinner for their husbands simmering on the hob. We hoped.

'Tomorrow, I suppose.'

Thank goodness for that. There was no point in driving through the suburbs in the morning.

'You'll need extra ice to preserve it,' I'd offer helpfully.

'Gosh, yes,' Patti would gush.

One of us would reach in the van, fill a scoop of ice from the bucket at the back, then seal the box to keep the freshness in. £100 later, the housewives would be gone and so would we.

Before they opened up their purchases and found that the boxes they'd handpicked had been switched for an identical package, filled with junk to make the weight.

Ah, happy days…

Twiggy, the "Shrimp", Butch Cassidy, not forgetting Italian Jobs and Midnight Cowboys. The year we sipped frozen orange juice and dabbled maraschino cherries in our Babychams, with the added joy of knowing that, however bad anybody's day anywhere, it could all be put right watching *Hawaii Five-O* on the telly.

For me, Stevie Wicks, it seemed the Age of Aquarius was dawning pink and rosy.

Instead, there was a very bad moon rising.

* * *

I first met Patti when I was working with Derek the Shell, an easy-going, curly-headed Welshman, with a smile as broad as his shoulders. Patti and Derek had just got married (nineteen? it would never last!) and I was going steady with a chap called Rob, who could double for Charlton Heston. The best thing about Rob, though, at least for a group of shysters, was his knack of being able to mimic any accent under the sun. Heady times, I tell you. And though the scam we pulled was as old as the hills, it was just a question of plying it right.

First of all, choose your pitch, and in 1967, when Scott McKenzie was urging everyone to go to San Francisco and wear flowers in their hair and The Beatles were getting by with a little help from their friends, that wasn't difficult. Petticoat Lane, Marble Arch and Portobello Road were overrun with tourists. Covent Garden was a banker, King's Road, Leicester Square and Soho just as good. But not Trafalgar Square. Too many crooks.

Derek was what's known in the game as "the shell man". He'd open up his black umbrella and prop it on the pavement. Then he'd lay out three bottle tops and a pea.

'Come on, lovelies. Find the lady.'

His rich Welsh lilt would draw the crowd.

'Who'll be first. You, sir?'

People laughed. Whether in red velvet jackets, kipper ties or hippie jeans, they weren't born yesterday, you know. But still they watched the caps whizzing back and forth across the brolly.

Then Rob, playing the Swedish tourist, would take the bet. He wins. Twice. No surprises there. But then he loses, and it's his own stupid fault. The crowd would have put their money on the middle cap.

'Would you, now,' Derek murmurs.

The Swedish tourist chews his lip. The crowd seem to be doing better than him, and his confidence wavers. He hands over a pound note and is about to point to the left bottle top, but the crowd are convinced the pea is under the cap on the right. The Swede changes his mind in line with popular thinking. He wins.

'Anyone else want to take me on?' Derek asks.

Well, of course they do. This guy isn't half as good as he thinks he is, the wally. Fivers fly cross that umbrella faster than you can say Ruby

Tuesday. The punters lose three times in a row.

Meanwhile, I have slotted in at the front.

Raymond Chandler wrote something about the sort of blonde that would make a bishop kick a hole through a stained glass window. Or was it Dashiell Hammett? Hell, it could have been Shakespeare for all I ever read a book. The point is, I might not have been quite up to that standard, but with my false eyelashes, bouffant hair and killer legs, I turned a head or two. Men always trust a pretty girl.

'I've just thought of a way to win,' I whisper excitedly to the punter standing next to me. 'I'm going to mark the cap with the pea under it with a smudge of lipstick. You watch. Ten pounds,' I announce, adding that first, though, I want to check the pea is actually under the cap Derek says it is.

'Of course it is, what do you take me for?' he huffs.

But he lets me lift it anyway, and I leave a miniscule coral pink blob.

Needless to say I win, and so does the punter next to me. Word ripples round the crowd in heated whispers. The bets increase. Except this time, as the tops get moved around, Derek notices the lipstick.

'Did you do this?' he asks one of the women in the crowd.

'I did not,' she says indignantly, looking daggers in my direction. I, of course, am looking back at her, pleading with my eyes, but she shops me all the same. That's women for you, eh.

'Right, that's it.' Derek packs up his caps and brolly. 'I'm not doing this if there's cheating going on.' He points an angry finger at me. 'I'm clever with my hands, but I'm no bloody cheat. You ought to be ashamed of yourself, young woman!'

Off he goes, muttering things like 'I can't believe anyone would stoop so low,' and that if I had been a man, he'd have punched me on the nose. I bubble up and apologise to the crowd, who melt away without realizing yet that he hasn't handed back their money, and what do you know. In half an hour we've pocketed the equivalent of a week's wages for an office wallah. Nice work if you can get it, wouldn't you say?

The Summer of Love rolled profitably on. Jimi Hendrix, Otis

Redding and Janis Joplin became imprinted in our brains. I fell in love with Cool Hand Luke, Rob picked up Dutch and German accents, Patti and Derek dressed like Warren Beatty and Faye Dunaway in *Bonnie and Clyde*, and amazingly didn't split up.

Then, while Christiaan Barnard was completing the world's first heart transplant and the Beatles were taking their magical mystery tour, the unthinkable happened.

Derek and Patti were driving through Wales to visit his parents, when his car careened off the road and down the side of a mountain. I don't know how well you know the Valleys, but take it from me, it can be treacherous at times. One minute you're driving along in bright sunshine, the next you're climbing, climbing, climbing up those narrow, twisty roads and suddenly you're in the clouds and can't see the front end of your bonnet. Patti had got out on a particularly vicious hairpin bend to walk the road and guide him. She was in no state to talk to anyone afterwards, even Rob and me, but we found out at the inquest that the police reckoned he'd been driving so slowly that the engine probably stalled. In trying to restart in damp conditions that played havoc with the spark plugs, he would have hit the accelerator too hard. Derek didn't stand a chance, while poor Patti was prostrate with grief and guilt.

The next day Otis Redding and six others were in a plane that crashed into a lake in Madison, Wisconsin.

Both he and Derek the Shell were twenty-six.

* * *

A year passed. By then, Rob found that picking up Dutch and German girls was a lot more interesting than just picking up their accents. Johnny Cash performed in Folsom Prison, Martin Luther King Jr. was assassinated on a hotel balcony in Memphis, and the Zodiac Killer claimed his first two victims in the States.

Oh, and the other big event of 1968 was that Stevie Wicks grew up.

* * *

I missed the old days, though. When I was ten, my father said, 'Don't forget. The world's your lobster, love.'

I giggled. 'You mean oyster, Dad.'

'No, girl, I mean lobster. Always aim big, that's the trick.'

That was the only piece of advice I remember him giving me. Three weeks later, he hit my mother one last time, packed his bags and left. I've never seen him to this day, don't know whether he's alive or dead and don't mind either way.

So when Patti turned up in the spring, wondering did I have any ideas on how to earn a decent living, I almost bit her hand off. Yes, I damn well did! With what was left of Derek's life insurance (she'd been living off the rest), we put down a deposit on a one-year-old white van, had the sign painted on the side in gold, then nicked the AA badge from a Rolls Royce. In broad daylight, too, with me strolling past, swinging my tote bag, and as I'm just about to cross the road, whoops. Down goes my handbag, contents everywhere. And while the chauffeur's leaping out to help me gather up my bits and bobs, Patti's whipped out her screwdriver, releasing the badge from the grille. Chauffeurs are always such gentlemen, I find.

After that, it was just a question of working out the best route to see the country and have a good time, working our fish scam as we went. I tell you, the cats in those towns did not go hungry when we left, though even now, if I so much as see a bloody prawn, my stomach heaves.

But as they say, all good things come to an end, though in my case, I swapped good for wonderful. Mr. Wonderful, in fact. And while Apollo 11 was busy landing a man on the moon, I was over it.

Do you remember Flight Deck? *Champagne Rain* and *Psychedelic Sunday* are probably the only songs of theirs that you can name, reaching thirty-eight and twenty-four in the Top 100 respectively. Anyway, Mick was the drummer, I met him purely by chance one night in a club, and we fell for one another. Hard. Looking back, I don't think my feet touched the ground for three years after that, and Dad was right. The world really was my lobster then. Flight Deck didn't play at major venues and they never broke into the States. But we toured Britain, Germany, Italy, Holland, hitting the ground running wherever we went.

We all knew it couldn't last, but while it did, Mick and I laughed and loved like there was no tomorrow, and even today, if I look at those photographs of Finland, Norway, Sweden, wherever, I still get a lump in my throat. When the crash came, it came fast. Part of the domino effect that swept right across the music industry, when creativity was so intense, so claustrophobic, that it was always destined to implode. Not so much a case of "Turn on, Tune in, Drop out," to quote the hippie mantra. More "Move on, Grow up, Burn out."

Randy, Flight Deck's songwriter and vocalist, suddenly found God, and without the booze and pills for inspiration, his work became anodyne, unappealing, but most of all unsellable. This made it as good a time as any for Boz, the flamboyant bass guitarist, to decide to study architecture, while Davey-J on lead guitar did a Brian Jones and died in a swimming pool at the age of twenty-seven. The difference was, he was so high on drugs he thought he could dive into it from the top floor of the hotel with the mini-bar strapped firmly round his waist. It said a lot for the scum he hung around with that they let him do it, too, and the only reason his death comes as news to you is because it coincided with the "Rumble in the Jungle", in which Mohammed Ali knocked out George Foreman to regain his heavyweight boxing title in Zaire.

See? That's the only bit of news you remember from that day.

Not much of a consolation for Davey's mum.

For Mick and I, it wasn't the break-up of the band that rang the death knell on our marriage. The killer was routine. Hardly in the same bracket as the Beatles, the Rolling Stones or even Herman's Hermits, Flight Deck still made good money at their peak, but, like kinky boots and beehive hair, the songs were quickly dated. Royalties dried up faster than puddles in the Sahara, and by the mid-Seventies, good drummers were two-a-penny on street corners, while the managers of any new bands wanted new faces to front their publicity campaigns.

Don't get me wrong, I'm no snob, and I wasn't ashamed of Mick going back to plumbing. Quite the opposite, in fact. Not every man who'd tasted freedom and the high life could settle back again, and he was a bloody good plumber. I was proud of him. I'm just not cut out for nine-to-five, or working in an office. The passion faded like a lightbulb on a psychedelic strobe, and while Mick was happy living on memories and U-bends, I moved on to selling timeshares.

Florida, Majorca, the Canary Islands, Cyprus. I made a tidy packet, I can tell you, with shoulderpads, big hair and *Miami Vice* helping me survive the dips and troughs.

So you could have knocked me down with a feather when Patti strolls up my path one bright and sunny morning, and it's not a lie to say I bubbled up for real. We cracked open a bottle of champagne, and never mind it was only twenty to eleven. We sank another, laughed, cried, swapped stories over chocolate cake and chardonnay, and agreed we both looked bloody good for women in our thirties.

By this time, of course, Michael Jackson was beating it, Elton John was still standing, and Joe Cocker was well and truly up where he belonged with Jennifer Warnes. Sean Connery had reprised his role as 007, and though I still carried a torch for Paul Newman, I was sharing him with Tom Berenger now. Though it was Mick's photo I slept with underneath my pillow.

'I need your help, Stevie,' Patti said at last. 'There's no one else I can ask.'

'Hell, Patti.' I opened another bottle. 'We've been pulling scams through Vietnam, the Cold War and the Falklands. What's it to be this time?'

'No scam,' she said, setting down her glass. 'It's Dan. My husband. I think… I think he's seeing other women.'

Some people call it puppy love, and I daresay if the roads had been fog-free that day in the Valleys, she and Derek would have gone their separate ways and not looked back. But at nineteen, colours are that much brighter, the pace of life much faster, and what I'm getting at is that it took her a long, long time to get over him. She'd married again, far too quickly the second time, she said.

'I was lonely, Stevie, like you can't imagine. First, Derek dies, then you go off with Mick—not that I begrudged you having fun, don't get me wrong. But suddenly the fun was gone, the nights were long, and when Norman popped the question, I just jumped.'

I'd never heard of Norman until that morning, but one thing's for sure.

Anyone calling himself that was doomed from day one. Norm, Nobby, Noz. Crikey, any bloke with an ounce of spunk would have changed his name from Norman. I saw why that relationship didn't last the year.

'I don't learn, do I?' Patti laughed. 'Two years later, I'm walking down the aisle, or at least the Register Office corridor, with Charlie on my arm and a wedding band on my finger. Another empty marriage heading for the rocks.'

'But Dan,' I prompted. 'Dan is different, eh?

Her face lit up. 'For the first time after Derek, I fell hook, line and bloody sinker. The full nine yards this time, and no mistake.'

She whipped out a photograph from her Louis Vuitton handbag. Never let it be said we girls did not invest our winnings wisely.

'Isn't he just gorgeous?'

Well…let's just say, he was no Paul Newman or Tom Berenger, and bless him, he was already balding from the forehead. But he had a lovely, open smile, and honest eyes that had security written all over them. He didn't look the type to fool around, and I told her so straight out.

'I know, but he's rich, Stevie. I mean super, stonking, million-billion rich, and people in that stratosphere see things differently.' She knocked back another glass and blew her nose. 'I don't think these tarts mean anything to him, and he swears he loves me and that we'll be together for ever and a day…' Her voice trailed off.

'Why not let sleeping dogs lie?' I asked gently.

'Would you?' she shot back. 'Would you sit back while your husband slept with other women?'

No, of course I bloody wouldn't, what was I thinking of. I told her that straight out, as well.

'Exactly. And I don't want to hire a private detective in case Dan finds out. You'd be surprised how money in those circles talks, believe me.'

I did, but all the same I'd have quite liked a shot at finding out myself. 'Where do I fit in?'

Patti couldn't be *certain* he was fooling around, she said. He'd told her he was playing poker with the boys, which explained the erratic hours, and maybe it was true. 'I just have this gut feeling,' she said, choking up again. 'I thought that maybe if you followed him… I mean, he doesn't know you. He wouldn't suspect anything. It would put my mind at rest once and for all.'

Absolutely. Hustling Joe Public is one thing. Being on the receiving end quite another.

'Just tell me when and where,' I said.

* * *

To be honest, he looked a whole lot better in the flesh. Perhaps that's just the effect of having super stonking millions, though. I wouldn't know. And in any case, she was exaggerating. Millions-billions, definitely not, but Dan Daniels wasn't on the breadline, either. He was Managing Director of Treble-D Holdings, some kind of property development company according to the plaque outside. Of course, property development was nowhere near as common in 1983 as it is today, but judging from the house on Richmond Hill and the E-type Jag, it was every bit as profitable. I drove a Golf Mk.1 Cabriolet (Ice Water Blue) thanks to flogging timeshares. I knew about these things.

Luckily, the London traffic was relatively light, and pretty blondes can get away with anything, providing they flash the right kind of smile when they cut you up or jump the lights. I followed him to the Dorchester on Park Lane, where he handed his car keys to the valet and headed for the bar like a homing pigeon. Then again, when Patti's suspicious instinct was on overdrive, who in their right mind would doubt it?

The one thing you need to hustle well is an ability to read people and situations, and when Derek plied his shell trick with Rob and me, Patti acted lookout. A keen eye will always spot trouble long before it starts, as well as keeping watch for the police.

'Cinzano and lemonade, please,' I told the waiter.

If it was good enough for Joan Collins and Leonard Rossiter, it was good enough for me.

I found a booth where I could watch him, but where he'd have to turn round to see me, then settled down with a paper spread out on the table. Funny what sticks in the memory, isn't it? One, *Terms of Endearment* was scooping Oscars like they were going out of fashion. Two, Sting was making the hairs on the back of my neck prickle with every breath I took. And three, a zoo in Singapore put five lionesses on birth control, after the cub population jumped from two to a mind-boggling sixteen. That's right. Lions on the pill. Who'd have thought it, eh?

I was still taking this in when a stunning brunette in a white lycra skirt took the seat next to Patti's husband at the bar. They seemed to know each other. Very well, in fact. I recognized her as his secretary. She kept looking round. He kept looking round. Furtive was the watchword of the day. He offered her a drink. She declined. She leaned close, whispered something then slid a room key across the counter. (Bearing in mind keys weren't exactly on the subtle side back then, being brass and weighing half a ton.) A minute later, off she went. A minute after that, a smug looking Dan left the bar and pressed the button for the seventh floor.

Hot damn.

Breaking the news to Patti wasn't easy, but she was getting quite adept at taking knocks. She called him names. I called a lawyer. She called me the best friend she'd ever had.

'Once this divorce is finalized, no more men,' she vowed. 'Maybe you and I can hit the road again?'

There was very little magic, only money, to be gained from selling timeshares.

'Let me close the deals on Rhodes and Malta, then I'm yours.'

* * *

Rhodes, yes. Malta, yes. But then Spain really starts to bloom, and with those things it's always best to get in on the ground floor while you can. After all, this was my pension fund I was saving for, and I had both experience and contacts to kickstart the boom in Spain. Plus, any excuse to get away from Spandau Ballet and Duran Duran. I'm guessing the best part of eighteen months, two years, must have drifted by, flogging holiday homes to expat felons in Marbella, before I packed up my spiel and headed home to Britain in case our two countries signed an extradition treaty.

To be fair, I didn't expect her to have kept the fancy house on Richmond Hill. Divorce is one thing, taken to the cleaners something else. But not for the first time, Patti and I had lost contact numbers, so I had no choice. I rang the bell.

'Mrs. Daniels? No, love, not for a while.' Why is it cleaners always like to gossip? 'Sold the place straight after the funeral, I think.'

Funeral?

Dan Daniels, it seemed, had been the victim of a mugging. Parked on a plot of waste ground, presumably with a view to developing it, he was found shot three times in the chest, his watch and wallet missing.

'Here's her new address.' The cleaner tutted sympathetically. 'Such a shame, innit?'

Shame for who, I wondered? Because suddenly I was starting to see black insects with eight legs, and sure enough. A little investigative work—well, a lot of investigative work, actually—revealed that it began right back in '67. I should have guessed. Derek taking out a life insurance policy? Pigs would fly. At twenty-five you're armour-plated, and what's more you live for ever. He wouldn't have wasted money on "the future," and now I saw what held the marriage together after all.

Greed.

The bitch guided his car over the edge, and it only took a year before she'd spent the money and was looking for new ways to earn a living without actually working for it. I conveniently provided the fish van scam.

Norman? Well, the name frankly said it all. Not wealthy, but steady income, steady life. No one had even suspected he suffered from depression when he put his head in the gas oven. The widow was distraught. Blamed herself for hiding his problem from the world, but hey. He'd made her promise. Blah-blah-blah, more bouts of guilt, and thank God the insurance companies hadn't tightened up the net regarding payouts on suicide.

Charlie was not her darling, either, it transpired. Another closet depressive, who ran the hosepipe from the exhaust into his car.

How come, I wondered, I was the only person joining up the dots?

Then I went back through the files, and saw she'd picked her marks with care. No close family to ask questions at either the beginning or the end. And we all know how good Patricia is at weaving stories.

As good as weaving webs to draw them in.

* * *

'You lied to me,' I told her on the phone. 'Derek, Norman, Charlie, Dan…'

'Not all lies,' she said, completely unrepentant. 'I *was* lonely after you left, though I admit Dan wasn't anywhere near as rich as I made him out to be.'

I knew that.

His secretary was still working for the company. We had a nice long chat. Mostly about how Dan Daniels had been planning a surprise anniversary present for his wife, after Patti had been dropping hints like mad about a romantic weekend in what was, at that time, the poshest hotel in London by a mile. He'd got his secretary to set it up, arranging champagne and roses in the room. No wonder he looked smug, going up to check.

In the end, though, the surprise was on him. Far from being at the pictures like she claimed the night he died, Patti would have driven with him to that waste ground he'd been hoping to develop, the gun primed and ready in her bag.

Lulu Guinness, knowing her.

'Yes, but when you talked about another empty marriage heading for the rocks, I didn't think you meant diamonds,' I laughed back. 'Let's meet.'

'You have another scam?'

'The best yet, girl.'

'Good, because I'm lousy with money.' Patti's sigh echoed down the phone. 'Can you believe the bank coughed up half a million pounds on Dan's insurance, and there's hardly any left?'

Easily. Patti couldn't put aside to save her life.

'Consider your financial worries at an end,' I told her. 'I've been perfecting this for months. It really is the best scam in the world, but this time the split is sixty-forty in my favour.'

I deserved something for being jerked around, I said.

* * *

There's an old saying when it comes to fraud. If it looks too good to be true, then it is.

There's another one, as well. That the definition of fraud is a crime perpetrated by the greedy on the greedier.

Patti was so engrossed with hustling and making money that she never stopped to think she might actually be the mark.

A walk along the cliffs to discuss the workings of the scam without being overheard. My friend slips. I ring the police, the ambulance service, the fire brigade—don't forget, always pitch close to a telephone box—screaming at the top of my lungs, because it's my best friend.

Did I lose a wink of sleep over this? Not one. I'd never met Norman or Charlie, but I'm guessing they were both decent blokes. Dan Daniels was, you could see it in his face. And it wasn't just that she'd used me, twice, to work her black widow payouts, even to staging the phoney adultery business to make me trust her next time she came calling.

It's just that Derek was my friend.

And while she was plunging head first to the rocks, I hoped he was up there, somewhere, watching this last game of Find the Lady.

* * *

There is a postscript to this story. Two months later, while Foreigner were still wanting to know what love was and Tina Turner was your private dancer, a dancer for money, I'm walking past the house I shared with Mick after Flight Deck had disbanded. The van outside read

Mick Robinson

Plumber & Central Heating Engineer

Well, I wonder… It's early evening, he is obviously at home. Along with three kids, a mumsy wife and lots of muesli and yoghurt in the kitchen, no doubt, but what the hell. I can't keep sleeping with that photo under my pillow.

'Stevie!'

Ten years drop away like water swirling down a plughole. No, he isn't married. No kids. No ties. He's never really settled.

We take a walk. We drink cappucinos, we eat pasta, we drink wine. I wake up next morning in his bed.

Our bed.

'Come to think of it,' he said lazily, 'we never actually got round to fixing that divorce.'

He packed in plumbing. I packed in hustling. We did what we'd always talked about. We cut loose. Today we live in southern Spain. If hustling pays well, it's kids' stuff compared to what a plumber earns. We have a nice house with a pool overlooking the sea. He sings and plays in clubs and bars, Dylan, Paul Simon, Phil Collins kind of stuff. Starved of culture, and unable to go home, the Costa del Crime crowd tip pretty big.

I can't believe I'm sixty, when I only look and feel forty-five. Or that I am an artist now, with my own gallery in Marbella that sells for pick-a-number add a nought.

God willing, Patti's also watching us, eaten up with envy. I sincerely hope so. So every now and then I raise a glass, and say, 'Here's to me, Mrs. Robinson. Jesus loves me more than I will know.'

Damn right he does. Rock on.

667, *Evil and Then Some*

The devil went down to Georgia. Everybody knows this, because Charlie Daniels wrote a song about how he was looking for a soul to steal and was in a bind, 'cause he was way behind, and was willin' to make a deal. Obviously there's poetic licence here. Hell, as you'd expect, is not exactly short of applicants, all of whom are processed with commendable speed and efficiency. Nor do we make deals.

What was true, though, was that when the devil came upon that boy playing on a fiddle and playin' it hot, he did jump up on a hickory stump and say, 'Boy let me tell you what: I bet you didn't know it but I'm a fiddle player too, and if you care to take a dare, I'll make a bet with you. I'll bet a fiddle of gold against your soul, 'cause I think I'm better than you.'

Or words to that effect, the devil not really being one for poetry; whereas, Mr. Daniels probably needed it to rhyme. But the point I'm making is that the President does like to get out of the office every once in a while, see how the world of sin is shaping up. Which is pretty nicely, as it happens, but when he's gone, Hell doesn't run itself. So while he and this Johnny character were taking bets, souls versus fiddles and all that, it was noses to the grindstone for the rest of us.

Leastways, it should have been.

Was it Georgia specifically, which always gets as hot as Hell in August? Or pure bad luck that the minute the competition started, the pitchfork sharpeners went on strike? In no time, the brimstone workers had walked out in support, with the stokers of the hellfires downing pokers in sympathy. I felt beads of sweat trickle down my horns. As the

President's right-hand demon, it was my job to relay status via his personal hotline, and I wasn't looking forward to that, I really wasn't. He tended to have what I suppose you'd call mood swings when it came to bad news. Messengers rarely volunteered for the job. In the end, of course, it was immaterial. The weather forecast showed that it was a rainy night in Georgia. I couldn't make a connection.

'Don't worry about the strikers.' The Head of Inhuman Resources patted my shoulder reassuringly. 'I used to teach in kindergarten, so I'm well used to tantrums,' he breezed. 'I'm off to start negotiations straight away.'

'Good, because it would have put the Old Man right off his playing,' I said, remembering how very attached he was to that golden fiddle of his. And quite honestly, I had enough problems to contend with, without my boss venting his spleen.

The thing is, you see, before he left, he'd tasked me with conducting a feasibility study on the future of Hell.

'After all, if the Universe is expanding,' he'd argued, 'we need to know what's going to happen to us.'

He was big on economic forecasts, was the President, and like any major corporation, tended to invest heavily in research, development and marketing. Once, he set me writing slogans in his absence and I thought that was a pretty tough assignment.

The devil's in the detail, that was one of mine.

Hell to pay, another.

Damned if I know, probably the best.

But slogans, I quickly discovered, were a piece of cake compared to feasibility studies. I mean, where do you start? After kicking at the edges for a while, I eventually pressed the button in the elevator for three thousand floors down to the Finance Department, where every thumbscrew, prod and drop of boiling oil has to be accounted for. Exactly. If taxation is hell, then Hell itself is truly taxing. But thankfully, between Accounts and the Admissions Office, I managed to gather enough statistics to fill a football stadium. And having waded through them, began to see a problem.

'Dr. Faust.' The nasal voice of the tannoy echoed through the sulphur. 'Dr. Faust to ER immediately. Dr. Faust to ER.'

Another emergency in Eternal Retribution, then? Any other time I'd have been curious to see what was so urgent that it needed to drag the good doctor away from the Golf Course. Someone else selling their soul to the devil, and starting a fight because they couldn't get a discount? Or was the Irritating Ringtone Punishment Squad failing to get a signal again? Whatever the crisis, though, I decided it wasn't my problem. What I'd discovered, on the other hand, was. And it was big…

'Dr. Lecter,' boomed the disembodied tannoy. 'Dr. Lecter to the canteen, please.'

Poor old Hannibal. Ever since he'd been appointed Director of Pain & Misery, he kept forgetting lunch, and another time I'd have made some wisecrack as he hopped into the elevator about taking his work home with him. That day, though, I had weightier issues on my mind, and even when I got the spiky bit of my tail caught in the doors, I barely noticed the bruise.

'Good news, good news!' The Head of Inhuman Resources was grinning as he rounded the corner. 'Arbitration's going swimmingly. With luck, the strikes will be over before the President returns.'

I wished I could have returned his smile, or even confided my suspicions, but for the moment, I held back. I had to be sure—I mean really sure—of my findings.

Meanwhile, up in the foothills of the Appalachians, the devil opened up his case and he said, 'I'll start this show.' And fire flew from his fingertips as he rosined up his bow.

Soon, though, it would be Johnny's turn to play.

I was running out of time.

* * *

'Boyle's Law?' My friend, Stanley, looked up from where he was updating the Liars, Cheats and Swearers database, and frowned. 'Since when have you been interested in thermodynamics?'

'I'm not,' I said, crossing my fingers in the hope that my name wasn't about to be added to the register. 'Learning the twenty-three laws of gases is a new punishment being introduced for those who didn't eat their greens.'

Stanley used to be in second-hand car sales, so he didn't query my explanation. Instead, he reached for a piece of paper and wrote $PV = k$ on it in thick red ink.

'What's that?' I asked.

'Boyle's Law.'

I must have looked as stupid as I felt, because he pointed with his trident.

'P denotes the pressure, V is the volume of the gas and k is a constant value representative of the pressure and volume of the system,' he explained. 'So long as temperature remains constant at the same value, the same amount of energy given to the system persists throughout its operation and therefore, theoretically, the value of k will remain constant.'

I was hoping he'd give me a moment to take this in, preferably ten years. But, just as if he was selling a ten-year-old Chevrolet with dodgy brakes and leaking radiator, Stan was in his stride.

'Due to the derivation of pressure as perpendicular applied force and the probabilistic likelihood of collisions with other particles through collision theory,' he said, 'the application of force to a surface may not be infinitely constant for such values of k, but will have a limit when differentiating such values over a given time. Forcing the volume V of the fixed quantity of gas to increase, keeping the gas at the initially measured temperature, the pressure P must decrease proportionally. Conversely, reducing the volume of the gas increases the pressure, got it?'

'Got it.'

Like you, I hadn't the faintest idea what he was talking about. In fact, it was only later that I discovered he'd brought up the Wikipedia article on his computer and was quoting it verbatim. Seems you can't trust anyone these days.

'You can also tell those cabbage-haters that Boyle's law predicts the result of introducing a change in volume and pressure to the initial state of a fixed quantity of gas. The "before" and "after" volumes and pressures of the fixed amount of gas, where the "before" and "after" temperatures are the same (heating or cooling will be required to meet this condition), are related by this equation here.'

My heart sank. Another piece of paper. Another red equation.

$P_1 V_1 = P_2 V_2$

I nodded knowingly, thanked him for his time and then, once I got back to my desk, cried my eyes out. Physics *and* feasibility? I was doomed.

* * *

'Boyle's Law?'

Of all the help in all of Hell, the last place I expected to find it was from my pedicurist. Don't get me wrong, Suzie does a great job, buffing, polishing, and getting a really even cleft between my hoofs. In fact, it was me who suggested she put the "love" in "cloven" in her advertisements, and turn the "o" into a heart. Even so, she was the very last person I expected to be familiar with physics.

'Oh, sure, honey.' Buff, buff, polish, polish. 'Pythagoras's theorum, Archimedes' principle. Ask me anything.'

I hadn't actually intended asking her one damn thing. I'd simply been grumbling about my problems over a soothing shod-rub to unwind, when suddenly she trots out with that little gem. Amazing. And though the prospect of more horrendous equations filled me with dread, when it comes to fact-finding, there is no such thing as too much information. I braced myself.

'Easy peasy, sugar.' She gave my scales an affectionate ruffle. 'Boyle's law simply states that the volume of a gas increases when the pressure decreases at a constant temperature.'

And there it was. Suddenly boiled down (boyled down?) to something I could understand. Everything I needed in a nutshell.

'Suzie, you're a star,' I said, hugging her.

'Aw, go on with you,' she said, blushing and pushing me away. All the same, she gave my horns a good hard burnish as a freebie, and when I left, I could really feel them glowing.

* * *

I know what you're thinking.

You're wondering why, if Hell doesn't make deals, the devil was cutting one in Georgia. Well, I'll tell you. Fun. He just went up there to have a look around and enjoy himself, because win or lose, Johnny's soul was his. It was only ever a question of time, since what people often don't appreciate is that everybody goes to Hell—and I do mean everybody. You. Me. Murderers, thieves, rapists (obviously), but where do you draw the line? Pickpockets? Exam cheats? People who exceed the speed limit while driving? Yes, you're probably thinking. There might be a case to be made for those, along with adultery, tax evasion, forgery and plagiarism. And you probably have a mental image of a panel of judges sitting in the Admissions Office, deciding who comes in and for how long, but you'd only be partially right. Sinners are indeed sorted according to category. But I repeat: everyone comes in.

Nobody comes out.

Surprises you, does it? It shouldn't, because in the end it all comes down to religion, many of which proclaim that if you are not a member of theirs, you will go to Hell. And since there are many of these religions, and given that people never belong to more than one, everybody ends up here by default. Factor in projected birth and death rates, and you begin to see that the clientele is increasing in direct proportion. Hence the need for a feasibility study.

But having done the analysis, the conclusion was chilling.

And frankly, it made telling the President about pitchfork sharpeners going on strike look very tame indeed.

You see, this is where Boyle's Law comes in. Once I'd got to grips with Wikipedia, I saw that if you look at the rate of change of the volume in Hell, you'll see that in order for the temperature and pressure to stay the same, the volume has to expand as more souls are added. Which means one of two things will happen.

Either Hell will expand at a slower rate than the rate at which souls enter. In which case, the temperature and pressure will increase until all Hell breaks loose.

Or Hell will expand at a faster rate than the rate at which souls enter. In which case, the temperature and pressure will drop until Hell freezes over.

Now who's going to tell the devil that?

* * *

The boy said, 'My name's Johnny and it might be a sin, but I'll take your bet, you're gonna regret, 'cause I'm the best that's ever been.'

He played: fire on the mountain, run boys run, devil's in the house of the rising sun, chickens in the breadpan, picking out dough, Granny does your dog bite? No, child, no.

Hmm, I thought. Fire on the mountain indeed.

Believe me, with what I'd just discovered, I was really starting to sweat.

* * *

The devil bowed his head, because he knew that he'd been beat. And he laid that golden fiddle on the ground at Johnny's feet.

This is a fact. I witnessed it myself.

Johnny said, 'Devil, just come on back if you ever wanna try again. I done told you once, you son-of-a-bitch, I'm the best that's ever been!'

He wasn't. The devil was just giving him his due, or at least an extension of it. 'Sucker,' he chuckled under his breath, and was so busy laughing at his own joke, that he failed to notice me.

And really, why should he?

When you leave the Great Underground Car Park, you adopt human form, and the first thing I did when I got back to earth was catch that midnight train to Georgia. You see, at heart I'm a coward. I knew what would happen when I showed the President the results of that feasibility study, and I didn't fancy being toasted over fire while having my liver ripped out as rats gnawed at my vitals. Not eighteen times a day for all eternity. No way.

On the other hand, I couldn't fudge the results, either.

So there was only one thing left to do.

I had to kill the devil.

* * *

Despite what you might think, murder isn't easy. Not that I haven't picked up a few tips over the millennia, of course. The Borgias had enough poison recipes to fill a cookery book. Genghis Khan was never short of ideas, either. Plus there was always Torquemada's bestseller to dip into, *Ink and Inquisition*, if I got stuck. But this is the devil we're talking about, and whilst silver bullets work for vampires, the President was bulletproof, and there was no heart to drive a stake into.

I resorted to the age-old tried-and-tested never-fails routine. My good friend, the peanut allergy. And since the devil has no soul, he won't be going back to Hell, and neither for that matter will I. No, sir. Not with that prognosis!

And in case you're wondering who I am, look up. Now whose is the first face that you see…?

Fire on the mountain, run boys run, devil's in the house of the rising sun. Chickens in the breadpan, picking out dough. Granny does your dog bite? No, child, no.

Cerberus, the three-headed hound that guards the gates of Hell, does tend to whine a bit, mind you. But that's only because he's missing his master, and no doubt once Hannibal takes over, he'll settle down again.

Petrified

Soaring on the thermals, high above the mountains, the eagle's view was clear. Soft peaks, blue and hazy. Olive groves that stretched for ever, shading flocks of sheep. Herds of cattle grazing on the plain. Directly below the eagle lay the citadel, bustling with the industry of shield makers, bronzesmiths, dyers and weavers, potters, perfumers and scribes.

The citadel was accessed by a long steep ramp, through a gate guarded by colossal lions, and protected by walls built from blocks of stone that weighed ten tons apiece. A defensive structure, because although the king had no stomach for killing or for war, he was not unwise enough to think that others shared his view. This city, the city he himself had founded, sat between the twin powerhouses of Corinth and Argos. Even peaceful men did not take chances.

From the rooftop terrace of his palace, the very pinnacle of this mountain on a mountain, the king surveyed his realm. His raiment was woven with gold thread, the rings he wore were heavy, and the wine he drank was of the very finest vintage.

But it had not always been so.

'Something troubles you, my lord.'

Perseus felt the tension slacken, for surely Andromeda had grown more lovely with every year since he took her for his wife. Why not? Liberation from the father who tried to sacrifice her to a sea beast had eradicated the worry on her face. Love had softened her frame. Motherhood had given her a bloom.

'I have received sad news, Andromeda. An old friend passed away.'

'Oh, Perseus.' She ran across and clasped both hands in hers. 'I am so sorry, my love. Who was it? Anyone I know?'

'No.' When he kissed her hair, he smelled the herbs she rinsed it in, to keep it thick and glossy. 'No, this was long before I met you.'

He turned away, his arm still round her shoulders, to fix his gaze upon the Temple of Poseidon far below. Poseidon, the Earth Shaker. Poseidon of the Seas.

And as the notes from the temple lyre mingled with the hammering of the bronzesmith, and the scent of ripe figs growing against the wall softened the cloying incense from the braziers, the years unfolded.

His mind drifted back…

* * *

'Who's Medusa?'

Perseus was young back then. Barely eighteen, standing in the hall of a different palace, on a different hill. This was the palace of Polydectes, King of Serifos, the little island in the Cyclades where he and his mother washed ashore when Perseus was a baby. But for all the years that had passed, for all the adventures and missions he had undertaken, Perseus could still picture the scene as though it was yesterday.

Red columns holding up a gilded ceiling. Battle scenes painted on the walls. Couches draped with lion pelts, musicians playing pan-pipes in the corner. And in the middle, like a spider in its web, was Polydectes, his beard oiled and curled, like some Babylonian princeling, strutting like a peacock. The sun was glinting off the ornate pins that held his tunic, he remembered, but there had been a glint in the king's eye, too. A smugness that made the hairs on Perseus' young neck rise.

'Not *who*, boy. *What*.' Polydectes took another slug of wine. 'Medusa is a monster. A thing. A vile creature, with fangs and tusks, and hair of hissing snakes. Her skin is scaly, she has claws of bronze, and one look from this abomination turns all living things to stone.'

Perseus' eyes narrowed. 'And you want *me* to kill it?'

'You asked my price. I named it.' The King signalled for a bearer to refill his goblet. 'Bring me the head of Medusa before the moon is full, I said, and I will take Hippodamia for my bride, and not your mother.'

Too late Perseus saw it was a trap. An impossible task.

But the perfect solution for Polydectes…

'Then so be it, my lord.' He bowed low. Partly to hide the sickness that came from his stupidity. But mainly because dignity was all that was left to him. 'Before the moon is full, I shall bring you the head of Medusa.'

Retreating from the hall, he could have sworn the king's smirk deepened.

* * *

'Have you taken leave of your senses?'

Dictys, when he told him, almost slapped him.

'Go back. Now. Humiliate yourself before him, Perseus. Tell him you are sorry, but you cannot accept this undertaking.'

'I have given my word.'

'To a man like my brother, a sworn oath means nothing.' Dictys threw his hands in the air. 'Summary executions are a weekly occurrence, justice is a word, not a code,. Last week he killed a man for calling him fat. If you will not renege, son—'

'I will not.'

'—then there is only one option. You and your mother must leave this island. Tonight.'

'Run? Dictys, you know I cannot.' But he'd wanted. Oh, how he had wanted. 'You took us in when the storm dashed our boat against the shores of this island. You raised me with decent values, values your brother does not possess, and as surely as the gods move among us, Dictys, you love my mother.'

'I would give my life for Danaë, it is true.' The older man's eyes filled with tears. 'But I would rather you took her far from here, and I never set eyes on her again, than see her married to a tyrant that she hates.'

'I am no coward, Dictys.'

'It is not cowardice to save your own life, and spare your mother from a life of suffering.'

'It is cowardice not to try. So.' From somewhere, Perseus mustered a weak smile. 'Tell me about this Medusa creature. What is it, and where will I find it?'

"It", according to legend, was once a ravishingly beautiful young woman, who could have had any man she wanted. Instead, she chose the mighty god Poseidon, and, in her arrogance, seduced him in the Temple of Athene.

'Athene's wrath is legendary,' Dictys said. 'Her shrine had been violated in the most heinous manner, and she could not forgive Medusa for the insult. As punishment, the goddess changed her once luscious hair to venomous, living snakes. She gave her scaly serpent skin, and made her features so vile, that any living creature who gazed on her would be turned immediately to stone.' He gripped Perseus by the upper arms. 'You see what the king has done, son? He dare not kill you himself, but by sending you to kill Medusa, he has sentenced you to death.'

'This is not the first time a king has been too scared to kill me, in case he risked the wrath of mighty Zeus himself.' A small amount of courage (bravado?) filtered back into Perseus' bones. 'And that didn't pan out too badly in the end.'

The kingdom of Argos was one of the most powerful in the Peloponnese, second only to Sparta. So when the Oracle foretold that the King of Argos would have no sons but that his grandson would kill him, the king took no chances. He imprisoned his only daughter, Danaë, in quarters that no man could breach.

In material terms, the princess lacked for nothing. But with no windows by which a man might enter, and a door of solid bronze, this was still a prison—the original gilded cage, where Danaë's only view of the outside world was through the opening in the roof that let the smoke out.

With only stars and clouds for company, she begged the gods to help.

'My daughter has WHAT?'

The eunuch bowed low before the king. Heard his voice tremble as he answered, for messengers bearing bad tidings weren't renowned for their longevity. 'Your daughter has given birth to a son, my lord.'

Recriminations, retributions, explanations came later. Mostly at the end of a sword. And though Danaë stuck to her story—that Zeus came to her in a shower of gold—the king, her father, did not believe a word. On the other hand, only a fool would risk the wrath of the most powerful deity on Olympus, and the King of Argos was anything but that. He cast Danaë and her baby son adrift, leaving their fate in the hands of the gods.

'We could have drowned. We could have been dashed upon the rocks,' Perseus said. 'Instead you opened your house and your heart to us, my friend. Maybe Zeus smiles upon me, after all.'

Under Serifos law, Danaë remained the property of her closest male relative, although no marriage could be contracted until Perseus reached maturity. At which point Polydectes, whether to spite his brother, or because Danaë was still a beauty and a princess, decided to make her his bride. Perseus objected. Told the king to name his price to free his mother from the contract. Walked straight into the trap.

If he backed out, he would be forced to leave Serifos in disgrace. And his mother to her fate.

If he agreed, he was signing his own death warrant.

'Hey,' Dictys called. 'Where are you going?'

'Medusa seduced Poseidon in the Temple of Athene.' Perseus had only straws to clutch at, and his voice carried far more confidence than he was feeling. 'Who knows, old friend? Athene might just be in the mood to help me win this quest.'

* * *

Darkness cloaked the island. A soft breeze was blowing from the south, bringing the scent of wild thyme from the hills, and lavender. In the temple precinct, smoke from Athene's fire swirled. The leaves of her sacred pear tree rustled, her sacred owl, a poor chained bird, hooted mournfully, and flames from the torches set high upon the walls danced and flickered.

'You come seeking guidance on how to kill Medusa.'

The priest stepped out of the blackness, his white robe fluttering round his ankles in the breeze. Perseus jumped.

'It will not be easy, my child. Her haunt is a cave far, far from here, in the Land of the Hyperboreans.'

The priest's bony fingers made strange shapes in the air, over and over and over. Perseus shivered.

'To reach the cave before the moon is full, you must travel on Hermes' winged sandals, wearing Hades' helmet of invisibility.'

'That's—impossible.'

'Nothing is impossible, my child.' Teeth showed white in the darkness. It might have been a smile. Then again, it might not. 'To kill Medusa, you must avert your gaze using Athene's mirrored shield, and you must—listen carefully—cut off the creature's head with Hephaestus' own sword.'

'Is that all?'

He'd meant it sarcastically. He did not expect the priest to say, 'No. That is not all.'

Weakness washed into Perseus' knees.

'You will also need gold, my child. Much gold.' He bowed. 'The goddess Athene has spoken. You may go.'

The priest waited until Perseus was well clear of the temple grounds before turning to the man standing in the shadows. 'Satisfied?' he murmured.

'More than,' Polydectes said, pressing silver into the priest's outstretched palm.

* * *

The house of Dictys was on the western side of the island, as different from the palace as Dictys was from his brother. Bathed by the setting sun and calmed by the lapping of the ocean, this was the only home Perseus had known. Not so Danaë. Imprisoned by the one man who should have cared for and protected her, she'd understood that her only chance of escape was to bear a son. Pregnancy was not enough. Her father would have force-fed her aborticides. Burning bush, stonecrop, hedge hyssop, any one of which could have killed her, along with her unborn baby. But if she had a child, a boy, then who else could the father be, except a god?

At first, watching the sun streaming through the opening in the roof, she had thought to claim Apollo as her lover. Then storm clouds darkened the sky, and Danaë knew that Zeus' thunderbolt was the most powerful weapon she could wield.

The gods had indeed answered her prayers, and all she'd needed was a willing male. Not the insurmountable problem that it seemed.

By balancing a stool upon a chest, the young princess had been able to climb out through the open window in the ceiling, skim across the roof, drop down into the palace and then into the city of Argos itself. She had, of course, considered running. But the King feared the Oracle's prediction so badly that he would have tracked her down and killed her. No. The son of an innkeeper, dark of hair and light of eye, was Danaë's escape route. Concealing her pregnancy under her voluminous robes, praise be to Hera, the child was a boy.

'Hermes? Hades? Haephestus? *Athene?*' She watched her son pace the courtyard in despair 'To seek one item is absurd enough, but four? And gold? "Much" gold? I've failed before I've even started, and the moon will be full in less than two weeks.'

Danaë looked from Perseus to Dictys, and her heart ached. Perseus, as dark of hair and light of eye as the innkeeper's son, couldn't wring a chicken's neck, much less slay a monster. Yet he would lay down his life for her. Not, of course, that she would let him! She could drug him. Take a boat. Flee to some place Polydectes couldn't find them, and he was, in any case, too fat and lazy to even try. But the other man she loved, dear honourable Dictys, could not flee. As the king's only male relative, he was responsible for the people of Serifos, should anything befall his brother.

She leaned forward.

'Tell me again, Perseus, everything the priest said to you in the temple.'

* * *

Tonight the moon would reach its zenith, and the wedding preparations were in full swing. A public banquet in the *agora*, where an ox and five sheep had been slaughtered in readiness, along with a wild boar that Polydectes had hunted down and killed himself. Actually, that wasn't strictly true. His spear had missed its mark, but the lackey who'd stepped in to kill it for him was in no position to contradict the story, since his tongue had been ripped out.

In honour of his new queen, the king had garlands hung, commanded rare scented oils for her bridal bath, and indeed was feeling so generous, that he had spared this week's prisoners the traditional slow death by strangulation. Instead, he'd had them buried up to their necks in sand and run a chariot race across. Those who lived would be pardoned, he'd decreed. No one was the least bit surprised when none survived.

Meanwhile, in the run up to the ceremony, while Danaë prayed to Zeus and Hera like she'd never prayed before, Polydectes prepared for the nuptials in the time-honoured manner of bridegrooms everywhere. He and his cronies—sorry, ruling council—locked themselves in the king's own private quarters and set about getting very, very drunk.

So perhaps it was not surprising, among the fanfares, drums and trumpets, that, at first, no one noticed the little boat slipping into the harbour.

On the other hand, a cry of *'I have it! I have the head of Medusa!'* tended to capture their attention.

'The King!' Perseus was out of breath from running to the palace. 'I must see Polydectes!'

'Sorry, sir. The King's orders.' The guard's hand hovered over his sword in warning. 'He is not to be disturbed.'

'I can vouch for that.'

Dictys had been sitting by the door, head in his hands, when Perseus came rushing up. His cheeks were hollow, his chin unshaven. There were dark circles beneath his eyes, and if Perseus did not know better, he'd say that was the outline of a dagger beneath his old friend's tunic.

'I've been trying to seek an audience with my brother for several hours. Wait, wait, wait! Did you just say—?' Dictys jumped up. 'You really bring the thing my brother asked? You bring the head of Medusa?'

'I do.' Perseus held up the leather sack, which was far heavier than he'd imagined a human head to weigh. Then again, the monster wasn't exactly human, was it?

'Then let him pass,' Dictys ordered the guards, and there was an authority in his voice Perseus had not heard before. 'Let him pass at once!'

The soldiers knew the story. Everybody did. Polydectes had been bragging for the past fortnight about the fool's errand Perseus had run. Journey to the Land of the Hyperboreans? The Hyperboreans were Celts, for Hades' sake. The very name meant Beyond the North Wind; that was a two-week trek to start with. Plus he'd need Athene's mirrored shield to complete his quest, along with Hermes' own winged sandals and the smith god's personal sword. *After*, ha, ha, ha, journeying through the Underworld to bring back Hades' cloak of invisibility. Oh, and did the King mention the gold the Oracle said he'd need? *Much* gold? Ha, ha, ha, and ha again.

The guards exchanged glances.

'Hercules was set twelve seemingly impossible labours,' one ventured nervously. 'He completed those without a hitch.'

'The gods on Olympus *are* capricious,' another guard acknowledged. 'They've been known to help mortals in their quests more than once.'

'Hercules a case in point,' the first one said.

'Jason, when he went in search of the Golden Fleece.'

'Odysseus, on his return from Troy.'

The list went on.

No, the sticking point, as the guards saw it, was the gold. But hey. If the gods were with Perseus on this venture, gold would hardly be a problem, would it? Look at Midas.

'Very well.' The guards stepped aside, knowing, realistically, they had little choice. If their decision to admit Perseus displeased the king, they were dead. If they failed to admit him, they were dead.

Perseus pushed through, vaguely aware that Dictys was holding back the soldiers who'd tried to follow.

'This is my brother's business, a private issue,' he commanded. 'Keep back, men.'

When the soldiers did finally fling wide the door to Polydectes' quarters, the sight was not what they expected.

At the far end of the chamber, Perseus was stuffing something heavy back into his leather sack.

Around the table, piled high with figs and fish and bread and wine, the king and his drinking cronies sat as stiff as starfish.

'Holy Hades,' Dictys gasped. 'They've all been turned to stone.'

* * *

'Oh, my love.'

The past snapped away. Perseus was back on the roof terrace of his palace, high above the citadel with its long, steep ramp and Lion Gate. The voice was that of his wife, Andromeda.

'I knew you slew the Gorgon. Heavens, the whole world knows the story, just as they know you saved me after my father chained me to the rocks to feed some dreadful sea monster. You are, after all, the son of Zeus.' She planted a tender kiss on his cheek. 'But this is the first time in all our years together that you have ever spoken of your heroic deeds.'

Heroic? It was all Perseus could do to stop from laughing.

If only she knew…

Knew the sea monster was nothing more sinister than a series of harsh storms that had been battering the coast where her father was king. That his arrival coincided with its passing, and that his rescue of a naked, terrified young woman was what any man would have done.

Or that he was the son of a humble inn-keeper, not the King of the

Olympians.

Much less that the truth about the monster was a far cry from the story that had passed into the history books…

* * *

'Tell me again, Perseus, everything the priest said to you in the temple.'

Even in the face of adversity, his mother remained calm. That, he'd thought, was the true mark of beauty and of courage.

And so he'd repeated his encounter in the precinct, over and over, down to the finest detail. For several minutes afterwards, maybe as long as an hour, Danaë sat in silence. Finally, she said, 'It is as I thought. The priest is our friend. He was feeding you clues.'

The shield of Athene, she said, proved that.

'It means the priest is protecting you. That you wear Hades' helmet of invisibility suggests you leave under cover of darkness, and Hermes' winged sandals means you should make haste. Signifying that the king's men will be waiting in ambush if you do not leave tonight.'

'Even so,' Dictys protested, 'the Land of the Hyperboreans lies in the cold lands to the north. Assuming the lad managed to reach it before the full moon, where would he start looking?'

'When the priest talked of a mirror, I think he was saying, *look behind you*, and the part about the gold? *Much gold.* He stressed the point.'

Danaë believed he was alluding to the shower of gold in which her son was conceived.

'He's telling you, go back to Argos.' She slipped the gold medallion from around her neck, the talisman that proved she was the King of Argos' daughter. 'On the southern corner of the *agora* you will find an inn with the sign of two triangles above the door. Ask for Krios. If anyone can help you, he will, and take this.' She pressed the medallion into his hand. 'This will smooth your path.'

Of all the scenarios Perseus had imagined when he set sail that night—and to be honest, there were so many, he lost track—seeing his own image when he walked into the Inn of the Two Triangles was not one of them.

'Danaë?' Krios asked, when he showed him the medallion. 'She's alive! Is she well? Is she happy?'

Perseus found himself lost for words. Krios was his father, and Krios had loved her. He could hardly believe it. This son of an inn keeper, now keeping the inn himself, had known the identity of his mystery lover all along, yet kept her secret for almost two decades! Of course, he was married by then. Had two strapping sons and a pubescent daughter. But the feelings he'd had for his first love never dimmed. Of course he would help!

Because who hadn't heard rumours of the fearsome creature who lived up in the hills, in a cave surrounded by creatures she'd turned to stone..?

With an embrace that left both men moist of eye, Krios gave him directions.

* * *

After saying goodbye to his mother on Serifos, Perseus embarked on an adventure that offered more new experiences in six days than he'd had in his lifetime.

It was, for instance, his first time aboard a fully fledged merchant ship, rather than a fishing boat or island hopper. Unlike most ships, this galley sailed by night (by night!) and, built to transport dispatches and cargo such as fresh food and horses that required rapid transportation, it was very much designed for speed. Standing on the prow, face to the wind, Perseus felt this was the closest he would ever come to flying.

There was also his first experience of a big city. A great city. Wide avenues, soaring temples, apartment blocks five storeys high. The market was sprawling, and bustling, offering delicacies he'd only heard about, like smoked sturgeon's eggs, larks' tongues, and spices from beyond the Black Sea. The squares were shaded by plane trees, populated by so many men in fine clothes and fancy footwear that he'd felt underdressed—and the theatre! Oh, my. How many people could cram into that? What dramas were played out on the stage?

But there was no time for sight-seeing. Following Krios' directions (another new experience, coming face to face with his father!), Perseus set off into hills, as far removed from barren little Serifos as could be imagined. Vast green meadows opened before him, brimming with wild flowers and herbs, their scent as heady as any incense. He negotiated precipices, rivers, canyons and forests, heard wolves howl in the distance, smelled wild mountain sage, watched eagles soar above peaks capped with snow.

Something else he'd never seen.

As the track opened into rugged, scrub-strewn hills, the trees changed. Oaks became feathery pines. The air became thinner. The wind sounded like a young woman singing.

There was a bend in the path. A clearing. A stream. A place of such unimaginable beauty that he didn't immediately notice the grey stone image of a man. A man in the battle dress of the Spartans, right down to the helmet and kilt…

Perseus' heart jumped to his mouth. His skin became clammy. His tongue dry. To his shame, his sword was shaking in his hand.

What madness was this? Whatever possessed him to think he could kill a fiend that turned the world's most hardened warrior to stone?

Run. There is no shame in defeat. Shame comes from suicide, which this must surely be, if he—

'You are sick?'

The wind had dropped. Too late he realized the sound was no breeze, but a song. A siren song, luring men to their deaths—

'N-no.'

He dared not turn round.

'Are you sure now?' Her voice was heavily accented. 'Your face is whiter than chalk, and your poor teeth are chattering. Fever, is it?'

'The c-climb. It's s-steep. I'm sorry, you must excuse me. I…I must be on my way.'

'Is that so?' Her laugh was light and teasing. 'And where exactly might that be, up in these hills leading to nowhere?'

As she stepped forward, he saw the creature's shadow reflected on the stony ground. The mass of wild snakes that was her head.

'I…um.' His knees could barely support him. 'Lost.'

That's right. He had lost. And because of his stupidity, his mother had lost everything. Dictys, too.

But Polydectes? Polydectes had won. As he knew he would, when he'd laid down his terms.

'I don't know which land you're from, stranger, but where I come from, men who tangle with unfamiliar forests and ravines don't usually carry unsheathed swords.' Her lilt was mesmerizing, even while she mocked him. 'You look to me more like a man in need of a drink. Come on.' The shadow beckoned. 'Inside with you.'

From the corner of his eye, Perseus made out a stone dragon, a stone porcupine, children, birds… If only his shield was polished metal, not leather. Mirrored to deflect her gaze.

'Come along with you, now. I don't bite.'

His last thought, as he turned to face the inevitable was, *until now, I hadn't believed in dragons.*

* * *

'Me, neither.'

'Excuse me?'

Something rushed past him, lithe and slim, and flung its arms round the stone creature's neck. 'You said, you didn't believe in dragons, I said, me neither. But this is what I imagined they'd look like.'

Perseus didn't know what surprised him the most. That he'd spoken his final words aloud.

Or that they were not his last words.

'I don't understand,' he blurted. 'Why am I not turned to stone?' The sun through the trees blinded him. 'Are you not Medusa?'

'The name's Mettalise, but no one round here seems able, or willing, to pronounce it properly. Medusa will do fine.'

Shielding his eyes with his hands, he saw they were not snakes at all. Rather, they were wild curls that tumbled over her shoulders, copper red in colour. And she was—or had been—very lovely indeed.

'Sweet Hera in heaven.' He sheathed his sword. 'What happened to you, girl?'

For yes, her skin was every bit as scaly as folklore said, but Perseus had seen such scars before. These had been made by fire.

'Oh, it's my life story you're wanting now!'

'It is,' he said, and there was no reciprocal laugh in his voice. 'Because I want to know why Polydectes sent me to kill you.'

* * *

The story was bad. As bad as it came.

Mettalise was on a ship bound for Athens, when a storm blew up. The helmsman spotted a light. Put into what he thought was safe harbour, only to discover that what he'd seen was a wrecking beacon. Even as the crew and her tribespeople stumbled ashore, she knew it would end badly. She was right.

'Every man cut down. My father, my brothers, my grandfather, too.' Her voice was barely a whisper. 'Ten years on, and the screams of the helmsman still haunt me.'

As the only woman on board, she was spared slaughter. Her fate was to be dragged to the city, along with the gold and treasures looted from the ship, and thrown at the feet of the king.

'Polydectes decreed that I should serve the goddess Athene in her temple, where he would seek pleasure whenever he felt like it. Starting,' she added, 'that night.'

Perseus tried not to think of his mother with this man—

'Resistance only enraged him, but I had to fight back.'

In punishment, he smashed her face against one of the stone pillars, breaking her cheekbone, her nose and her jaw. Punched her so hard, her ribs broke, then threw her head first into the cauldron in which burned the eternal flame.

'Left me for dead, he did, but we Celtish women do not die easy. The young acolyte who found me said the coals cauterized the wounds and most probably saved my life. At the expense, though, of permanent disfigurement.'

An understatement, if ever there was one. What was left of her face was twisted and withered. The skin, like her hands, neck and arms, was shrivelled and scaly, from the pattern of burns.

'The acolyte also said the king would finish the job if he knew I'd survived. At great personal risk, he put me on a boat early next morning. That boat was bound for the Peloponnese. And without health, help or finance, here, as you see, I remain.'

The young acolyte eventually took over as priest, but that night clearly stayed with him. Was it he who'd started the legend? Put it to people that, in retribution for seducing Poseidon in Athene's own temple, the goddess changed Mettalise—Medusa—into a hideous creature? Reptilian-style burns could easily lead to curls being transformed into living snakes, and to further protect her, spread the rumour that Medusa made her home in the Land of the Hyperboreans?

Of course, he could not possibly have foreseen that the girl herself would have added to the legend, by sculpting rocks round the cave she'd made her home.

Polydectes would not have swallowed the story. On the other hand, he would not trail such a distance to silence her, but when the opportunity arose, he grabbed the chance with both hands. He knew Perseus would kill Medusa to save his own mother. Equally, he knew he could not possibly journey to the Land of the Hyperboreans and back in two weeks. There could be no better outcome. The witness to his brutality would be eliminated. No less than the King of Argos' daughter would be his wife. Her bastard brat exiled for ever.

'How do you manage up here, all alone?' Perseus asked.

'You think I'm not happy? Look around. Have you ever seen a lovelier spot? My cave is warm, even in winter. I hunt small game, I fish. But also I heal people, using the old Celtish ways, though for obvious reasons, I wear a mask. Made of kidskin', she added. 'In return, they leave food for me. Clothes. Sometimes animal pelts to snuggle under.' Her laughter rippled through the pines. 'They believe their offerings prevent them being turned into stone, and who knows? Maybe they're right.'

The stone was soft, she said, and easy to carve. 'It's incredibly therapeutic. You should try it.'

Then the laughter died, and a tear trickled from her one good eye.

'The king is the monster, Perseus. Not me.'

'He is,' he said, taking her hands. 'And I need to save my mother from him, as well as other young women like you.'

Not to mention people executed on nothing more than a whim.

'Do you indeed?'

Medusa led him inside her cave, where the walls had been painted with bright vivid dyes, and garlands of fresh flowers scented the air. She poured wine into a vessel shaped like a bull's head, complete with gilded horns and gold ring through its nose. Not all the locals were poor, then?

'The question is, Perseus.' She poured the wine over an altar at the mouth of the cave, and the libation trickled like blood. 'How far are you willing to go?'

* * *

How far indeed?

Standing on the terrace of his palace, looking out across the city of Mycenae that he had founded personally, Perseus pondered the morality again.

His compassion for the woman whose family was butchered, while she herself was raped, beaten, vilified and disfigured, was uncontested. But his loyalties, then as now, lay with his family. The only thing that would save his mother from a life of horror was Medusa's head. He could not afford to let sympathy stand in the way of her suffering, or betray the friend who'd opened his house and his heart to them. Dictys deserved more. Danaë certainly did.

There was only one thing he could do.

Give Polydectes what he'd asked for—

'Is that who you grieve for?' his wife asked, sensing the sadness that engulfed him. 'Your old friend, Dictys?'

In spite of himself, Perseus smiled. 'I sincerely hope not.'

To the best of his knowledge, Dictys was still ruling Serifos, wisely and kindly, with Danaë at his side.

'It is as I told you, Andromeda. Someone I knew long before I met you.'

There was an ache in his heart. In his stomach. Poor, sweet Mettalise…

'I can give you poison,' she'd said. 'If that is what you truly want.'

'It is,' he'd replied.

A coward's weapon, perhaps. But effective. On every level.

He had needed help administering it, of course, but slipping into Serifos under cover of darkness, the priest needed little persuasion. For had it not been his own idea? That the monster be slain with Hephaestus' own sword?

In other words, turn Polydectes' own viciousness upon himself.

The king trusted the priest. He'd paid him handsomely to betray his bride's son. Had no reason to doubt the wine that he brought, or the herbs he had added to increase the king's potency.

With Dictys stationed outside the door, an unsuspecting accomplice, who could doubt the truth of what happened? He, the guards, they'd seen it for themselves.

Perseus sailing into the harbour, a heavy sack in his hand.

His bursting in on the king and his cronies.

All six turned to stone.

Who would even *suspect* their corpses were already in the throes of rigor mortis?

Or that his entrance was timed to perfection?

With Dictys ruling the island, the people of Serifos would be well served. Danaë would be happy. Medusa could live the life that she wanted.

A life that brought the peace that she craved.

Perseus' fame had grown after that. Son of Zeus, killer of monsters, rescuer of sacrificial maidens, how could it not? By the time he was twenty, he'd apparently travelled through Hades, tamed Pegasus the winged horse, and killed his own grandfather with (of all things!) a quoit, thus fulfilling the Oracle's prophecy, which was hogwash. He was in Athens when his grandfather died.

But throughout everything—his marriage, his sons, his founding Mycenae—he'd remained in touch with Medusa. Sent presents, food, soft boots. New chisels!

And now she was dead. Passed away in her sleep. And while Perseus mourned, there was still one task left to him, to ensure the tale passed into legend.

For as much as he'd love to lay her to rest here, in a magnificent tomb outside the city, he knew he must travel south, three days' march. To bury her in an anonymous pit.

Where only eagles would watch over Medusa's grave.

And stone dragons stand guard over her bones.

The Longboat Cove Murders

Dan Trelawney was the first. A kind-hearted, hard-working father of three, he was the landlord of *The Fighting Cocks*, a 17th century coaching inn complete with beams, stables and a resident ghost, who died foiling a robbery in the early hours of a bitterly cold January morning. The most popular man for miles around, practically the entire population of Longboat Cove turned out for his funeral.

Arnold Warne was next.

Arnold was everything Dan Trelawney was not. For one thing, he was seventy-four to Dan's forty-three. He was also foul-mouthed, unkempt, miserly and bad-mannered, a man firmly of the opinion that not only did the world owe him a living, but that the world consistently welched on its debt. No one—not even his son who'd moved as far away as humanly possible, to Brisbane, Australia—mourned Arnold's passing.

Having said that, it was still pretty rotten luck that he'd happened to disturb a burglar ransacking his cottage during Dan's funeral (sadly, an all too common occurrence), and fell headlong down the stairs in his rush to confront the intruder.

In fact, it was only when nineteen-year-old Jenna Kestle was killed that the residents of Longboat Cove began to wonder.

* * *

Set in the land of King Arthur, Camelot, Merlin and magic, Longboat Cove was typically Cornish. A small, hilly peninsula jutting into the Atlantic, it boasted a harbour with stone piers on the eastern side and a sandy beach to the west, both protected by rugged black cliffs topped by swathes of sea squills, sheepsbit and tufts of pink thrift. With the surf pounding the rocks and puffins bobbing like corks on the water, Longboat Cove was just about as picturesque as it came.

A profusion of megaliths testified that settlement here stretched back to the late Stone Age, with nearby tin having been mined from around 2,000 BC, and a port that was probably built by the Romans. The present-day town remained the same tangle of steep, cobbled streets from Medieval times, many of which were way too narrow for cars. Planters and window boxes spilling geraniums, petunias, phlox and lobelia were happy to encroach on the precious space even further.

Popular year-round with tourists, bird watchers, history buffs and walkers, the town was dominated by the solid, square-towered Church of St. Piran, and fronted by a bustle of gift shops, tea rooms and creaking inns catering for the thousands of visitors entranced by clotted cream teas, the sound of gulls shrieking overhead, cats snoozing on what seemed like every other windowsill, and ancient stonework that was virtually obscured throughout the summer by wild froths of wisteria, clematis and rambling roses. A fragrance, incidentally, that was engaged in permanent battle with the fresh, salty sea air.

Longboat Cove's other claim to fame—indeed its main claim to fame these days—was a vibrant artistic community, who found its traffic-free isolation almost as appealing as its sunsets and the quality of its light.

In fact, until Dan Trelawney died, life here had been good to the point of idyllic.

'Bollocks.' Ellen Pascoe slammed down her coffee cup. 'What planet have you been living on?'

Tamara continued to stir her sugar—three lumps—without looking up. 'What do you mean?'

'I mean, Tam, that we've been battered by freak storms three years running. Record tidal surges flooded the waterfront twice last month, a metre deep each time.' Ellen ticked the disasters off on her fingers. 'Landslides swept away a massive section of cliff path, leaving two cottages teetering on the edge of oblivion and rendering eight more uninhabitable.' Hers included. 'The post office and police station have closed thanks to government cutbacks, the Sandpiper Gallery caught fire, and if that's not enough, we've seen more violence in ten days than we've seen in ten years. If that's idyllic, I'd hate to see what horrible looks like.'

A broad shadow fell over the table and pulled up a chair. 'What am I missing?'

'Nothing, Davey. Absolutely nothing.' Tamara selected another lump of sugar, dunked it in her coffee until the bottom half turned brown, then popped it in her mouth. 'My sister's riding her usual hobby horses of politics and global warming.'

'Climate change,' Ellen snapped. 'And it wasn't your home that went skidding into the sea.'

'Wasn't your home, either. You were only renting it until your divorce comes through, and excuse me, but that cottage didn't skid anywhere. Well.' She licked the sugar off her fingertip. 'Not until the next landslip.'

'You think it's funny, do you?'

'Girls.' All their lives, it seemed Davey Calloway had been pulling them apart. In the playground, on the tennis courts, on the dance floor, on the beach. Dark and rugged as the Cornish cliffs, Ellen could never understand why his wife walked out on him.

Or why Tamara never married him.

'Once again, my little sister missed the point,' she said, pouring him a cup of coffee from the urn. 'I was merely saying what a rough ride it's been lately, and what with Dan dying the way that he did, and then Jenna, suddenly this town feels—' She broke off.

'Unsafe?'

'Cursed.'

That was the word she was looking for. Cursed.

Her eyes scanned the back room of this tiny town library. Stone built, low beams, stepped floor, a hundred years ago this used to be the schoolhouse. Now it was just another institution hanging on by its fingertips.

And another fight they'd probably lose.

'There's more than weather eroding this land, Davey. There's a sense of evil pervading the Cove, I can feel it.'

'Oh, please.' Tamara rolled her heavily kohled eyes. 'Bad things happen all the time, Ell. It's called life.'

'Armed robberies, burglary—'

'Without a police presence, criminals see us as a soft target. Right, Davey?'

'Doesn't explain Jenna Kestle, Tam.' His face clouded. 'Poor kid.'

'Exactly,' Ellen said. 'Robbery gone wrong, burglary gone wrong, now sex attack gone wrong.'

'Over on Ibiza, for Chrissakes.' Tamara took a sip of her coffee and grimaced. Barista it most certainly was not. 'You can't legislate for getting strangled, trying to defend yourself from a rapist.'

'Don't be so bloody flippant,' Ellen began, but this time it wasn't Davey Calloway who stopped her.

'Morning, me handsomes.' The broad accent and gnarled old face were at odds with the sharp tailored suit, but when pilchards were called pilchards, there was no money in fishing. Call them sardines, and it's a whole different story. 'Not started without Clacky Bill, have ee?'

Clacky was Cornish for the sticky, chewy foodstuffs to which William Bolitho was partial.

'Not a chance, Bill.'

Once a month, local business owners gathered to debate issues to lay before the Town Council. Antique shops, cafés, beachwear outlets, pubs, even Davey Calloway's motor mechanic shed were represented. A casual Rotary if you like, with attendance varying according to commitments. Most times, though, the turn-out averaged at around a dozen, giving it the nickname of the "Jury Room".

Ellen poured another cup of coffee and handed it over. 'We were discussing Jenna.'

'Tragic, tha'.' Bill shook his grizzled head. 'Young maid can't e'en go on holiday and be safe.'

'Jenna? Last time I saw her, poor love, she and I were pulling paintings out of the Sandpiper like it was the first day of the January sales.'

Rain or shine, cold or hot, Maggie Bawden wore white from her swan neck to her toes. Of indeterminate age, immaculately made up and Spanxed to within an inch of her life, what better advert for the family dry-cleaning firm?

'Oh lord, it's so sad.' Tears welled in remembrance. '*Would you look at us, Maggie!* Jenna was giggling like a schoolgirl when she said that, wasn't she always? What a live wire, that girl.'

Pretty with it too, Ellen thought, picturing Jenna's streaming red hair, legs like a colt, and with the same profusion of freckles on her nose, she was the spitting image of her mother, in the days when Ellen used to sit next to Kath in geography, swapping homework and boy stories, toffees and mags, before the ferryman's son got her pregnant and Kath had to drop out of school.

'*We look like a pair of chimney sweeps!*' Maggie's lips pursed. 'That was the last thing Jenna said to me, because then the Dutchman came rushing downstairs with the fire extinguisher, face like bloody thunder, shooing us out as though we were stealing his precious daubs, instead of saving them from the fire. It's his fault I never had a chance to speak to Jenna again. Lousy, rotten bastard.'

'Cummas zon, Maggie.' A calloused hand covered hers and squeezed. 'Thee can't be blaming no Dutchman for that.'

'I damn well can, in fact I damn well do. He never even *thanked* us, Bill. How ungrateful's that? Just a nod and a growl, then he's locking the door behind us and running round like a dog chasing its tail, while we stand on the street, coughing and shivering and covered in soot, and now Jenna's dead and his paintings are safe, where's the justice in that?'

'Here.' Tamara passed her a tissue. Maggie blew.

'Stress brings out the worst in people,' Ellen said gently. 'Artists tend to pour their souls into their paintings. The effort drains them and makes them moody. I'm sure Mr. Reynders didn't mean anything by it.'

Her job—more accurately, her vocation and her passion—was art restoration. Mostly Victorian oils, since these were the most plentiful. But cleaning portraits and restoring landscapes to their original glory gave Ellen a deeper insight than most into how passionate an artist could be about their work. And how volatile they became at times.

'The Sandpiper Gallery only opened at Christmas,' she reminded the group. 'After weeks of prep and restoration, to see all his hard work go up in flames must have been soul-destroying.'

'There you go, exaggerating again.' Tamara threw her manicured hands in the air. 'The gallery hardly went up in flames, Ell.'

'Electrical short, wasn't it?' Davey asked.

'Serve 'im right for rushing the job.' Bill ripped open a packet of custard creams and took two. 'If 'ee'd hired a proper electrician, 'stead of one of his Dutch friends, it wouldn't ha' catched fire in the first place.' He let out a contemptuous sniff. 'Electrics on the Continent inn't the same as over 'ere. Everyburdy know zat.'

'We weren't to know it wasn't serious.' Maggie eased her feet out of strappy heels that most women stopped wearing at thirty. And certainly not during the winter. 'Jenna and I were shooting the breeze—ever the chatterbox, her—when we saw the smoke in the gallery.' She began massaging her bunion. 'Soon as we realized there was no one inside, we ran over and started yanking the paintings off the walls, yelling our bloody heads off to raise the alarm.'

'Ay, and thanks to 'ee two, it were catched in time.'

Their shouts alerted Maarten Reynders, who'd been doing what he always did. Locked himself away upstairs while he worked.

Another couple of local business owners trickled in to take their places at the table. Ellen hardly noticed.

'Jenna's dead and his paintings are safe, where's the justice in that?' Maggie said, but that was the trouble. When was life ever just? It's not like TV. More often than not, the good guys lose, because evil is strong and black hearts are determined.

In this case, there was no good and no bad, and, thanks to the reactions of two bystanders, damage was so minimal that it didn't even warrant a claim on the insurance.

But then, a few days later, Dan Trelawney was stabbed, Arnold Warne fell down the stairs, and Jenna Kestle was murdered on a little Spanish island.

Rarely, Ellen thought, had the scales of justice balanced more unevenly.

* * *

Contrary to what most people assumed, the town was not named after the boats that were stowed or towed by sailing ships to ferry crew, supplies and water to shore and back.

Not that Longboat Cove hadn't seen its fair share of *those*. From the early 1700s to the late 1800s, when taxes on imports were so exorbitantly high that smuggling became a way of life, contraband was discharged with such regularity, it was a wonder the wagon tracks weren't worn six feet deep. Particularly when rocky coastlines were such a magnet for shipwrecks, rendering lonely little peninsulas perfect for clandestine landings in a nimble rowing boat.

But, as Hamlet said, 'therein lies the rub.'

Because when you're a Viking longship, looking to make a nice, juicy raid on an unsuspecting community to sack their lands and pillage their treasures, those rocks must have come as a nasty surprise.

As, no doubt, did the hospitality of the locals, who didn't take kindly to having their village burned, their women raped and their treasures carried off by a bunch of uncouth strangers. They slaughtered every Viking who staggered from the wreckage, then set their dragon carvings at the far end of the headland, like heads upon a pole, to deter any future Norsemen who might have it in their minds to come a-calling.

None did. And even though this was down to Viking raids being confined to northern Britain for reasons of logistics, it made these people heroes.

Twelve centuries down the line, standing beside the scaled longship, low winter sun gleaming off the bronze, Ellen had never been more conscious of her heritage. Or more proud. For three thousand years, her ancestors had lived and died on this peninsula. Fishing, mining, even smuggling to survive and then, in more recent times, tourism and art. Now the baton of responsibility had been passed to her generation. The weight was heavier than she imagined.

'I remember the day they unveiled this sculpture.'

'Davey?'

'You'd been married a year by then, and were living the high life in London.'

His hands were deep in his pockets, his collar was turned up, and his breath was white on air that was rich with that uniquely Cornish blend of fudge and pasties, crabs and seaweed, all mingled up with oak chips from the smoke house.

'Early August, though you wouldn't know it. The wind was howling off the Atlantic like it was March, the rain slanting in sideways like you wouldn't believe. The band, poor sods, were soaked to their marrow, the ice cream stalls had to be battened down before they took off to the moors, and the sky was blacker than the bottom of a coal mine. Those hardy souls who'd turned out for the unveiling took shelter in the pub, cheering from the window while the Mayor struggled to cut the ribbon. Before a power cut took out all the lights, leaving us toasting the occasion with warm beer.' He smiled. 'See what you missed?'

She watched the acrobatics of the gulls following the fishing boats as they returned to harbour. Stamped her feet against the cold. When you're young, small towns are stifling. You want—*need*—to break free of their grip. See exactly how bright those lights are out there. Feel the world's pulse throb through your veins, and show this inward-looking bunch there's something better beyond these suffocating boundaries.

Then prove to them, of course, that you were right.

'I missed a lot of things, Davey.' She returned his smile. 'That's why I came back.'

'And the good folk of Longboat Cove are very glad you did. Some—

' he leaned his shoulder against the plinth and crossed his arms '—more than others. Now suppose we go in out of the cold, I buy you a pie and a pint, and you tell me what's putting that ugly frown on your face?'

* * *

Fronting the harbour, the *Crab & Lobster* was a quintessential smugglers inn, all higgledy-piggledy stone flag floors, oak beams, exposed brickwork and roaring log fires. With its heavy thatched roof, whitewashed walls and tiny windows, the only thing it lacked from the outside was a rumble of illicit barrels and the clack of a wooden leg on the cobbles.

Inside it was fast forward six centuries, with the stables converted into five-star luxury accommodations featuring marble vanity tops and high four-poster beds, and a restaurant that employed a world-class chef.

'What happened to the pie and a pint?'

'Wine goes better with a hearty Cornish *bouillabaisse,* don't you think?'

She did think. Especially a crisp, dry sauvignon.

Davey had wangled a table by the fire, and, warm as toast, Ellen pushed up her sleeves. The place had come up a lot in the eight years she'd been away, and to her delight, the menu was as sophisticated as it was varied, with the food locally sourced, perfectly showcased and excellently priced. Not too bad on the tastebuds, either.

'So then. This is my end of the bargain.' Davey tucked into his stew of lobster, red mullet, mussels and prawns. 'Your turn.'

Ellen turned her eyes to the crackling logs. Watched flames lick round the splintered edges and sparks fly up the chimney. 'Outsiders.'

The spoon paused midway to his mouth. Only tourists tackled *bouillabaisse* with a fork. 'Of all the issues I thought might be responsible for that ugly frown—things like, y'know, homelessness, marriage break-up, coming back, starting over—somehow "outsiders" didn't make it to my shortlist.'

She pulled off a chunk of crispy baguette and challenged the laugh in his eyes. 'Shouldn't ask the question, if you're not going to like the answer.'

'Funny, your father said exactly the same thing to me once. Right after I told him I'd proposed marriage to one of his daughters.' It was Davey's turn to stare into the glowing amber logs. 'Don't suppose you even remember.'

Oh, she remembered right enough.

That was the night David Calloway broke her heart.

'There were twenty, thirty of us down on the beach,' he said. 'The usual suspects. Someone, I think it was Gary, had brought his guitar, and we all sang and drank beer and told jokes and swapped stories while sausages sizzled on an open bonfire. Then there was a lull. I took you to one side.'

Yes, he did. And the stars were twinkling brighter than diamonds, and the light of a three-quarters moon reflected white on the sea.

I have a mind to ask one of Joe Pascoe's daughters to marry me. I've known her all my life, for God's sake. Loved her as long as I can remember.' He'd paused at that point. Grinned. *'Even if she does fight like a cat with her sister.*

No one forgets that conversation in a hurry.

So what do you think, Ellen? I said. *If I asked one of Joe Pascoe's daughters to marry me, what do you think she'd say?*

For all it had been a warm summer's night, everyone in t-shirts, vests and shorts, a chill had crept into her bones.

'Long time ago,' Davey was saying. 'Wouldn't expect you to remember your reply, but I do. I remember it clearly. You said—'

'I said, *Don't worry, Davey. Tamara will snap your hand off.'*

'Right.' He laid his spoon carefully on the side of his plate. 'Then you turned your back and walked away, and ten minutes later you're standing on a wooden crate, catching everyone's attention by tapping on an empty beer bottle with a fork, and announcing your engagement to some city slicker I'd never even met. Which was when I told your father I'd just made the most pitiful proposal in the history of marriage—'

'*What?*'

'To which Joe Pascoe said, shouldn't ask a question, boy, if—'

Her? Wine spilled on the cloth. Not Tam..?

'—you know the rest, of course, and the daft thing was, I thought City Boy was just some casual date. A lame duck you'd asked along, because he was at a loose end on holiday.'

Ellen wanted to scream. She wanted to cry. She wanted to slap David Calloway till he was red in the face, kiss him, kick him, throw his dinner in his lap. Hold him tight and never let him go.

Damn those Cornish genes that mean you never let it show.

'Yes, poor you. So heartbroken that—remind me again, how long before you married that librarian from Dublin? Five weeks? Six?'

'Marrying on the rebound was the worst thing I could have done. *I'm not sure you ever loved me*, she said the night she dragged her suitcase from the loft. To tell her I never had would have been hurtful, and I'd hurt her enough. But stacking her books and boxes in the back of her car, I knew I'd never see her again. And the saddest part was, I didn't care.'

'Which brings us back full circle.' Ellen waved a saffron potato on the end of her fork. 'To outsiders. And what bothers me about them, Davey, what really bothers me, is that we still view them as Vikings. Intruders, invaders, not to be trusted. People who we can lay the blame on for our troubles, instead of taking responsibility for our own actions and facing up to our shortcomings.'

'Hello…? Anybody listening out there…?'

'I was quick to blame my ex. He was the one who had the affair. He was the one who walked out, so of *course* it was his fault. He was an outsider, I should have known I couldn't trust him. But yesterday, Maggie's outburst in the Jury Room got me thinking.'

How men who work in the City can't be expected to understand why Longboat girls would hanker to sleep beneath the stars, or have the salt air licked off their cheeks. How they could lose themselves in art restoration to the extent that they forgot appointments and mealtimes, much less why they'd want to listen to the taped sound of seagulls and crashing waves, when their husband had three thousand songs loaded on to his computer, because where was the rhythm in that?

'He wasn't a Viking, but I killed him just the same.' She stabbed a mussel with venom. 'Metaphorically speaking.'

'My wife was Irish, but I never blamed her. Which you'd know, if you'd been listening.'

'I was listening—' sort of '—but you're the exception. Maggie blames Maarten Reynders for not having the chance to say goodbye to Jenna. Something she'd never have done, if that had been your gallery, or mine.'

'So there's two of you. Happy now?'

'Laugh all you like, but hostility in Longboat Cove is endemic, that's a fact, and Arnold Warne was one of the worst offenders. *That stuff they wuz draggin off the walls? That weren't no Dutchman's.* Remember that? *Can't paint for toffees, him,* he'd tell anyone who'd listen. *Has loads of 'em lined up on their easels, just so's he can practice, and it's crap. Nothing like the stuff downstairs,* he'd say. *Kids daubs, that's what Dutchie paints, with green stripes down the middle.*

'Arnold Warne's prime motivation in life was stirring up trouble. Passing on gossip when he could, making it up when he couldn't.'

'Agreed, and you don't need an eye for art to appreciate Maarten Reynders' talent.' Her face softened. 'I've watched him paint, Davey. The attention to detail is amazing, and his passion for bright colours verges on *fauvism—*'

'Whatever that is.'

'Derain, Matisse, Jean Metzinger? No?' Sometimes she forgot he spent his life tinkering with engines. 'Anyway, because Maarten's an outsider—from the Netherlands at that—Arnold had no compunction in rubbishing his work. *Bleddy fraud, that's what he is.* He wouldn't have dared to slander any of the other gallery owners.'

'Reynders being the closest thing to a Viking?'

'I knew you'd come round eventually.'

'Round?' Davey gulped a mouthful of sauvignon to stop the choking. 'Jesus, Ellen, I'm not even close! Arnold was a poisonous little prick, who took great delight in telling Maude from the riding stables that her boyfriend, Jack, was cheating, when he was nothing of the sort. He accused Clacky Bill's grandson of shoplifting, old Mrs. Galloway of stealing, and if that wasn't enough, he swore blind the vicar of St. Piran's was an alcoholic on the quiet.'

'And the irony is, if Arnold Warne hadn't boycotted Dan's funeral out of meanness and spite, he wouldn't have disturbed the burglars and would be alive today. Instead, he's dead, Jenna's dead, Dan Trelawney, too. Which is why I say, Longboat Cove is cursed.'

Dark eyes rolled. 'For a professional woman, Ellen Pascoe, you put forward some of the most irritating, irrational, unfounded arguments of anyone I've ever met, and if you don't come outside and kiss me this minute, I'm going to have to lean across this table and do it.'

'Last time you kissed me, I didn't leave your bed for a week.'

'We were teenagers back then. Experimenting. You'll find I'm not in such a hurry these days.'

They were still laughing, arms wrapped round each other's waists, when they noticed the sprawl of white at the foot of the cliff steps. Ellen's first thought was, parachute. Paragliding was a popular pastime in the summer, and in the winter too, if it was mild.

Then she saw the blood. A glint of gold. A broken stiletto halfway down the steps.

White and strappy.

The sort of shoe most women stopped wearing after thirty—

* * *

For three nights, Ellen hardly slept, and when she did, her dreams were of slashed paintings, violent colours, blood and smoke and screams. She saw Dan Trelawney's children crying tears that stained their little faces green. She saw Clacky Bill throwing pilchards on the fire, and ancient standing stones running red with Maggie's blood. The nightmares merged. She dreamed her sister pushed her rented cottage over the edge of the cliff, laughing as she sang *he's mine, he's mine, he's a fraud, a bleddy fraud, but Davey Calloway is mine,* while the locals burned a longship on the beach.

'Maarten Reynders.'

The duvet groaned. 'Always a good start to a new relationship. Calling your lover by another person's name.'

Ellen sat bolt upright in bed. 'This is hardly a new relationship.'

'Teen romances don't count.'

Don't they? At the time, she thought it would last for ever. Then different universities came along, and before you could blink, Romeo and Juliet had become brother and sister, her forging a career in art, him dropping law to dabble in mechanics. Time passed. And though he always seemed to be hanging round their doorstep, like a feral cat on the scrounge, mostly it was because he was baling Tamara out of trouble. A puncture here, a shelf up there, a lift to the station if he wasn't busy. Any excuse, it seemed, to see her baby sister.

Or so she'd thought…

'Maggie, Dan, Arnold and Jenna.' Ellen prodded Davey's ribs. 'The link is Maarten Reynders, which means they're not coincidence, which means the town's not cursed.'

'You do know that three hundred years ago, they'd have burned you as a witch? Or perhaps just for being a pain in the arse. What time is it?'

'Six o'clock, give or take.'

'Give or take how much?'

'An hour.'

'Jesus, Ellen. You woke me at five in the morning to tell me something I already know?'

'Seriously? You knew the deaths were connected?'

'No. That we're in the 21st century and there's no such thing as cursed, and by the way they're not. Connected, that is.'

'The hell they aren't.' Just in case he wasn't fully awake, she switched on the bedside light. 'Jenna and Maggie Bawden rescued the paintings at the same gallery Arnold Warne bad-mouthed, and now all three are in their graves.'

'What are you suggesting? Death by Dutchman?'

'There's something fishy, Davey. I can feel it.'

'You have no idea how much I wish I hadn't given up smoking.' One eye swivelled round to face her. 'I'd stuff two in my ears right now.' With a heavy sigh, he sat up. Spiked his hands through his hair. 'Ellen. Listen to me, then we can both get back to sleep. Dan Trelawney was killed when someone broke in and tried to rob him in the night. No—repeat, no—connection.'

'Maybe he—'

'No connection, Ellen.'

There was an edge to his voice that brooked no argument, and to be fair, she couldn't make a case for the opposition either.

'Arnold Warne was in the wrong place at the wrong time. Shame, but these things happen, love. The stair carpet was frayed, his slippers were worn. The police investigated both cases thoroughly, if you recall—'

'So thoroughly, they haven't caught anyone, or even come close.'

'That's not unusual in robberies.' He smacked a kiss on the top of her head. 'But can we please be objective about this? You said it yourself. If Arnold hadn't stayed away from Dan's funeral, he'd still be alive. Jenna was strangled on a Spanish holiday island and, like it or not, if Maggie hadn't insisted on wearing the most unsuitable shoes in Christendom, she'd still be around, too.'

'This had nothing to do with shoes.'

He twisted his lip. 'Muesli.'

'Too sweet for me,' Ellen said, 'and besides. There's only cornflakes in the cupboard, with a sell by date of 1866.'

'Not breakfast. You.' This time the kiss was tender, more meaningful. 'Flaky and nuts. And excuse me, Ellen Pascoe, but exactly where do you think you're going?'

'Nothing's changed with me, Davey. I still like to be up with the larks.'

'Nothing's changed with me, either.' He pulled her back on to the duvet. 'I still like to stay in bed for one.'

* * *

Ellen couldn't fault his logic concerning the recent spate of tragedies. Which was not to say she accepted it, either.

She just needed to figure it out.

Luckily, the fey side of her nature was balanced out by good, solid Cornish practicality and she immersed herself in cleaning up a portrait of an 18th century dignitary, whose image had turned greyer than his periwig after languishing in an attic for a hundred and twenty years.

'You've made Blackbeard look almost handsome.'

'Tam.' She caught the pot of linseed oil before it hit the floor. 'You made me jump, and if you don't mind, he's a privateer, not a pirate.'

'That's like sticking a sheriff's badge on a gunfighter. Just because it's legal, doesn't make it right. What's with you and Davey?'

'Do you mind we're back together?'

'Would it matter if I did? Besides, everyone in Longboat Cove knows Tamara Pascoe's footloose and fancy free by choice.' She flopped down on a chair. 'What they don't know, of course, is that the choice isn't mine.'

Ellen laid down her brush. 'You've been dumped, haven't you?'

The word "again" hung in the air.

'Same old story. He said he loved me, wanted me to have his babies, spend the rest of our lives together, blah, blah, blah.' She bit back the tears. 'But hey, I'm getting better. For once, this one wasn't married, just a live-in lover. But when Maude's horse threw her—'

'Riding stables Maude?'

'You knew?' Tamara buried her head in her hands. 'Omigod, I thought we'd kept it secret. Instead, everybody knows, how humiliating is that? Because when Maude fell, and for God's sake she only broke her collar bone, Jack dropped me like the hottest coal in hell, and now the whole *town* will know I'm—'

'Green.'

'What?'

'In my dream the other night, Dan Trelawney's kids were crying green tears that stained their faces.'

Tamara's eyes bulged. 'Seriously?'

'God's truth. Plus there were fires on the beach and on the—'

'Not your bloody dream, you selfish cow!' She jumped up. 'Tell me you listened to a single word I said.'

'Of course I did.' Sort of. 'And in my other dream, you were pushing my cottage down the cliff—'

'Dammit, Ell, you do this every bloody time!'

'Do what?'

'Just like when we were kids. You disappear into your own little world, and sod everybody else. I should have known better than to come to you for help!'

Standing in her tiny studio, winter sunlight pooling on the portrait of the smirking privateer, Ellen was torn.

Should she console her sobbing sister?

Or run straight down to the church?

Because now she knew the motive for the murders.

* * *

Summer transformed Longboat Cove. The scent of sticky fudge, homemade ice cream and honey from the moors replaced the earthier smells of the little fishing fleet. Tanned legs and sunglasses paraded round the cafés, shops and harbour like the South of Cornwall was the South of France. Surfers rode breakers, old ladies scribbled postcards and, down on the beach, new defences were built to repel the Vikings. Castles made from sand.

Watching over the town, the church of St. Piran, patron saint of tin miners, stood proud. Every March, the children of Longboat Cove filed through the narrow streets waving the flag of Cornwall and St. Piran, the white cross on a black background, to celebrate the saint's day. Daffodils would be laid in the nave, their life expectancy doubled thanks to the church's fridge-like temperature, and rousing hymns sung as a means to keep warm. Today the doors stood open to let the heat out, instead of in, and light through the stained glass windows twinkled jewel-like on the ancient flagstones.

'I hated wearing the Cornish tartan when I was a kid.'

'Davey.' Somehow he always knew where to find her.

'Felt a right prat. Ten years old and forced to wear a "skirt". But now? Now I'm proud of it. Of who I am, and where I came from. I just wish I'd told my grandparents before they died. They were the ones who pushed me into wearing it for the parades.'

Ellen smiled. 'What's this? A kilt trip?'

His laugh echoed round St. Piran's, causing five middle-aged flower arrangers to look up sharply in rebuke. The smile faded from his eyes. But not from that.

'I still don't know how you did it. Linking the deaths and proving they were murder, rather than four tragic but isolated incidents. The good folk of Longboat Cove are proud of you, Ellen Pascoe. Some—' He leaned his weight against the pillar and folded his arms across his chest. '—more than others.'

She'd liked to have said she was proud of it herself, but that was a lie.

'You have my line of work to thank for that, not me.'

Restoring paintings bridges the commercial world with the artistic.

'Having a foot in both camps meant I was familiar with what goes on in the art world, but have a practical side at the same time.'

'Does "cursed" fall in the practical, arty or just-plain-loopy category?'

'Laugh all you want, but back then, you weren't the one living in a caravan, waiting for your divorce to come through, trying to find your feet after eight years away with a sister who's had four husbands and not one of them her own.' She calmed down. 'OK, cursed might have been a bit OTT, but the point is, too much tragedy in such quick succession isn't normal. Especially in a small town like Longboat Cove.'

Should she tell him that talking it through with him also brought the answer?

'The sticking point was Dan Trelawney.'

Maybe later…

'Maggie, Jenna, Arnold, they were all connected to the fire at Maarten Reynders' gallery. Dan Trelawney was not, and yet he was killed just two days later.'

Four days after that, Arnold Warne *supposedly* tripped downstairs. The next day, Jenna *supposedly* died fighting off a sex attacker in Ibiza. Then Maggie Bawden *supposedly* lost her footing on the cliff steps.

'Then I remembered Arnold accusing the Dutchman of not being able to paint. Kids' daubs, he called them, with green stripes down their faces, all lined up so he could practice.'

'Which made the link to favouritism.'

'*Fauvism*, you philistine!'

She aimed a mock punch at his arm as they sauntered into the sunshine and the sound of children's laughter. Down on the harbour front, Clacky Bill's grandson grilled fat pilchards—sorry, fat *sardines*—over an open fire, where they were being snapped up as fast as he could cook them. Good to see him in proper employment, away from the gang of losers he used to hang around with. Where, yes, shoplifting was indeed a rite of passage.

Because that was the thing. Mean as Arnold was, dripping poison to cause hurt, spreading malice for its own sake, it seemed the old man's intel was spot on. His delight in other peoples' pain—and Ellen subsequently found there was a word for this, *schadenfreude*—meant that no one took any notice of his ramblings. If you don't listen, you can't hurt.

'A fact outsiders aren't aware of.' She stressed the word outsiders, before he jumped on it. 'I'd watched Maarten Reynders paint. I told you, didn't I, how he'd lose himself in his work? The detail was amazing, and the colours! The colours, Davey, took your breath away.'

Which meant that if Arnold Warne was right about Maude's boyfriend cheating on her (and with Tamara, dammit), Ellen wondered what else he'd been right about.

'I know you think I should have comforted Tamara, instead of belting down to the church—'

'When did you ever hear me say that?'

'You must have thought it, though.' Or maybe that was just her conscience. 'But it was important to ask the vicar if he really was a struggling alcoholic, because if the answer was yes, which it was, then it meant more lives were in danger.'

What was that wartime slogan? Careless talk costs lives? In this case, that was exactly what cost four people theirs.

'After talking to the vicar, and then I'm sorry to say, tackling Mrs. Galloway about stealing flowers from her neighbour's garden—which, by the way, she only took to lay on her husband's grave, because she couldn't afford to buy them from the florist—I scoured the internet.'

Matisse. That was the link. As the leader in *fauvism*—all primary colours and passion, bold brush strokes and spontaneity—one of Matisse's most famous portraits was of his wife. In an orange dress, with her dark hair in a chignon, flattering it was not. Poor woman looked almost mannish. And not a little bored. But he'd separated light from shadow with a vivid slash of green, and called the piece *La Raie Verte*. "The Green Stripe". A technique he'd used in "Woman in a Hat", even a self-portrait.

Now, hadn't Ellen read about a Matisse being stolen from a private collector late last summer?

Thank heavens for Google. Within five minutes, she'd confirmed that a New York socialite had indeed reported "Man with Violin" stolen from her mansion in the Hamptons. Estimated value? A whopping £30 million.

On the black market, of course, that value would be a mere fraction. Assuming there was just the single copy—

That stuff they wuz draggin off the walls? That ain't no Dutchman's, Arnold had said. *Can't paint for toffees, him. Has loads of 'em lined up on their easels, just so's he can practice, and it's crap. Nothing like the stuff downstairs.*

He'd called them children's daubs. With green stripes down the middle.

Bleddy fraud, that's what he is, Arnold Warne had said, but on this point, Arnold Warne was wrong.

The Dutchman was no bleddy fraud.

He was a bleddy forger.

* * *

'That's why he insisted on having his own people wire the gallery,' Ellen said.

She and Davey were sitting on a clifftop bench, watching children dabble in the rock pools far below, fascinated by the tiny shrimps and crabs. Two of the boys were trying to prise off barnacles that had closed tight with low tide. And having as much luck as they had catching seagulls on the beach.

'And the reason he didn't claim on the insurance.'

This was a sophisticated job, a long time in the planning, with everything worked out to the nth degree. Right down to choosing a sleepy English backwater, where one more moody artist would easily pass unnoticed. Not that Reynders could have pulled it off alone. Forgers aren't thieves. No, his role was to make reproductions not just of the Matisse, but of a Sisley, a Pisarro and a rather lovely little Degas that were taken at the same time. And when you're part of a gang looking to net anything from twenty to thirty million pounds apiece, the cost of keeping a professional hit man on standby was negligible.

'Arnold had seen what Reynders was doing, but didn't twig—'

'How?' Davey passed her a piping hot pasty. 'According to the police report, the Sandpiper Gallery had a pretty sophisticated alarm installed.'

'Which, like every other alarm system, was designed for conventional break-ins.' Ellen bit into the crumbly pastry, oozing with spicy beef and vegetables. 'What he couldn't have legislated for were the old rat-runs that dated back to smuggling times.'

Arnold Warne was born in that building seventy-three years ago, when it used to be the old post office run by his grandfather. Curious to see what alterations this latest owner had made, he'd sneaked in through the secret panels when he knew Maartens would be out.

'Once Reynders heard Arnold shooting his mouth off, he had to shut him up.' Davey wiped a flake of pastry off her chin. 'Which is where Dan Trelawney came in.'

The most popular man in Longboat Cove, Maarten knew the whole town would turn out for his funeral. Except for one.

'Dan's death was simply a means to an end.'

Collateral damage, wasn't that what Reynders called it? Suddenly Ellen wasn't hungry. Try explaining "collateral damage" to Arnold's devastated wife and children, she thought, tossing the pasty to the gulls. Try explaining that to his broken-hearted parents.

'Jenna was such a chatterbox, he couldn't be sure Arnold hadn't told her about the paintings, or that she hadn't put two and two together herself.'

Which she wouldn't, her mind didn't work that way, and that was the Dutchman's mistake. Jumping in too fast. If he'd sweated it out, let things lie instead of resorting to murder, he'd have got away with it.

Except greed has no warmth.

Greed has no compassion.

Certainly greed has no compunction in pushing an old woman over a cliff, just because he'd overheard Maggie talking about the fire.

'Another thing he hadn't legislated for.' Davey sighed. 'An electrical short.'

'Or two good Samaritans.'

Who paid for their kindness with their lives.

And once Ellen realized Reynders was eliminating anyone who stood in the way of his financial gain, she knew that logic was already out the Dutchman's window. He would just keep on staging accidents, whether people were connected to the gallery or not, to safeguard his own avaricious interests.

'So then.' Davey tipped his dark head on one side. 'Did talking it through with me help you find the link between the deaths?'

Ah, those stubborn Cornish genes.

'Let's forget all that tragic stuff, shall we? Six months have passed, summer's here, and life's pretty bloody good.'

'Is it?' He laughed. 'You're still living in a caravan, waiting for your divorce to come through, trying to find your feet, and fighting with a sister who's had four husbands and not one of them her own.'

One day (maybe next month), she'd move in with him.

One day (maybe next year), she would marry him.

But she didn't want him to think she was easy…

'Race you to the bottom of the cliff,' she yelled over her shoulder, already skipping down the steps. 'Last one in the *Viking* buys the drinks.'

Glasses they would then raise to Dan Trelawney, Arnold Warne, Jenna Kestle and Maggie Bawden.

Yehes ha sowena whath dhewgh why ha 'gas henath!

Health and prosperity to you and your descendants!

Ellen Pascoe drank to that.

The Way It Is

I see things other people don't, and hear things they often miss. This is neither an asset nor a liability. Just the way it is.

Home for me is a narrow boat on the Leeds & Liverpool Canal, one of the longest canals in the country, and by far the longest in the north. Slicing through the mountainous backbone of England, this gentle waterway flows past castles and moorlands, rivers and meadows, and more sleepy stone villages than you can count. Add on aqueducts, tunnels, and ninety-three locks, and you have a pace so slow, it makes snails tut with impatience. A tempo which suits me down to the ground.

What is this life if, full of care,
We have no time to stand and stare?

What indeed. They say you see more by standing still than running, and from the *Firecrest*'s red painted deck, I see it all. Spring unfolding in a fanfare of lambs, tadpoles, cuckoos and apple blossom, not to mention endless vistas of bluebells that carpet the beechwoods. Autumn carries the tang of ploughed soil and wild mushrooms, and in winter the countryside is white with crunchy, sharp frosts. A rolling spectrum of colour and mood, peppered with the song of the nightingale, the scent of wild flowers, and the jewel-bright flash of kingfishers.

But there is more to the Leeds & Liverpool than mere picture postcards. For its entire hundred and twenty-seven mile length, the canal is stalked by the ghost of its industrial past. A past that long ago stopped clogging the lungs of its workers, thank God, driving them to paupers' graves ahead of their time. But you'd be surprised at how many of these towering breweries, woollen mills, chimneys and tobacco warehouses remain. Restored, resplendent, elegant even. But a potent reminder, nevertheless, of a history that was as dark and satanic as it was prosperous and dynamic. The golden age that was Victorian Britain.

These days, the narrow boats carry tourists, rather than cargo. On holiday, where time loses all meaning, no one minds being squashed into a vessel less than seven feet wide. That's right. Six feet ten inches most narrow boats, and around seventy feet long. In the old days, they were drawn by black, blinkered Shire horses, famous for their white feathers and blazes, as much as the brass plaques that embellished their harness. Indeed, many a fireplace and beam of the pubs lining this route gleam with these intricate brasses. At least, I believe that's still the case. I don't drink anymore, so pubs hold little appeal, and all in all, given my disability, it's easier to stick within the confines of home.

Narrow boat, narrow life? I can't argue the logic, but the odd thing is, I'm content with my lot, and how many people can say that?

Looking at the flowerpots brimming with phlox and geraniums, the castle scenes painted on the cabin doors, and the array of watering cans decorated with overblown roses, it's hard to imagine that such flair evolved from poverty and was inspired by defiance. But when horse-drawn transport became no match for steam, bargees were forced to seek freight wherever they could along the complex network of English canals. Unable to afford hired hands, their wives and children laboured as crew, and instead of a cosy warm cottage at the end of the day, home was a tiny box cabin. Despite being pitched into a harsh gypsy lifestyle, the boating community responded with brio and flair. They painted their woodwork with bright colours, splurged hearts and spades over the hatches, set trends with decorative rope work, and introduced a distinctive white lettering on the side of the boats. They even adopted their own style of clothing, and I ask you: With a legacy that is as humbling as it is uplifting, who couldn't be happy?

With little else to occupy me, since I no longer work, my powers of observation have become finely tuned with the passage of time. Details become absorbing in their own right. For instance, I know the date on which the first swallows arrive. March 23rd, the same every year. These are the males, the advance guard, coming to inspect last year's nest sites. I know where the squirrels bury their acorns—a piece of knowledge I happen to share with the jays that dig them up! I've watched ducklings hatch, and you can forget this nonsense about swans mating for life. True, they pair up, but take it from me, those birds indulge in the same adulterous liaisons as their human counterparts. (Only without the nuclear fallout.) And if you blithely imagine all swans are the same, think again. In nature, nothing is replicated. Not a bird, not a fish, not a tree, not an insect. The differences may be microscopic, but, after a while, you learn not only to tell swans apart, but to understand your own species a lot more.

'Dad? Dad, can we go to McDonald's after?'

'What kind of a question's that, Harry? Don't we always?'

Now that, funnily enough, is a case in point. Father and son cycling along the tow path are two a penny on Saturday mornings. No one gives them a second glance. But if, like me, you've little else to occupy your mind than learning how to read body language and recognizing behavioural patterns, you understand that here's a dad who only sees his boy at weekends, possibly not every weekend at that. As a result, he indulges the kid in a way that will, sure as hell, deepen the divide between him and his ex, but what does he care? For today, tomorrow, he is the hero. The man who never says no.

A small example, but it shows what happens when you have time on your hands. The kind of detail you absorb through your pores.

Like the lock-keeper's wife, near the famous double-arched bridge at East Morton. No matter what time of year, she'd be sitting under the oak tree surrounded by hordes of children, and only two of them were her own. If she wasn't doling out picnics or making daisy chains, she'd be playing hide and seek, bouncing balls or pelting snowballs. That lock positively rang with laughter and song. Until one autumn day, when the tow path was a deep, amber carpet of leaves and a soft mist shrouded the valleys, and the silence hit like a punch. When we passed through the lock the following spring, the oak tree had gone. It was old, overhanging, and quite probably dangerous, but when I looked into the lock-keeper's eyes, I knew that wasn't the reason. The memories were simply too painful to live with, and although that happened long before they built the golf links, my heart still breaks each time we pass.

But then what is life, if not sunshine and shadow?

Before the accident, my life wasn't what you'd call a bed of roses. Whereas now I'm trapped in this…this…shell, where I can't walk, can't feed myself, can't even feel pain—a limbo of paralysis where you'd expect misery to come with the territory—I'm more content than I've ever been. Even those Victorian mill workers, slogging from dawn to dusk in dangerous and deeply unsanitary conditions, made their own spots of sunshine. Friendship, banter, religion and love gave them the strength to survive. And trust me, the human spirit knows how to endure.

If that sounds jaded, I'm sorry, but under the circumstances, it isn't surprising. Last month, you see, I watched a man die. Well, no, that's not strictly true. The word "die" implies heart attacks, epileptic fits, even stumbling into the water on a dark night and drowning. There was nothing natural about this. What I saw was a killing.

And yet—

And yet—

Despite the severity of my disability, I do my bit whenever I can. Take that incident on the tow path a year or three back. An old lady walking her dog would be the obvious cliché, robbed by a thug in his teens. If only! This was a little girl of eight, maybe nine, on her way home from school. Was she habitually bullied by classmates? No idea; I'd never seen her before. What I do know is, another girl wearing the same yellow and grey uniform snatched her school bag and ran down the path, laughing her red curly head off. Which makes you wonder about this next generation. What can possibly be funny about pushing your fellow pupil in the canal? As it happened, the kid was a strong swimmer, but this other little madam didn't know that. She ran off without looking back, swinging the bag like a trophy.

What most yobs lack in intelligence they make up for in cunning, and this little yobette was no exception. She'd seen her window of opportunity and pounced, knowing everyone's attention was diverted elsewhere. She almost got away with it, too.

We were just entering the Foulridge Tunnel, a pitch black passageway with no tow path, and only wide enough for one boat at a time. In the days before engines, men would "walk" the boats through by lying on the deck and propelling it along with their feet. It's still three times darker than Hades in there, which tends to concentrate the mind somewhat, as you'd imagine. But back in 1912, a cow called Buttercup (I kid you not) fell in the canal and somehow ended up swimming the whole mile through the tunnel. In fact, there's a photo of her on the pub wall at the far end, being revived, of all things, with French brandy. Anyway, the day this little girl got mugged by her classmate, there was even more of a distraction than usual.

I don't know whether it's because cats are notoriously hostile to infirmity, or whether it's because the boat is on the move too often for comfort. Either way, they flat out refuse to stay on the *Firecrest*, but dogs, now. Dogs are happy-go-lucky creatures, everyone's friend, who like nothing better than to stand at the prow, like some hairy figurehead, their noses into the wind. Except this particular day, the stupid mutt jumped in just as the traffic light control turned to green. So there he was, this big soppy labrador, splashing through the canal like his bovine predecessor, with everyone laughing, pointing, and taking videos on flashlight for *YouTube*.

Except me.

God knows how many times I've been through that tunnel, I know the Buttercup story inside out, and of course it's hardly unusual for dogs to take to the water. But for desk-bound holiday makers, such moments are rare, and the girl on the tow path was banking on that.

She had revelled in her trophy-taking for perhaps half a minute before she noticed me on the *Firecrest*'s deck. Her jaw dropped. I made a pointing gesture directly at her, then crooked my finger to beckon her to me. She turned whiter than the lambs in the field behind. Did I save her from descending into a life of violence and crime that fine day? God knows. I never saw her again. But my intervention was enough to make her run back, pull her struggling victim out of the water, and apologize to the point of grovelling almost.

There have been similar incidents along the way. Some large, some small, and not one of them likely to tilt the earth on its axis. All the same, considering my limitations, I chip in where I'm able. Only sometimes my best isn't enough—

Like last month. It was a Saturday night, the usual thing. Pubs might shut at eleven, but the desire for drinking goes on. Armed with bottles and cans, gangs of youths regularly congregate under the bridges and binge themselves into the ground. Lord knows, it's a common enough sight along any canal, not just this one, and Sunday mornings always dawn over bobbing bottles, debris and litter. Mostly these youths are harmless. Loud, I agree, and every now and then boisterous high spirits explode into aggression and fights break out, sometimes with knives. But honestly. We're talking schoolboy scuffles, not Wild West showdowns. Insults get traded, punches get thrown, then it's back to the vodka.

Unless Fate throws a spanner in the works.

Wrong place at the wrong time, you could argue. That a homeless man, used to dossing down for the night, ought to have seen the carpet of crushed glass and broken syringes and looked for somewhere better to sleep. Except when you're down on your luck, it's cold, and it's raining, a bridge offers shelter, and in any case, time has no meaning. The fact that it's Saturday is neither here nor there. Just one more night to get through.

So when you're curled up under a lice-ridden blanket, no home, no food, no future, no past, is it too much to ask to keep the noise down?

'Hey, grandpa, think that's loud?'

Buoyed up by too much beer, too much cider, the one on the left pumped up the volume.

'How about this?'

The one on the right bounced a can off the blanket. The others roared with approval.

'What's the matter, old man? Can't you sleep?'

The jeering and taunting continued for—I don't know, maybe another two minutes. Then the blanket moved and the homeless man got to his feet, I thought, if he's got any sense, he'll move on. But I suppose we all have our limits, and who knows? Perhaps he'd been pushed once too often. Instead of collecting his blanket and carrier bags and shambling off, he booted their i-pod dock into the water.

I think, at that point, they simply wanted to jostle him, hustle him, shove him around. Show him who's boss around here. Being young, of course, they didn't understand that homeless isn't the same as downtrodden.

'Jeez!' The blond kid reeled backwards, his fleece covered with blood. 'He's broken my nose!'

'Nope,' the tramp growled, swinging a second punch to the boy's head. 'Now I have.'

'Whoa, grandpa.' The group weighed in. 'Someone needs to teach you some manners, old man.'

'I'm not your grandpa, and I'm not old,' he said, breaking loose from the scrum. 'I was fighting in Kuwait before you were born, sonny. 1st Armoured Division. Now get the hell out from my bridge.'

'*Your* bridge?' Apart from the kid cradling his broken nose, they all laughed. 'We'll show you whose bridge this is. Grandpa.'

Right from the outset, they'd seen the *Firecrest* moored a hundred yards up, curtains closed and in darkness, reasoning there was no one on board. They were wrong. I was there. I was there, on the deck, with the rain hammering down, willing the ex-soldier to look round. I couldn't shout, I couldn't throw anything, but hell, I could point. I could jab my thumb in a gesture that said, *go*. Show him there was no need to make a stand against six drunken louts. Call it a tactical retreat, if you want. But whatever it is, it's not weakness.

The trouble is, I haven't experienced life on the streets. Don't know what it's like to sleep rough, be permanently dirty and cold, have to wade through litter bins for something to eat. Most of all, I can't imagine how a man from an outfit whose insignia is a charging rhinoceros, could spiral into this pit. Gulf War syndrome? Post-traumatic stress? Failed marriage, repossession and debt?

What I do know is that, if I felt powerless, he did not. He let them think their beating had weakened him to the point where he submitted. Then with a roar, he broke free, and suddenly the rhinoceros charged. I saw the flash of steel. Heard a cry. Then a groan. Watched a body crumple and fall…

That was the moment I could have—when *maybe* I could—have intervened, had I been able. It depends on one's definition of justice.

I am not, and never have been, a hero, and my philosophy has always been that it's the job of the police to catch criminals, not mine. Don't get me wrong. I don't condone murder, even if it was provoked. But there are always options, and walking away from a fight is just one. Also, a trained soldier knows how to kill. A thrust to the heart under the rib cage. Yob or not, the kid stood no chance.

By the time the boys realized it was too late for their friend, the soldier had gone. That's when I could have intervened, I suppose. Held my arms out, maybe beckoned him forward. Any small act that might have slowed him down enough for the youths to catch up and hand him to the police. I could already hear sirens closing the distance. Instead I chose to do nothing.

Too many things happen in life that we can neither change nor undo. We are all spectators at some point.

This wasn't my fight.

This wasn't my right to judge.

I watch the clouds pass in front of the moon, follow the swoop of a barn owl as it scoops up a vole, track shooting stars as they fizz through a sky unhampered by the pollution of light from the cities. And I look at them all with peace in my heart, knowing my sleeplessness is not caused by a conscience. Most likely, the soldier would not have seen me, even if I had tried to intervene. Most people don't.

As the *Firecrest* navigates gentle bends overhung with willows and alder, I no longer look in the mirrors that hang in the cabin. What's the point? I have long since ceased to cast a reflection, because one hundred and twenty-nine years ago, I, too, was a victim of the industrial age. Crushed between the lock gates near Skipton, when I stumbled and fell from the deck in the fog, transporting limestone to Leeds.

A hundred and twenty-nine years in which to fine tune my powers of observation, which is why I see things other people don't, and hear things they often miss. Like I said, this is neither an asset nor a liability.

Just the way it is…

A Taste for Ducking

'Duck the witch!' *Clap hands*. 'Duck the witch!'

Dawn was breaking cold and grey, as the procession chanted its way through the little village of Farringham in the South Downs. Hoar frost sparkled on the roof of the church. Wind rattled the tavern's windows. The bare branches of willows reflected like cracks on the frozen duck pond. Betsy didn't notice. The quicker this business was over and done with the better, that was her view.

'Duck the witch!' *Clap hands*. 'Duck the witch!'

With her hands tied behind her, she stumbled and slipped down the icy path—past the dairy—past the smithy—down to the miller's place.

'Far enough.' Parson Dale held up a hand that had turned blue at the fingers with cold. 'Let the Ordeal of Innocence begin.'

Most of the faces that had crowded round were a blur, but Betsy did notice the parson's wife leading the clapping while Tommy Collins elbowed his way to the front for a good view. She was sorely tempted to tell him that he, a master carpenter of all people, ought to be ashamed of himself, jeering in public like this. Who was it taught him his numbers, eh? Who showed him how to tie knots in a rope? The best way to harden a conker? When this was over she'd clip his ear, that's for sure, and never mind he was thirty-seven years old!

'Duck the witch!'

The clapping was constant now, fast and eager. Perhaps, she thought, the villagers needed to keep themselves warm.

'Duck the witch, duck the witch!'

At the front of the crowd, the hard lips of Betsy's daughter-in-law were pursed in smugness, and malice glittered from her green eyes. Betsy shook her head in bewilderment. All right, Mary wasn't the wife she'd have chosen for her son, but, though they'd never got on, she'd accepted the girl into her family and gave way on everything Mary had asked. Trouble was, and try as she might, nothing could please her, nothing was ever enough. It had reached the point now where she slept in the kitchen and acted as a servant in her own home, yet *still* Mary wasn't satisfied. She wanted Betsy out, that was the problem, and the truth was, she would have gone and willingly so—had she had some place to go.

By her daughter-in-law's side, Betsy's only child fixed his gaze to his boots. Not his fault the lad was weak, she supposed. Took after his granddad on his father's side, did poor Robbie—only soft men were always grist to a shrew's mill. Every time Betsy tried to put her foot down, it was Robbie who caught the sharp edge of Mary's tongue. Robbie, who found no comfort in his wife's bed for a week. Betsy couldn't let her son pay the price for his mother's resistance, so she gave way. Shooting him a thin smile of encouragement, she felt a pain in her heart when he didn't once lift his eyes to meet hers.

'Betsy Bellingham, you stand accused of unnatural compacts with Satan.' The parson's voice droned through the February bleakness. 'Of placing the Devil's familiar at your disposal—'

As though no one else in Farringham kept a cat!

'—and performing whatever vile service Satan demanded of you. Betsy Bellingham, how do you plead?'

'Not guilty, as you well know!'

The priest's black brows joined above the bridge of his nose in a frown. 'You deny causing Farmer Preston's bull to turn into a toad?'

Betsy rolled her eyes at the gate that had been left open all night. 'I certainly do.'

'You deny summoning the dead last Halloween?'

'Of course.'

'Of making magic at the crossroads? Conjuring demons? Bringing calamity upon the mash in the brewery?'

'Parson, Nathan Stokes has had a reputation for brewing bad beer for the past six-and-a-half years. What other nonsense do you put forward?'

'How do you plead to the charge that you were seen riding a broomstick over Bramber Down three weeks ago last Wednesday night?'

'With my arthritis?'

The laughter that rippled round the crowd was quickly quelled by the glare of the priest. 'Very well, if you persist in denying the charges levelled against you, we will proceed with the test.'

Betsy heard a snip and for the first time in three days her wrists were unbound. Numb and leaden, she shook them to bring them back to life, but the action only brought fire to her hands. And it was because of this distraction that the parson had to repeat his request.

'Strip? Naked?' The pain in her fingers was instantly forgotten. 'How dare you even ask!' She scowled at the priest. 'At my age, as well!'

'You admit to the charges then?' This voice was softer. Like melted lard oozing over a ham.

'I most certainly do not.'

'Then I urge you to submit, the quicker we might record your innocence.'

Sharp-featured, bearded and with his head cowled, the stranger could have been a monk with all those crosses on chains. He was not. Any time an accusation of witchcraft was bandied, the Witchfinder General sent out an agent. A brodder, whose task was to prove or disprove the allegations.

'And if I don't?'

Where was the ducking stool? Betsy wondered. She'd expected it to have been wheeled down by now and hoped someone would send for it soon. Her limbs were shaking with cold.

'If you don't, we will hang you and bury your body in unconsecrated ground in a grave that will never be marked,' the brodder replied softly. 'So why not let the Officer of the Ordeal disrobe you that we might be certain there is no mark of the Devil upon you?' He paused. 'Dame Bellingham, I assure you this really *is* for your own good.'

Behind his shoulder, Mary folded her hands over her chest in grim satisfaction while her mother-in-law shivered with cold and humiliation.

'Let the record read, there is no mark of the Devil upon Betsy

Bellingham.'

Half the crowd seemed relieved. The other half itched for more entertainment. They were in luck.

'Crouch the candidate, please.'

The brodder's voice was politeness itself, while Betsy's teeth chattered too loudly for her to protest.

'Proceed as we discussed, Parson Dale.' He might have been overseeing the trussing of a goose. 'Right thumb to left toe, nice and tight, now.'

'What about the ducking stool?' she finally managed to splutter.

'Ducking stool?' The priest paused from blessing the millpond. 'My dear lady, we're ducking witches, not scolds.'

'We need to test your innocence,' the witchfinder lisped. 'For this, we throw you into the waters and if you are, as I truly believe, innocent of these vile allegations, you will sink.' A soft hand indicated two stout men standing by, stripped to the waist and ready to dive in and save her. 'If, on the other hand, Satan has put lies on your tongue to deceive us, your body will reject the baptismal waters, so have faith in God, my child.' He patted her head reassuringly. 'Have faith in God.'

Betsy did. She always had. And as two pairs of strong arms lifted her over the millpond, His was the only name on her lips.

Of course, she had no way of knowing that the distinctive tying of her bonds was the result of years of painstaking research.

Even when her body plunged beneath the icy waters, Betsy Bellingham firmly believed that her innocence was a foregone conclusion.

* * *

Blackestone Manor, with its chimneys and gables, wings and half-timbers, was by far the grandest building for miles. Like Drake and Raleigh, Sir Francis Blackestone had been one of the late queen's most resourceful pirates, and even though his cut represented a mere fraction of the plundering he'd done for the Crown, it had allowed him to purchase what seemed like half the land between Chichester and Brighton and, of course, half the population who lived on it. But despite profits from his farms and forests that more than offset the profligacy of his lavish lifestyle, it was not in cold, dull England that Sir Francis Blackestone made his home.

Preferring the warmer climes and even hotter native maidens, he settled in Jamaica to a routine that his only son and heir took great pride in inheriting and which, by all accounts, was set to shorten his life by approximately the same amount as it had his father's.

As a result, Blackestone Manor had remained unoccupied for virtually its entire existence. Occasionally, before his death, Sir Francis would come to England for a month (but no more) to sort out his affairs, gamble away the odd thousand or two and impregnate as many chambermaids as he was able, and, to his credit, his son even made the effort to attend the new King's coronation. But the point is, Jamaica was the place the Blackestones called home. The Manor House was merely the mark of their success.

So when the staff went into a flurry of airing and warming at a time of year when no Blackestone in his right mind would make the crossing, not on those seas, the curiosity in nearby Farringham was relentless. Was young Sir Roger coming home for good? Was he touting at long last for a wife? Would those lazy buggers employed at the Manor finally have to earn their damned wages? Eventually, it was the footman who told the laundress who told the parson's wife who, in fine civic duty, passed it on to everyone else that in fact the house had been lent to a distant cousin of the Blackestones. More pertinently, it appeared that it had been lent to the young wife of that distant cousin, a certain Eleanor Dearborn, who, despite claiming she needed nothing more than a few weeks of rest and recuperation after a heavy winter's cold, was obviously in "a certain condition". Farringham (in the form of the parson's wife) knew this because, dear me, the whole *world* knew that Geoffrey Dearborn had taken a wife thirty years younger than himself in his desperation for an heir to his fortune. Why else would the lovely Eleanor be here on her own, Mrs. Dale reasoned? And since Sir Geoffrey enjoyed a reputation for fairness and honesty in these parts, Farringham rejoiced for them both.

'Seven years is a long time to wait for the rock of the cradle,' the parson's wife told the newcomer, waiting no time at all herself before popping round with a basket of eggs.

'Indeed it is, Mrs. Dale, indeed it is.'

My word, the staff had had to move to get those rooms in order, the parson's wife thought. No dust, not a speck, and with that roaring log fire you'd think the chimney had been swept every year.

'You must have been terribly worried,' she prompted, once she'd realised that nothing else was forthcoming and that gossip doesn't spread by itself.

'Not at all.' The firelight shone on Eleanor's auburn curls as she laid a hand on her visitor's plump forearm. 'I put my faith in God,' she said, squeezing gently.

'Quite right,' Mrs. Dale said briskly. 'With Him watching over us, the Devil cannot gain a foothold. I must go.'

Eleanor glanced at the window. 'Won't you stay for tea and crumpets?'

By the time the parson's wife finally made to leave, the sky was purple and heavy with storm clouds, but, bursting with more news than she'd heard in a six-month, she failed to notice the downturn in the weather. Eleanor Dearborn waved her off with a kerchief embroidered with violets.

The stitching, she mused, fingering the petals as she waved, was far from expert. But then she'd only been nine years old when she'd embroidered the thing, and how well she remembered sitting in the tiny kitchen behind her father's tailor shop, legs crossed on the floor just like him, while his sister taught her to sew. The laughter, the cuddles, the hilarious unpicking came flooding back, as did the smell of bread baking in the oven, the songs that floated up to the beams and the rays of golden sunlight that streamed through the window while the needle flashed in her amateur hands. Then a thunderclap overhead banished childhood back to memory and, as the rain began to hammer against the window panes, Eleanor watched the parson's wife leaning into the wind, her skirts sodden and her hair dripping wildly beneath her cap as she battled her way down the broad, open driveway. Tossing another log onto the fire, Eleanor Dearborn tucked the kerchief back inside her gown and reflected on how far she'd come from those happy days of embroidering violets.

And sighed.

*　*　*

'That was the house where the witch lived, down there.'

In his early forties with rugged features and prematurely grey hair, the stranger cocked one long lean leg after the other over the fallen tree trunk on which Eleanor sat and settled himself beside her.

'Which one?' she asked. 'That one?'

'No. The one you were looking at before I arrived.'

'I was watching a squirrel.'

'Unusual to see one about on a cold day like this,' the stranger replied, crossing his arms. 'Lucky you.'

She said nothing. He made no move to leave.

'Tom Jordan,' he said after a while.

'Eleanor Dearborn,' and as she turned towards him she could smell pinecones and hay.

'The witch was called Betsy,' he said after another long while. 'Betsy Bellingham. Wicked woman by all accounts, too. Fornicated with the Devil and his cloven-hoofed spawn.' He ticked the points off on his long bony fingers. 'Cast evil spells over the village. Kept a familiar that sucked babies out of the womb. Wicked,' he added with a cluck of his tongue. 'Wicked, wicked woman.'

'Is that a fact?'

'Indeed it is fact,' Tom Jordan said with a crack of his knuckles. 'The old dame confessed to everything, it's all written down. Bewitching horses, bewitching cattle, turning her neighbours' food inedible, and that was just the beginning. If you read her confession, you'll see she cursed James Buckle to bring on rheumatics, gave his wife Janet an ulcer, dosed the carpenter with megrims and gave little Kitty the dairymaid cramps. Oh, and she confessed to night flying over this very hill, too.'

'Don't tell me, with the Devil riding pillion on her besom.'

Eleanor turned her eyes back to the small thatched stone cottage nestled at the end of the lane, the one with a pheasant made of straw on the roof. She pictured the cottage three months from now, when the garden would be filled with cabbages and peas, parsley and roses, and where chickens would peck and lay eggs.

'That old dame ran quite a coven,' he continued easily. 'Eliza Crowe, Margaret Drabbe, Jane Parcival, Annie Thomas and her daughter Bess,

Katherine Pearson and old Lucy Hewitt. They're all listed in the records, in the brodder's own distinctive hand. Thirteen of them in the end.'

She studied the craggy face and dark violet blue eyes.

'I was in Milord's courtroom earlier,' he explained cheerfully. 'Thirteen trial accounts laid open for all to see.'

Not just to be seen, Eleanor thought. To be seen and *feared*. For only the crimes of murder, robbery, arson and rape were tried by the Assizes. Everything else was tried by the local JP. His courtroom carried more traffic than Farringham High Street.

'Still, they say the brodder's work is nearly done,' Tom Jordan said.

Over his head, rooks cawed their territories around their nests while the buds of the blackthorn were thickening nicely. In the valley, a pair of hares boxed.

'Apparently, rumours of witchcraft have surfaced in Stoughton and so now, having rooted out all the witches in this part of the world, he'll be wanting to curb their black arts elsewhere.' He pointed towards the far hills. 'Another two days I give him, no more,' he said, nodding thoughtfully, and then smiled. 'The King's agent is nothing if not thorough.'

The King's agent, she thought. The King's agent…

Witchfinder, witchpricker, jobber, brodder, his was a profession that carried a multitude of names yet was charged with but one single task. To confirm or refute allegations of witchcraft. To drive out sin and the Devil.

'Thou shalt not suffer a witch to live,' the stranger quoted softly, staring up at the cloudless blue sky. 'It is written in the Bible. Exodus, Deuteronomy, Leviticus, Samuel, Galatians, Revelations and at least twice in the Acts, I believe. Our King is a deeply religious man.'

How true. Translating the Bible into English and taking a Danish wife to strengthen his commitment to the Protestant cause, James had even survived a plot last November to restore Catholicism to the land. A good man, the English cried! A good king! Intellectual and learned, he'd not only taken up Elizabeth's cultural baton, he had positively run with the new flourish in art and literature, whilst continuing to encourage science and the Virginian colonies. To be sure, long live the King!

But there were two sides to every coin. Eleanor wriggled deeper under her furs. Before sitting the English crown on his richly dyed curls, James had researched extensively—some might even say passionately—the subject of witchcraft. Indeed, respected and talented scholar that he was, he was considered an expert on the subject and under him, hundreds (sic, hundreds) of women had been put to death. But of course that was while he was king only of Scotland, which was a long way, a lifetime, away.

Or was it?

The law that he had introduced over here was pretty recent, and what did it say? That it was *a hanging offence for the devilish act of witchcraft and, by the force of the same, killing or laming their neighbours or harming their cattle*? Ah, but the King is a fair man, everyone said so. A just man. He doesn't simply act on somebody's say-so. He sends agents of the Crown to investigate these allegations. A brodder, who carries with him a bodkin which he prods into the accused person's flesh—and if the flesh doesn't bleed, only then has he had found a true servant of Satan.

And in Farringham's case, Eleanor mused, thirteen true servants who had duly choked to death on the gallows.

'Who are you, Tom Jordan?' she asked quietly. 'Why did you seek me out here this morning?'

His grey head turned and his face twisted in a crooked smile. 'Seek you out? You have me quite wrong, I fear. I am just passing through.' He indicated the cage at the edge of the clearing. 'I am the rat-catcher, see?'

'Which is what you were doing in Milord's courthouse? Catching rats?'

'Big 'un, too.' His hands spanned a gap large enough for a cat.

'It could be a trick of the light,' she said, 'but that cage looks remarkably empty to me.'

Tom Jordan's chuckle came from deep in his throat. 'Dead rats need no cage, Eleanor. It's the live ones you need to keep hold of.'

Tipping his cap, he bade her good day and was gone before she could ask why the rat-catcher carried no bells.

* * *

Down in the village, ducks dabbled in the melted pond water, primroses lifted their heads to the sun on the roadside and a bearded man with sharply pointed features walked with his cowled head held high. On his chest, several gold crosses dangled on chains. The brodder was proud of each one. Tomorrow morning, when he left this village for Stoughton, he would add another gold cross to his collection.

Another victorious medal in his fight against evil.

* * *

'It's Robbie, isn't it? Robbie Bellingham?'

A flabby young man, no more than thirty, whipped off his cap and turned pink. 'M-ma'am.'

'Do I have smuts on my nose, Robbie? Or do you stare at all the gentry as though they're chops on the butcher's block?'

'No. No, no of course not, begging your pardon, but for a moment there, I thought I recognised you from somewhere.' He wiped his hands down the sides of his pants. 'No offence, ma'am.'

'None taken.' Eleanor glanced up at the pheasant made of straw on the roof. Doubted it would last the spring storms. 'The thing is, Robbie, since your mother was convicted of witching—'

'I didn't know anything about that,' he cut in quickly. 'She practised it on the quiet, did Mother.'

'Indeed she must have done.' She studied the weak chin and blinking pale eyes. 'For you not to have noticed any of her abominations in such a small cottage.'

The silence was as brief as it was uncomfortable, at least on his part.

'Well, I knew about the cat, of course.' He wrung his cap in his hands. 'Saved it myself when it was a six-week-old kitten, once Farmer Preston said white cats were deaf and therefore no good as mousers. He'd have drowned it, you know, if I hadn't stepped in.'

'That was a very noble gesture, Robbie.' Pity he didn't mention it at Betsy's trial. Perhaps it slipped his mind.

'And I saw the candles,' he said, 'but I didn't think anything of it. I mean to say…candles? *Everybody* has candles.'

'Except these were different?'

'Not to me, they weren't.' Again, he was quick to distance himself. 'Looked like any other candle to my eyes, only how was I to know Mother shaped them into human form during the night, melting them so the victim sickened and died?'

'Did someone die, then?'

'No,' he said, frowning, 'but the parson got toothache and Tommy Collins started getting the megrims, and like I said at the trial, I didn't think anything odd about Mother's rags, either.'

'Rags?' Eleanor queried.

'Aye. She told me it was an old north-country custom, keeping rags to make into a mat. In fact, I can remember as a child her often telling me that she'd been shown how to make rugs with the clippings, only never had the time to make one herself. But the brodder got the truth out of her in the end. She'd been making rag dolls to burn and cause pain, she had. That's how James Buckle got his rheumatics and that's how Farmer Preston's best milking cow came over sick.'

'She admitted it?'

'Oh, yes.' He seemed almost proud of the fact. 'But I'm sure you didn't come all the way down here to talk about me, ma'am.'

That's funny, she thought they were talking about Betsy. 'No, indeed. As a matter of fact I came because I'd heard that you've been down on your luck since that unfortunate trial, and as it happens, I am in need of help at the Manor.'

'That's mighty kind of you, ma'am.' He turned a different shade of pink. 'I won't deny folk don't come near us these days and as a result times are a bit hard, but though I'm a mason by apprentice, I can turn my hand to any job you—'

'Actually, Robbie, it was your wife I was hoping to employ.'

'Mary?'

'Mrs. Dale assures me that she is a dab hand with a needle, and in my condition—' she gave a delicate cough '—well, suffice to say a good seamstress would not go amiss.'

The cogs of Robbie's brain turned slowly, but turn they eventually did. He remembered now how the rumour mill said Sir Geoffrey's wife had only wanted a few rooms brightened up at Blackestone Manor, at least for the time being. Summer, she insisted, was the time for the bulk of the work. Not March, when she risked a chill from the workmen's comings and goings, and Robbie, who yearned for a baby himself, understood all too well that she wouldn't want to harm a much longed-for child.

And what did it matter, she could see his mind reason, who got the work, as long as food came to the table?

Oh, dear. After ten years of marriage, Robbie still did not know his wife.

Or his mother.

* * *

'That's the spot where they buried the witch,' a familiar voice rasped in her ear.

'Where?' she asked, squinting.

'The mound you were staring at before I arrived,' he said, coming to stand alongside her. 'Unconsecrated ground, not blessed by the church, and forgotten by everyone else.'

'I was watching the rabbits.'

'Unusual to see them out at this time of day,' Tom Jordan replied, crossing his arms. 'Lucky you.'

She said nothing. He made no move to leave. He still smelled of pinecones and hay.

'Did you hear about the parson?' he asked after a while. 'Took sick during the night with skin rashes and blisters, vomiting and diarrhoea, while this morning he lapsed into stupor interspersed with delirium.'

'I had not heard the news, although it sounds a lot like baneberry poisoning to me.'

'Exactly the physician's diagnosis. He is of the opinion that his wife, whilst still suffering the effects of the chill she caught from the storm, must have muddled them up with sloe berries, but at least she can rest easily. The malady is not fatal.'

True, Eleanor thought, but convalescence is invariably lengthy.

'The other twelve members of Betsy's coven are also spread around in unmarked graves,' he said, returning to the subject of the mound with a nod of his head. 'Fat lot of good their witching did their families, though. They're nothing short of pariahs in this village, and when rents and prices are rising faster than wages, poverty stares a lot of Farringham in the face. It was kind of you to offer Mary Bellingham work.'

Eleanor thought of the speed with which King James was going through the realm's finances while standards continued to plummet.

'Children should not be visited with the sins of their parents. It's hardly Mary's fault that her mother-in-law sold her soul to the Devil.'

'Indeed no.' His nod was tight lipped. 'Though there are some who claim Mary was the first to accuse her.'

'That business about turning Farmer Preston's bull into a toad?'

'Rumour has it Mary was seen at the gate that very night.'

'Nonsense,' Eleanor said. 'No respectable seamstress hangs round farm gates at midnight.' She tutted loudly. 'Next people will be saying she was part of the coven!'

'No, no, the brodder is convinced he has got to the root of the witchery. The number thirteen has a nice ring to it, I suppose. How is Mary's stitching, by the way?'

'Excellent. She is busy embroidering a night gown with violets right now, as it happens, and I have to say her workmanship is faultless.'

'Good,' Tom Jordan said, and there was an expression in his eyes that she couldn't identify, though it looked for all the world like a twinkle. 'I'm sure you two will get along famously.' He bowed. 'But if you'll excuse me, I have rats to catch.'

'Big 'uns?'

He spanned a gap between his two hands large enough for a dog. 'Huge.'

And with a chuckle that came from low in his throat he was gone.

* * *

Sitting alone in his finely appointed quarters, a bearded man with sharply pointed features pushed back the cowl from his head and belched loudly. As the King's agent, the brodder was in a position to command the best accommodations and the finest foods, and, best of all, he never needed to dip his hands in his purse. Not for this flagon of fine, golden malmsey. Not for the succulent capons, nor the dainty sweetmeats, nor the crusty pies bursting with apples. And most *certainly* he did not have to pay for services of that broad-hipped, buxom beauty who did things that his poor wife would faint at. But the hour was late, and tomorrow the brodder was setting off for Stoughton, his work in this village all done. He wished to savour his success with the best company he knew, and he knew no better company than his own.

From the corner of his eye, he thought he saw something black and furry dart across the floor, but when he rubbed his bleary eyes it was gone. He must have been mistaken, rats don't infest such sumptuous accommodation, so he returned to the task of counting his crosses.

And licked his lips at the prospect of collecting another in the morning before he left.

Solid gold, they'd be worth a fortune one day.

* * *

'Why, Mary, this night gown is exquisite.' Eleanor held it up to the lamp light. 'You've done a truly excellent job.'

'Thank you, my lady.' Her thin lips pinched in pride. 'Like I told my husband, good skills will always find an outlet.'

A picture formed of a young couple sat either side of the fire, him flabby and pale as he stared into his ale, her hard to the marrow as she carped and gloated in equal measures. Squawking like a magpie as she stitched and sewed, reminding him how she had found work when the man of the house had found none, eroding his confidence with her nagging and bullying, undermining him whenever she could.

'Indeed they do,' Eleanor said, linking her arm with Mary's. 'Now let us take a walk.'

'At this time of night?' Green eyes flashed in distaste. 'It's cold out.'

'As cold as the grave,' she agreed sweetly. 'But here. You may borrow a fur. I wouldn't want you catching a chill.'

Torn between making excuses or hobnobbing with gentry, the furs swung the balance for Mary. Obviously, you could see her thinking as they strolled through the village, Madam was lonely. And as they climbed Bramber Down with the aid of a lantern, you could see the calculations going on inside her head at how much a live-in companion might pocket.

Above them, the moon rose full and yellow.

'It was good sport, wasn't it?' Eleanor said at last. 'I mean a *bull*, for heaven's sake. How the village must have laughed when Farmer Preston found that toad.'

'Can I go back now, ma'am?' Mary asked.

'Soon.' And even though the smile was warm and reassuring, the hand that clamped her upper arm was like a vice. 'Only there's something we need to do first.'

Mary looked at the night gown Eleanor pulled out from under her own furs. 'I—I think I'll turn back, miss, if it's all the same with you.'

'But it is not all the same to me, Mary.' The voice had an edge to it. 'You see, by accusing Betsy of turning a prize bull into a toad, you thought you'd found a way to drive your mother-in-law out of the house. Her house, I might add.'

'I don't know what you're talking about.'

'Because even though you knew she hadn't done it, you also knew that allegations of witchcraft are always taken seriously. But just to be on the safe side, I'm sure you dropped a word in the parson's wife's ear that you'd heard Betsy cursing the brewer's mash, and wasn't it a coincidence that it was around the same time the parson got a toothache?'

It only took one drip of malice for the poison to take root. Mrs Dale was a glutton for gossip, and in no time the carpenter's megrims and someone's sick cow had turned into a full-scale blight on the village.

'You're a sensible girl, Mary Bellingham. Have you ever come across rheumatics, or for that matter ulcers, that come on overnight? And I wonder who planted the notion in Kitty the dairymaid's head that her cramps were caused by something other than the onset of her menstruals.'

'You don't know what you're talking about,' Mary said defiantly. 'Betsy confessed to everything, the parson heard her and the brodder wrote it down.'

'What would you expect from an old woman who'd been stripped naked in front of the entire village then trussed up in such a way that sinking's impossible.'

Bastards.

Green eyes narrowed. 'What do you mean, impossible?'

'Exactly what it sounds like,' Eleanor said. 'And because of one selfish bitch's bid to turn an old woman out, tragedy rippled right across this village, causing pain, distress and hardship to more people than anyone could imagine.'

'It's not my fault.' She tossed her head. 'I thought ducking the witch meant using the ducking stool. Betsy thought so as well.'

'Of course, it's your fault! All of this is your fault!' Eleanor's eyes flashed in fury. 'And don't tell me what you thought, because the only thing you thought about was yourself, and dammit, you revelled in Betsy's humiliation. When she was stripped naked, you laughed, and when she was tossed into a freezing cold millpond and floated, you wallowed in satisfaction. Ah, here we are.'

She held up the lantern to reveal a freshly turned mound in which a shroud glowed below in the moonlight.

'Betsy's grave.'

Mary stared. 'You're mad, you are. You ought to be in one of them asylum places.'

'Even when the woman who welcomed you into her family was tied in a sack that the brodder strung over the gallows tree, you didn't think about Betsy. You didn't *once* stop to wonder what fear was in her heart when the god she believed in rejected her body on waters that had been blessed by the priest. Shame on you.'

'I thought she'd be found innocent,' Mary protested.

'If you tell me once more what you thought,' Eleanor hissed, 'so help me I will leave your body in this grave and no one will be any the wiser.'

Imagine the terror of being tied in a sack, knowing it was to swing from the gallows. The knowledge of innocence mixed with holy rejection when the brodder set the sack swinging. Swinging and swinging, back and forth, back and forth, imagine what it must have been like…

The rocking motion causes disorientation.

The victim vomits but has no room to move.

She's gagging, but trapped in her own vile stench.

And still the sack keeps on swinging—

'How long did you stand there laughing at her, Mary? How many hours did you watch an old woman struggle for breath and for dignity, until she finally confessed to her sins?'

The brodder had recorded it in delicate detail, insisting the witch give up the name of her accomplice, who in turn, of course, gave up the names of others.

'They call it the witch's cradle and, just like the tying of bonds for ducking the witch, it was designed with great care,' she told Mary. 'The dice are suitably loaded.'

Often the victim suffers hallucinations as well, which was how Lucy Hewitt, eighty-two years old, admitted convening with the coven at the crossroads at midnight, conjuring the dead round the compass of death as they copulated with Satan in turn.

'That's not all.'

Anger was rising like a rip tide inside her. She could no more hold it back than turn push back the sun.

'Before hanging, it is the witchfinder's solemn duty to wash away corruption and redeem the soul, and do you know how he does that? Do you, Mary? The brodder ties his victim to the boards naked—oh yes, naked, he's a sadist to his core—and then he pinches their nose until they can stand it no more, and when they frantically open their mouth to gasp for air he stuffs a funnel in it and pours scalding water down their throat.'

Mary gulped but quickly recovered. 'All right, I admit it got out of hand, but I don't see what this has to do with you—'

'No? Well, that's the interesting part, Mary. You see, if you're going to accuse someone of witchcraft, you really ought to know who and what you are dealing with.' Eleanor smiled. 'Me, Mary. I'm the real thing.'

Mary's face went white and her mouth dropped. 'Dear God in heaven!'

'Somehow I doubt that. In the same way that I can't accept cloven-hoofed monsters prancing around waving pitchforks, I find it difficult to believe in a god who idly stands by while decent women suffer the most abominable torture in his name, either.'

'So—' For the first time, Mary was worried. 'Are you going to make a wax image of me and burn it slowly to twist up my body and make me suffer pain?'

'Worse,' Eleanor said, because there was no point in telling the girl that witchcraft had nothing whatsoever to do with the black arts, but revolved around health and wellbeing. 'My curse upon you is a conscience. Every day for the rest of your life, Mary Bellingham, you will wake up with a body every bit as sturdy as it is today, and every day you will relive Betsy's torment, your role in it and the tragedy you brought upon not just thirteen innocent women, but also those who had loved and depended on them.'

For as the brodder himself proved, if you plant an idea in a gullible brain, that idea will quickly take hold. And now that Mary had been told she'd be fit and healthy for the rest of her life, as a result, she probably would be. The stronger to relive and repent the wickedness she had done. The damage she had done to them all.

'Now get down into that grave, and wrap the poor woman in a decent shroud,' she told Mary.

Aunt Betsy had always had a fondness for violets.

* * *

What is witchcraft? Is it the worship of evil for evil's own sake? Is it flying on broomsticks, cooking toads in their blood, whispering spells of cruelty and malice?

In the eyes of King James, witches served the Devil's apprenticeship, causing harm by unnatural means. Through their dark magic and Satanic rites, he saw them conjuring demons and inflicting disease, mixing sorcery that couldn't just bring on death, but was capable of raising the dead. To be fair, his obsession was rooted in personal acquaintance. When the ship on which he was bringing home his Danish wife was caught in a storm, he didn't stop to question how a group of ordinary people could possibly have conjured a tempest, much less what their reasoning might be. He simply attended their trial, believed what he'd heard, then promptly set about protecting himself and his kingdom through the simple expedience of wiping out witchcraft.

Poor James. An intellectual, yet he couldn't see that saintly relics were no different from protective amulets. A scholar, yet he didn't comprehend how the Church was manipulating paganism by propagating tales of demons and witchcraft to deliberately instil fear for its own ends.

Or did he?

If people turned to the Church for support in such dark, turbulent times (and eventually became dependent on it), would the same not be true of the King? That by extending the law to make witchcraft a capital offence—especially without benefit of clergy—might his own influence not grow, too?

But how does one define it? Certainly, Geoffrey Dearborn's wealth and influence could have secured him a wife among the landed gentry, yet it was the full-breasted, auburn-haired daughter of his tailor that he had chosen and adored from that day onward. Bewitched? Possibly, for the feeling was far from mutual, and poor Geoffrey. Seven years and still no sign of an heir. But then the rhizomes of water lilies had that effect, even if he didn't know.

A long night of drinking.

A wife who sighs the next morning, tells him he was remarkable.

Oh, no, Geoffrey would never denounce his red-headed love, even if the thought crossed Mary's mind later.

'I'm sorry, but you simply can't keep going round accusing witches; people will think you're a laughing stock,' Eleanor tutted, as they wheeled Betsy's corpse down the hill to the undertaker's workshop. 'And if my own cousin didn't recognise me, who'll believe you, and trust me, the brodder won't be pointing his bodkin in my direction, I assure you.'

The one thing about money is that it can buy you just about anything. Alibis actually rate pretty low on the scale.

'Go back to the stone you crawled under from, Mary.' With a soft click, the padlock on the door of the workshop sprang open. 'And may you have a long life with the husband who backed you over his mother.'

Now both parties get what they deserve.

Prising the lid off a cheap wooden coffin, Eleanor thought back to the tiny kitchen behind the tailor's shop, stitching her violets to hoots of laughter from her aunt, who sang songs and baked bread while her sister-in-law rested from giving birth to the twins, and taking time out between washing and scrubbing to teach the young Eleanor her letters. Covering Betsy's face with her violet kerchief, she hoped that Seth Mabbett, whose coffin this was, didn't mind sharing, but it was important Betsy Bellingham was laid to rest in hallowed ground, and the fact that her niece had no faith in God didn't matter.

Betsy had, that was the point.

* * *

Blackestone Manor had only just got used to having visitors under its roof before Eleanor was packing her bags, and wasn't it a scandal that the parson's wife had raised poor Sir Geoffrey's hopes by suggesting it was more than convalescence after a cold? Where *did* she get the idea from, that's what people wanted to know, and now they thought about it, wasn't Mrs. Dale always exaggerating?

Dear me, she'd even hinted that she'd been deliberately held back at the Manor in time to catch her death from the storm, but why should Sir Geoffrey's wife do a wicked thing like that? It was nothing but a cover for poisoning her husband, if you asked them. Accidental, of course, but all the same. Fewer callers knocked on the parson's wife.

'That was the old man who lived over the road from the witch,' a voice said, as Eleanor paused in the lych gate.

'Which one?' she asked. 'That one?'

'Not graves. The funeral you were watching before I arrived.'

'I was admiring the church steeple.'

'Unusual to find the gentry with such a keen interest in gargoyles,' Tom Jordan replied, crossing his arms. 'Lucky you.'

She said nothing. He made no move to leave. The smell of pinecones and hay hung between them.

'Did you hear about the brodder?' he asked after a while. 'They found him dead at the table, slumped over his crosses and chains.'

Eleanor looked round sharply. 'Did they indeed?'

'Drank too much, ate too much, it was bound to catch up with him in the end, I suppose.'

'More than likely,' she said, though it was strange that baneberries were often used as rat poison, and that the rat-catcher had been setting traps in Milord's courthouse at exactly the same time as the parson was checking the records. Just as he had been eliminating vermin from the brodder's personal quarters—

She looked at his long, craggy face and prematurely white hair, and his words floated back across time.

Another two days I give him, no more.

They had been discussing the witchfinder's imminent departure for Stoughton, to root out the truth of the accusations over there.

The King's agent is nothing, if not thorough.

James might have an obsession with demonology, she reflected, but Parliament wasn't so sure. And since too many allegations were going round for their liking, other agents were also dispatched in the King's name. Men who followed the witchprickers/brodders, call them what you will, to ensure that fair play was done…

'It's too early for them to be plentiful yet, but I thought somehow you might like these.'

As the funeral procession stopped at the graveside, he pressed a posy of violets into her hand. By the time the mist had cleared from Eleanor's eyes, he was gone, but there was something else with the flowers, she noticed.

A bodkin.

Yes indeed, she thought shivering. The King's agent was nothing if not thorough.

And in the lych gate stood an empty cage.

The Great Rivorsky

It's not easy being The Great Rivorsky. Take Milan, for instance. Now, had I not already made an elephant—a fully grown bull, if you please—vanish before their very eyes? Was it my fault I couldn't make the wretched beast reappear? Sometimes I think the audience hoard their kitchen waste for just such an occasion, and it didn't help that the creature *would* keep on trumpeting. I might have got away with it, otherwise—pretending its disappearance was part of the act—were it not for that ear-splitting racket.

Not that the elephant had ever brought me anything but bad luck. Three days out of Milan, didn't it drop dead? Just like that? The local authorities, I can tell you, did not take kindly to a three-ton carcase dumped on the roadside—although that, my friend, wasn't the worst part. The worst part was, temperamental to the end, the despicable animal crushed a very good keeper in the process. Nikko had been with me right from Stamboul.

After that, of course, Vienna was a disaster. This was only to be expected. Even in 1909 a magician can't get his hands on an elephant at just a moment's notice and, although I used a few of those distorting fairground mirrors to—if I may so myself, a truly spectacular effect—you can't fool an audience standing as close as they were that a horse painted grey is an elephant. The Viennese must have been hoarding *their* waste for months.

What? You think I joke? Please! Please, I am Russian. I do not joke. What I say is the truth. The Great Rivorsky ever speaks *only* the truth! What was that? Ah, you point out that I am not Russian. Well, no, strictly speaking I am Hungarian in origin. But The Great Rivorsky *has* played before the court of the Tsar—see here. On the posters. It says so. That earns me the right for a bit of flexibility on the name front, don't you think?

Oh, you've finished your drink. Another Vodka, perhaps? I could use a top-up myself.

I told you about Paris, did I not? No? Not about Michelline—my assistant before last? (Or was it the one before that?) You are already aware that Paris was worse than Berlin and that Berlin made Vienna look good, but I could have sworn I told you the reason. Your good health, by the way. Or rather, what is it you British say? Bottoms up. Very appropriate, under the circumstances I am about to relate.

Obviously I had given up on the elephant by Paris. In fact, you will observe that I've written it out of my act altogether, at least until I have sufficient time to get hold of a decent replacement, which won't be before my world tour is over and that's not for another six months. In consequence, you will sympathise, I am sure—the disappearing elephant being my star act—when I tell you that I was forced both to cut the price of admission and take a smaller, shall we say less prominent, theatre in Montmartre. And that was the problem, of course. You just can't rely on the staff in these little backstreet establishments.

What happened was this. I had just finished sawing Michelline in half and had swung the two boxes apart, thereby assuring the audience that they had not wasted good money to watch some cheap trickster at work, when suddenly the footlights started to smoke. The stage manager (imbecile!) thought this was the signal for the next act—my Houdini-style underwater escape—and yanked the trapdoor lever one act too early. I suppose you can guess what happened next. Here I am, happily showing the audience the Mechanical-Twitching-Foot box, when from the corner of my eye I see poor Michelline, bent double in the other contraption, going *fsssst!* Straight down the shoot.

I tried passing it off as a comic turn—who would not? —but alas,

Michelline sabotaged my attempts to salvage the show. It's not as if she was hurt, either. The box bounced only the once, but oh my! Have you ever heard so many profanities falling from such sweet rose-red lips? And she, the minx, led me to believe she was from a respectable family, too.

Well, at that point, I confess I would have welcomed an onslaught of distressed vegetable marrows. Because you see the audience, being Parisians and therefore without mercy, did not waste their time jeering or hurling missiles. The scum demanded their money back…

Which is why you find me today, my friend, in this shabby little theatre in the back of beyond. No place for The Great Rivorsky, I admit, but until I can overturn my run of misfortunes, what else can I do?

Now tell me. What is it you wish to see me about?

No, no, I'm fine. Honestly. It was the vodka. Went down the wrong way. Nothing to do with your proposition, I assure you. Just give me a minute to get my breath back.

That's better. Now let me just get this straight in my mind. You are willing to pay me one hundred pounds, yes, to let you and your good lady wife take part in my show? One hundred English sterling pounds, cash? And all I have to do to earn what is effectively one night's full takings is to teach you, sir, how to stick the swords in the basket and to teach your good lady wife to act as assistant, is that right? It is. I see…

Well, actually, no, I don't see. After all, it is obvious from your generosity as much as your attire that you are a gentleman, sir, and whilst you did explain how you wanted to put on a special performance for your friends, a sort of amateur dramatics with magic—I mean to say, one hundred pounds…? Oh, one hundred and *fifty*. In that case, sir, your reason is none of my business.

However.

If I might make a suggestion? Nancy! Nancy, come over here, will you, I want you to show this gentleman here how to levitate. Pass me the hoops, dear. Right, sir, if you could just watch Nancy a minute, this is how it is done. Curtains, please! Thank you.

Now first, you go through the motions of pretending to hypnotise your dear lady—we can practise that later—and get her to lie flat on the table. Then you say a few words of mumbo jumbo, there'll be drumbeats, a bit of smoke to add to the atmosphere, but the most important thing is that you position yourself here, right at the front of the stage, well away from the table. More words, a few hand gestures and, look, up goes Nancy. You pass the hoop over her body like so, like so, and like so, to prove there is nothing holding her up except the power of your mind—but, of course, as you and I know, it's all sleight of hand; there is a thin metal support between the curtains, attached to a winch which actually does all the lifting and lowering.

No, sir, I am aware this is not the trick you asked to be taught, but—how best can I put this? Oh, thank you, Nancy, you may go. The thing is, and excuse my whispering, but this is a *very* delicate matter. You see, the girls who assist in my acts are—how can I put it? —of a lower class than yourself. And they don't, er, object to…

To put it bluntly, sir, the other acts can only work with girls wearing the *minimum* of attire.

As for your wife, well, a well-tailored costume, whilst fashionable and no doubt much admired, is useless in any other act than levitation, which actually relies on long, heavy skirts to conceal the metal support and the winch. So I would certainly recommend—

But no, you are adamant. It has to be the girl in the basket with swords. And you would not consider…? No. I see. It *has* to be the girl in the basket with swords. Then allow me to demonstrate.

Ah, excuse me one moment. Pepé, how many times must I tell you? When you come down the rope, use your hands *and* your feet. Come down slowly. *Lente.*

A hundred apologies, but the dwarf, sir, he is Spanish. We have to use midgets for the Indian rope trick these days, since legislation prevents us employing children to climb up, but Pepé, he has not got the hang of it yet and a rope-burn between the legs is not a good thing for a dwarf. Now where were we? Oh, yes. The illusion.

Nancy, come back again, will you, dear, and fetch the basket and swords, there's a good girl. Right. You see my assistant climb inside. I cover her with this swathe of black velvet. Down she goes. On with the lid. These are the swords I use—test them yourself, sir, they are real and they are razor sharp. In goes the first one. You notice the angle? Then the next. Also at a sharp angle. Then the rest, one by one, and now it is impossible, is it not, for them not to have sliced through at least part of my lovely assistant? But just to make sure, we put the last one in here like so. Through the *lid*!

And you know yourself there is no monkey business with this trick. No trapdoors. Nancy is definitely inside, aren't you, dear? Louder, please, Nancy. Thank you. Out come the swords, in the same order they went in. Off comes the lid. I lay the black velvet over the top and climb inside to prove that the basket is empty. Out I come, The Great Rivorsky. Over goes the velvet again. I say some words, snap my fingers, and—well done, Nancy. This time you really are free to go.

The trick here is that the basket is much bigger than it appears, and at the same time my assistant scrunches herself up really small. But even though you tell me your good lady wife can be talked in to wearing the, ahem, minimum of attire and is able to make herself very small, I must warn you! This is a dangerous act.

Very dangerous. It relies on my assistant guiding the swords into place. That is the reason they go in so slowly. She steers them round her body herself. And, of course, it is pitch black inside. Even I, talented as I am, practise several times daily with Nancy.

But if you are sure this is the act you want to perform…?

Very well, then. I shall arrange for the blades to be blunted. What's that? Your friends are all officers, coming along with their families? I had no idea, sir. Mafeking, you say? Well, well, who'd have thought I would be sharing a vodka or two with a hero? Please. Have another. And a toast to you and, yes, another to your good lady wife.

But the thing is, sir, does it matter? Oh, no, not war. Please! I meant no slur, you being a colonel and all that. No, I was merely alluding to the matter of the swords being blunt. Well, yes, of *course* The Great Rivorsky always proves to his audience that the blades are sharp as well as deadly…

Very good. If that is what you desire. For the—what did you say—*two* hundred pounds you are now offering, be assured I will show you personally how to insert the weapons into the basket at the appropriate angles and speed.

When do you wish to start?

* * *

Ladies and gentlemen! Do not be alarmed! Due to unforeseen circumstances, we will have to close the show for tonight. Yes, yes, that is real blood, madam, seeping under the curtain, but if you would all leave the theatre quietly and in an orderly file, please? Thank you. Thank you. Good night. Thank you all.

Is the doctor here yet?

Oh, my friend, my friend, what can I say? Such a tragedy! Such calamity! But this is what happens, you see, when dangerous tricks are performed in amateur hands.

Please. Please step back, all of you. Give us room. Nancy, get the stage hands out of here and clear the theatre, there's a good girl.

After all, my friend, we don't want people around to hear our private conversation, now do we?

The doctor? No, no, he's not here yet, but then he's not likely to be, is he? If anything goes wrong, you said, make sure you send for Dr. Willis. Willis, you stressed, Dr. Willis. 48 Harley Street. But of course there is no Dr. Willis at 48 Harley Street—nor at any other number along that most prestigious of rows. In fact, I could not find a Dr. Willis anywhere in London except for a drunk charlatan down in Whitechapel. What's that? Did you not think I would check? *Please!* I am The Great Rivorsky. To make illusions work, a magician has to be thorough.

And any man prepared to pay an incredible two hundred pounds to put on a show in front of his friends is either a fool or a…

Well, there's no need for us to go into that.

So much blood. Dear me, I had not imagined there would be so much blood—

I'm sorry, you said something there and I missed it. But then it is not easy to concentrate. I am not as a rule squeamish, but… Excuse me, I need a bucket. Ach, that's better. Dear God, my friend, you look awful. That surprises me, because I confess, I didn't expect that.

We still have a few minutes to ourselves, before, as you British say, the balloon goes up. I think the stories are straight. The police will arrive, blowing their whistles now the emergency's over, and naturally I will tell them the truth.

That the colonel here staged a private show for his friends.

That most of the evening went exceptionally well, as one indeed would expect. I am, after all, The Great Rivorsky.

But I will go over it in detail for the police. How Pepé's Indian rope trick worked a treat. How Nancy was then sawn in half, your good lady wife was levitated by yourself, how Nancy was then sawn into three…

And then we come to the part of the terrible accident.

It happens, you know. In fact, it has happened three or four times to my certain knowledge, but then it is a very dangerous act.

Catching the bullet in the mouth.

Yes, yes, my friend, I know I assured you that it was a blank your good lady would be firing and that you simply kept the real one under your tongue until it was needed. Which I have removed, by the way. That's what made me sick a moment ago. Anyway, I apologise most sincerely for the deception, but you must remember: deception is my stock-in-trade. And it was obvious, was it not, what you wanted right from the start?

To murder your good lady wife and make it appear a tragic stage accident.

It is the old, old story, is it not? A plain heiress swept off her feet by a dashing, if penniless, cavalry officer—oh, how often do you ever see a lonely heiress? Tell me, my friend. How much did you stand to gain from her death?

What's that you say? Mon dieu, certainly not! What sort of a man do you take me for, that I would tell your good lady wife of your devilish plans? Did I not tell you at the outset that two hundred pounds buys the utmost confidentiality?

Mind you, when it came to explaining to that fine woman what she would be obliged to wear for the evening's entertainment, I admit that I *may* have steered the conversation somewhat. She does not lack intelligence, the lady, and was remarkably quick on the uptake. She confessed to me that she had been aware for some time that your ardour had cooled—indeed, as I recall, she gave the precise date as your return from honeymoon—and the bullet idea was entirely her own.

Huh? Oh, very well, then, yes. I admit she had a *little* encouragement, but then she was much more forthcoming in her finances. Five hundred pounds down and another five hundred once the police are satisfied in their enquiries. Which, of course, they will be. As I say, there are several precedents for this happening, and it really doesn't matter who fires the gun. Pistols are unpredictable creatures. Rather like elephants, in that respect.

So thanks to you and your wife's generosity, with twelve hundred pounds I shall be able to stage a show to rival Barnum's. Not just Europe, either. I see The Great Rivorsky touring America next year.

My, you *are* looking pale. And so cold. Here, let me cover you with my cloak. It is an old one, anyway. Now then, did I ever tell you about the time we toured Munich and my top trapeze artist eloped not just with Coki the Clown, but with the whole week's takings, and on two of my finest performing ponies as well?

Oh, I tell you, my friend. It's not at all easy being The Great Rivorsky.

Heaven Knows

'Come in, Frank. Sit down.' St. Peter waved me to the chair in front of his desk. It was deep and cushioned, like floating on air. 'Thanks for coming so quickly.'

'Didn't realize I had a choice,' I said. 'Only last time—'

'I know, I know. One minute you're driving down the M1 in thick fog. Next thing, here you are, with no recollection of that twenty-two car pile-up, much less the lorry that smashed into you at sixty miles an hour.' His mouth twisted. 'Sorry we couldn't cushion the shock, Frank. There's nothing I'd like better than to give everyone a heads-up on these things. Just doesn't work that way, I'm afraid.'

Better for me than for most, I supposed. No devastated wife throwing herself on my coffin. No traumatized kids growing up scarred. Even my parents beat me to it by thirty-nine years, after a car wreck claimed their lives on the north side of London. We O'Donnells are obviously magnets when it comes to twisted metal.

'If it's about being behind on my report—'

When you arrive, you're asked how you'd like to spend eternity. What would make you happy forever? *I was a detective in the police force before I went private,* I said. *Any chance of—?* Rhetorical question. Heaven always gives you what you want. Which means that, although my job is to reunite new arrivals with their loved ones, this is a big place and the issues are complex. Tracing them is not always easy.

'No, no, no, Frank, nothing of the kind. Any time you're ready, no rush.' St. Peter smiled. 'Time has no meaning here, and in any case.' He allowed himself a soft chuckle. 'It's not as if either of us is going anywhere, is it?'

'Glad to hear it. Because for a moment, I thought I was being reassigned.'

'Reass—? Oh, you mean expelled. Absolutely not, Frank. No way. Once you're in, you are *in*.'

'Funny, but I recall some bloke by the name of Lucifer was served with an eviction notice a while back.'

'History, schmistory.' St. Peter swatted it away as if a wasp had slipped in through the Gates. 'We've tightened the Admissions procedures since then, talking of which—' He leaned forward, elbows on the desk. 'Are you happy, Frank?'

'This is Heaven,' I said. 'Why wouldn't I be?'

No answer. He just sat there, stroking his neat, little Van Dyke beard, dark eyes staring into space. Through the Gate House window, I watched cherubs weighing the feather of truth, while angels read the newcomers' auras. Integrity. Loyalty. Honesty. Humour. Every human attribute splayed out in a vast spectrum of colour, like some celestial peacock, shaded according to strength.

'Thing is,' St. Peter said. 'We have something of a conundrum on our hands.'

A few taps on the divine keyboard brought up a photo on the big screen behind him. Blonde girl, pretty, laughing into the camera.

'Lucy Fuller,' he said. 'Twenty-four years old. Events organizer. Single. She sustained seventeen stab wounds close to her home in Winchester, where her attacker either left her for dead, or ran off when they heard footsteps approaching.'

A second picture flashed up alongside. Middle-aged couple with kind eyes and a springer spaniel at their feet.

'John and Susan Kincade were walking their dog in the woods, dog started barking, and bingo. Without Mrs. Kincade's nursing skills, a strong mobile signal and an exceptionally rapid response from the emergency services, Lucy Fuller would have died.'

'Except she obviously did, or we wouldn't be having this

conversation.'

'Now that, Frank, is precisely the kind of logic we're looking for on this case, so let me ask you a question. How do you feel about going back in the field?'

My stomach tightened. 'You mean earth?'

'We…don't actually think of it in those terms, but, yes. A temporary return to your old life.' He spread his hands. 'Sort of your old life, anyway. Technically you won't be alive, and you most certainly won't be allowed to contact your loved ones—'

What loved ones? An ex-wife who hated my guts so badly, she burned every item I'd owned, then posted a video of her bonfire on YouTube? Or my colleagues from the police force, who felt I sold them out when I opened up as a private detective?

'Can't say it holds much appeal.' An understatement, if ever there was one. 'Especially when I don't see a problem. I'm assuming Lucy Fuller died of her injuries?'

The Boss wouldn't be talking to an ex-CID officer if she'd slipped under a bus.

'Laceration of the renal artery led to delayed complications, but before she died, she identified this man—' A third photo flashed up, replacing Lucy's rescuers. '—as her assailant.'

Slim build, dark hair, easy grin. In his Coldplay t-shirt, two-day stubble and crumpled jeans, he didn't look the seventeen-stab-wound type. Then again, who does? I reached for the file, which told me his name was Craig Langstone, twenty-six years old, also from Winchester, where he worked as a media consultant. Somewhere in the file it probably told me what a media consultant was. I was too busy reading how, for almost a year, he and Lucy had been an item. Until she caught him in bed with another woman.

'What am I missing?' I flicked through the report a second time, in case I'd skipped a page. 'Says here, he committed suicide the day after she died. Hardly an exceptional event, in my experience.'

Guy has fling, guy regrets it, guy tries to win back girl, girl tells him where to go, guy gets angry, things turn nasty, girl ends up in hospital or worse. Overcome with guilt—or because the net is closing in—he tops himself. I'd seen it happen a dozen times, during the course of my career. Heard of it hundreds more.

'Well, now, that's where things get complicated,' the Boss said, leaning back. 'Craig Langstone turned up at the Gate House—'

Everybody does, this being the start point for the admittance/elimination process.

'—swearing black was white he didn't do it.' St. Peter grinned. 'Hardly an exceptional event, in *my* experience, either. Except.' He threw up his hands. 'When the cherubs weighed the feather of truth, it passed with flying colours, and when the angels read his aura, that also came out tops. To be absolutely certain, we had the seraphim put him through the Soul Scanner, but guess what? Not the faintest trace of evil to be found.'

'Then the girlfriend's lying. Or at the very least mistaken.'

'Our view exactly. In the end, we brought in the archangels to test her, that's how serious it was, but the thing is, Lucy's story never wavers. She was taking her usual Sunday morning run when Craig jumped out and struck her from behind.'

'She didn't see him?'

'No, but she recognized his voice, and, during the course of the attack, he referred to things that only the two of them could possibly have known.'

I want you out of my life, he kept shouting. *I want you out of my life.* The same words over and over, which at first she did not understand.

You've made a mistake! I'm Lucy Fuller, I live—

Remember that night we made love on the beach? When you lost your earring and we spent half the night searching for it, and it was caught on my shirt all along?

That was when she knew it was Craig. That, and various other things he brought up. Silly things. Insignificant things. Like their pet names for each other, the first meal she cooked him, that picnic by the river when his ice cream cone fell in the water, bobbing downstream like a raft. Even then, she'd thought it was just his fists he was using. The man she knew—the man she'd loved—would never lie in wait with a knife…

'Which leaves me something of a predicament,' the Boss said. 'She says he did it, and she's telling the truth. He says he didn't, and *he's* telling the truth. Until we get to the bottom of this, I'm not in a position to grant admittance, or exclusion, to either party.'

'Oh, no, not Limbo?'

'Now you see why I asked you here.' His face twisted. 'Uncertainty is ten times worse than Hell, Frank. In Hell, there's no false hope.'

Four contented years of reuniting children with parents, widows with husbands, lovers with one another, congealed like duck fat in the pit of my stomach. Memories flooded back. Of cold, lonely evenings. An even colder, lonelier bed.

'When do I leave?' I asked brightly.

* * *

Winchester, for those of you who have never been, is just an hour and a half from London and a completely different world. Bordered by lush water meadows on the east, golf courses on the west, it has a town centre lined with half-timbered houses, and boasts what was once thought to be the original Round Table from King Arthur's court. Turn any corner and you'll find a courtyard, arch or alleyway virtually unchanged from Chaucer's day, not to mention a 12th century castle, an alm's house built by William the Conquerer's grandson, and the longest damn cathedral in Europe. It doesn't hurt, either, that the river cuts right through the city, creating an oasis of calm and tranquility in a distinctly uncalm, untranquil world.

I stood beneath the statue of King Alfred, the one who burnt the cakes, feeling the spring sunshine warming my face for the first time in over four years. Despite countless visits to Winchester Prison during my spell in the force, this was the first time I'd stopped to listen to the voices of the Chapel choir drifting on the air, and suddenly it seemed a lighter, freer man who wandered round the Cathedral close, gazing up at the stained glass windows while the organ resonated round Jane Austen's grave. And as I walked through gateways that had stood for a thousand years, and passed mills that were almost as old, I felt an unexpected pull…

'Be careful,' St. Peter warned, once I'd been primed, updated and kitted out for travel. 'Don't allow yourself to become emotionally involved.'

'No worries there,' I laughed. 'Plug ugly flatfoots like me, we never get the girl.'

'Who's worried? Plug ugly flatfoots like you can take care of yourselves!' He paused, and the smile dropped from his face. 'Seriously, Frank. It's the living I worry about. Once they cross over, we can erase any bad memories, if that's what they want. But while they're still in the physical zone, there's nothing we can do to influence events as they unfold. Despite what some people think.'

'I'll be good.'

'I know, but—emotional attachment means someone gets hurt when it comes time to leave, and if it isn't the traveller we send back, it's the person they leave behind, and I've seen it happen too often. All chance of a happy future destroyed, because they're literally chasing a shadow.'

'Trust me.' I gave his shoulder a reassuring squeeze. 'Fifty-four's too old to start going off the rails.'

'Deny the Holocaust, deny paternity, deny the existence of God if you must,' he laughed back. 'But never, ever deny the male mid-life crisis!' He shook my hand. 'Best of luck, son. Those kids are counting on you, and remember. No diversions, no involvement, just facts.'

'No diversions, no involvement, just facts,' I promised.

Yet an hour into the mission, what do I do? I fall in love with a city.

Mind you, at least the girls were safe.

But now, with two carefree faces burning a hole in my conscience, it was time to leave the castles, crypts and tearooms and set to work, with the crime scene top priority. Hardly the freshest I'd ever worked, because, like St. Peter said, time loses its significance once you cross the

Threshold. Craig and Lucy's sojourn in Limbo might mean unchanging spiritual agony, but in earth times, seven years had drifted by. A lot of time for a murder investigation, but it was crucial to get a feeling for this peaceful, wooded hillside, where a young woman was ambushed, stabbed and left for dead.

I want you out of my life.

I closed my eyes, picturing Lucy, barely out of breath at the start of her run, thinking she'd tripped, until she felt herself being hit in the back, and heard a man spitting hatred into her ear.

I want you out of my life. Out of my life. Out of my life—

I opened my eyes, staring down at the spires and rooftops until the hatred faded. Right then. I drew a deep breath. Next stop Lucy's parents, and if you think it's tough standing on the spot where a girl was viciously attacked, it's child's play compared to questioning the bereaved parents. The only thing worse is breaking bad news.

I needed to tread carefully, too. If they got wind that my investigation wasn't kosher and contacted the police, they would also realize that neither Frank O'Donnell or his so-called agency existed. That in itself wasn't a problem. I'd be whisked back, they'd be confused, no one would be any the wiser. But if this mission was aborted, who knows when the next attempt would be made? In another seven years, memories would have faded to dust, witnesses might well be dead. What chance, then, of Craig and Lucy *ever* being released from their spiritual prison?

I am man enough to admit that my hand was shaking as I rang the Fullers' doorbell, the first of several interviews, and by the time night fell, my head was splitting after putting so many decent, wounded people through the wringer. Even after renewing my acquaintance with Chivas Regal—perhaps the only true friend I'd ever had—I still couldn't shake off their pain and suffering. Much less the guilt of forcing them to relive the blackest moments of their lives, probing memories they'd spent seven years trying to bury.

Somewhere in the early hours, I dropped into my hotel bed, no longer some distracted tourist revisiting a foreign land, in which so much had changed and yet so little.

My only thought was, shit. Tomorrow, I get to wreck some other poor sod's life.

* * *

'Mrs. Langstone? Frank O'Donnell from the D.I.A.' I handed her a card that looked every inch the biz. 'I wonder if I might have a word about your son?'

She handed the card back. 'I've never heard of the D.I.A.'

'It's a new initiative. Our brief is to clarify certain unresolved issues which—'

'You work for the Government?'

'A private corporation. May I come in?'

'No.'

Hostility's nothing new. Mothers either welcome you indoors, burst into tears, then swear their son's a good boy, an honest boy, who wouldn't hurt a fly. Or they hurl abuse because their baby's being victimized, those bastard cops had set him up, that he was at home eating pizza at the time. (And, of course, that he wouldn't hurt a fly.) Occasionally, though, they slam the door in your face, but what made me wedge my foot in this particular door had less to do with a murder investigation. More to do with the fact that, with her long blonde hair, tight top and skinny jeans, Craig's mum was one foxy looking woman.

'Five minutes, Mrs. Langstone. Please.'

Blue eyes scanned the clear blue sky and the stillness of the newly unfurled leaves. 'Very well, we'll walk. Give me a minute.'

Most men, I thought, would give her the earth if she so much as crooked her little finger.

Rather than stand, like some hapless vacuum cleaner salesman, at the glossy woodwork that had closed gently, but firmly, in my face, I leaned my elbows on the railings, watching the water gurgling past.

* * *

My home was the Victorian terraced house that I'd inherited from my parents. At the time of their crash, I'd barely turned fifteen, and my aunt—my father's sister—was appointed my legal guardian. In the face of ferocious opposition from my uncle to sell the house and put the cash in trust, she rented it out. In part, this paid for my keep. Mainly, though, the income gave me pocket money that most boys my age could only dream of, and a home of my own once I turned twenty-one. All of which appealed to the gold-digging virtues of my ex-wife, attracted to the money not the man. Not that I was rich, but when you're poor, comfortable equates to wealth, and that's about the best I can say in her defence. Sixteen years later, when I simply couldn't hack it any more, she became so enraged, when the court ruled in my favour about keeping the house, that she burned every single one of my possessions, including the few remaining photos of my parents. Needless to say, I haven't seen her since. In either dimension.

But roomy as the homestead was, it sat on a busy junction, plus I was never what you'd call handy with paintbrushes, screwdrivers or garden forks.

But this, this ancient flour mill, smack bang in the middle of town and converted into small, upscale apartments, was as far removed from tired and weed-infested as it was possible to get. Two hundred metres from the road, and you couldn't hear the traffic. Amazing. Just water rushing through the mill race, the quack of hungry ducks and a boisterous choir of birdsong from the trees. Times like this, I wished I could tell my willow warblers from my blackcaps. But at least I recognized the sparrows at my feet.

Just when I'd decided she'd had no intention of coming out, the front door opened and Craig's mother emerged, zipping up a leather jacket that half the women half her age wouldn't dare to wear. 'This way, Mr. O'Donnell.'

Yes, ma'am.

We followed the Itchen through the park, then out along the open water meadows, an artist's paradise of rolling downlands, wild flowers and waving catkins. We watched rainbow trout basking underneath the bridge, heard the occasional plop of a vole dropping into the water, and once caught the unmistakable—even for me—turquoise and orange flash of a kingfisher. On the way out, we discussed the weather, the economy, the problems in the Middle East. On the way back, we agreed that Pink Floyd were the best, stood in different corners when it came to politics, and discovered that we were both ambivalent when it came to Quentin Tarantino, which had to be a first.

'Well, that was a pleasant walk, Mr. O'Donnell.' You could almost hear the barriers go back up. 'Now perhaps you can tell me what exactly, after all this time, is unresolved about my son?'

I have a trick to break down barriers, and subtlety isn't it. 'His innocence,' I said.

'Oh, really? And what makes you such an expert?'

Everyone handles grief differently. There's no right way, no wrong way, though I wasn't sure brittle was helping. Still. If that's how she wanted to play it…

Sorry, Mum.' I'd read Craig's suicide note so many times, it was imprinted on my eyeballs. *'But the police don't believe me and I can't prove otherwise. If there is an afterlife, I can at least convince Lucy. Either way, we'll be together. Be happy for me, Mum. Love, C.'*

The clenching of fists was her only hint of emotion. I ploughed on.

'I spent twenty years in the police force, sixteen as a P.I., Mrs. Langstone, and contrary to popular belief, most suicides don't leave notes. Those that are, they're either short and abrupt, or they're long, rambling over-protestations of innocence by men who are as guilty as sin.'

'I don't follow you.'

'His letter hurt you, I know that—'

'Stop right there.' For all she tried, there was no snap to her voice. 'You know nothing about me, Mr. O'Donnell, much less how I feel.'

'Maybe I know more than you think. For instance, I know you don't trust me, and to be fair, I don't blame you.' All manner of shysters would have stepped forward after the tragedy, offering everything from psychic healing to seances and messages from "beyond". That was the reason for this walk. Establishing trust. Somewhere along the way, I must have passed the test, but these things cut both ways. 'I also know this cool-calm-and-collected manner of yours is an act.'

The mere fact that she didn't bat an eyelid when I turned up out of the blue showed the amount of effort she'd put in, keeping it all together.

'You didn't keep me hanging around on the doorstep, because you're cold or distant, or even suspicious. You needed that long to regroup.'

'Or I could just be another long-time single mum, who's used to being strong and in control.'

'You could,' I agreed. 'But no one's that tough.' I stared at the pavement. Ran my hands through my hair. Changed tactics. 'You had a son. Your only child. And when he died, you felt you'd failed him. *If only you'd phoned him more often— Talked more about it— Made him stay with you after he'd won bail, instead of letting him go back to his own flat—*'

The same guilt trip the bereaved always take. That, as his mother, she should have recognized the signs. Should have phoned the Samaritans. Should never have let him out of her sight…

'Mothers are supposed to protect their children, Mr. O'Donnell. They're supposed to fight for them. Kill for them. Die for them, even. Not let them slip through their fingers like water.'

'With hindsight, we'd all be heroes, Mrs. Langstone, but I can tell you now, you did not fail your son. You believed in Craig when no one else did, you believe in him still, and, for the record, so do I.'

Her expression hadn't changed, but tears began rolling down her cheek, splashing on to her jacket.

'Angie,' she said. 'My name's Angie. I think you'd better come in.'

* * *

The flat was as neat inside as out, everything tidy and in its place, smelling of coffee, fresh flowers and clean laundry. I used to think I had minimalism down to a fine art, but her beige sofas, floaty voiles and glass-topped tables added a sophistication that left me in the shade. There were no photographs, at least none on display, but a set of watercolours, a sketchbook and a pile of dog-eared paperbacks proved this was no sterile show house, but a refuge. Not just from the busy insurance office where she worked, but a means of escaping from the past.

Guessing she'd need a moment to compose herself, I asked to use the bathroom, and spent so long pretending to wash my hands that she probably thought I suffered from OCD. By the time I returned, I expected to find her plumping the cushions on the sofa, lip gloss and mascara picture-perfect, every inch a woman in control. The only thing I'd got right was the sofa. Face in hands, she was perched on the edge, rocking back and forth. Same as she'd probably done every night, every weekend, since her son hanged himself…

I scooped her in my arms and opened a floodgate. Bitter, silent tears gave way to anguished howls, which turned to wracking sobs. And while she heaved away seven years of pent-up pain, I wondered why Ken Langstone bothered getting married, if he intended to continue the bachelor life. Why men like him wanted kids in the first place, when they had no intention of hanging around to kick a ball, read them stories, go to school plays. And why more wasn't done to make feckless fathers keep up with the payments, instead of forcing their young wives to work two jobs to pay off their debts.

When Angie finally lifted her head from my shoulder, her eyes were puffy, streaked, bloodshot and red-rimmed. What stood out above everything else, though, and which surprised me above everything else, was that they were smiling. 'You have a tight grip, Mr. O'Donnell.'

'Had to. You've held things together for so long, I didn't want the pieces falling apart on your lovely white carpet. And it's Frank.'

'Well, *Frank*, thank you.' She blew into a Kleenex. 'No one's held me like that for a long time.'

She was lucky. No one had ever held me like that.

'I'll put the kettle on,' because if there's one thing a police officer knows, it's his way around a kitchen. More sympathy can be shown, more confidences drawn, sometimes even confessions, over a simple cup of—

'Are you kidding?' She reached down and brought out a bottle. 'After waiting seven years to clear Craig's name, I deserve something stronger than tea. Glasses are in the cupboard behind you.'

I picked out two crystal tumblers and thought, Chivas Regal, Pink Floyd, Tarantino. Wonder what else we have in common.

'Lucy was a lovely girl,' she said, sliding on to a stool and leaning her elbows on the black granite breakfast bar. 'Smart. Funny. One of those women who light up a room every time they walk in, you know? Until some psychopath comes along and wipes everything out, and the worst part is, Frank, the police didn't even *look* for anyone else.'

Not true. Extensive searches and lab analyses were carried out at the time, witnesses questioned to the point of exhaustion, the details distributed to police forces across Britain and Europe, in an attempt to link this crime with others. But between the paramedics, the Kincades and, bless them, their dog, any evidence that might have exonerated Craig, or pointed the finger elsewhere, was destroyed. On top of that, Lucy wasn't the type to make enemies, which meant there was no one else in the frame. Especially when she was a hundred percent certain.

'Have you spoken to her parents?'

'I have.'

A visit that hammered home—as if I'd needed reminding—that, in a murder case, it was never just the one life that was taken. The ripples of destruction stretch wide and cut deep, and the truth is, they never heal. The crusading, inspirational lecturer that used to be Roger Fuller had become a shuffling old man, whose wife slept in a separate bedroom, because every time she closed her eyes at night, the tears wouldn't stop welling.

Why? That's what I don't understand. Why?

Which was pretty much as far as that interview went. Roger Fuller repeating the question over and over, shaking his head, shaking his hands, as if the very movement would somehow give him an answer. Sarah, his wife, bringing out photos, mementoes, certificates, clippings, in a desperate attempt to keep her daughter alive, when the only thing she could think about was her daughter's death.

If Langstone couldn't face being dumped, why not kill himself and leave it at that? Roger spat. *This way, everyone suffers.*

He was right. Everyone did. But not on account of Craig Langstone.

* * *

'I had a long chat with the Kincades, too.'

At least, with Susan Kincade. Her husband, John, was in Winchester Hospital, in the final throes of pancreatic cancer.

It's ironic, she'd said, ruffling the ears of the spaniel I'd seen in the photo, just a little stockier now, with white hairs round his muzzle and eyes. *My training prolonged that young woman's life, but in the end, I was unable to save the person I love most in the world.*

Another irony was that if her nursing skills hadn't prolonged Lucy's life in the first place, Craig Langstone would never have been in the frame.

Is there anything else you can tell me about that morning? Any detail that struck you as odd?

The police always look closely at who's first on the scene, but in this case, you couldn't get two more law-abiding, upstanding citizens than a ward sister and her bank manager husband.

Nothing. Sorry.

The ultimate irony, of course, was that if it hadn't been for Susan, Lucy would have died on the spot and her killer would have got off scot-free.

You have nothing to apologize for, Mrs. Kincade. You did everything you could. We shook hands on the doorstep. *For both your husband and Lucy Fuller.*

When she smiled, I caught a glimpse of the woman on St. Peter's screen, before sorrow added two decades to her face and subtracted three stones from her body.

It wouldn't be long before John Kincade crossed the Threshold, and I knew what would happen. Eighty-year-old widows revert to twenty-year-old brides, to rejoin the husbands who died fighting in action. Spinsters revert to their childhood, so they can be loved unconditionally again by their parents. While every man with cancer opts for the lean, strong body of his youth—

For an instant, looking into her sadness, I was tempted to ask what she'd want for eternity, so I could reunite them that much quicker. Then I remembered the Boss's warning about becoming emotionally involved, and walked away.

In any case, who would believe me?

* * *

'I've also talked to Craig's friends, his old boss, his work colleagues.' I gave Angie a run-down on the interviews, partly because I knew she'd be interested, but mainly to satisfy myself that I'd left no stone unturned. 'Ditto Lucy's friends, her boss, *her* work colleagues.' I paused. Warmed the whisky between my hands. 'I had a long talk with the woman Lucy caught him in bed with, as well.'

An old flame called Nicole who worked in I.T., and I have to admit, having seen photos of Lucy, I'd been expecting the opposition to be something of a *femme fatale*. A huntress, a predator, someone I'd take one look at and go, wow. But that's why I'm a P.I. Good at tracking, good at detecting, bloody awful when it comes to reading women.

'I don't understand it.' Angie topped up our glasses. 'They saw each other a few times, sure. But once Craig clapped eyes on Lucy, ka-boom.'

'Love at first sight?'

She tipped her head on one side. 'You don't believe it can happen?'

I sipped. Slowly. 'On the contrary. I believe that it can.'

'Craig was devastated when Lucy accused him of cheating. He admitted bumping into Nicole, but that's it. He swore he never made any arrangement to see her again, and said he absolutely did not sleep with her.'

I know. His feather of truth passed the test on that, too.

'Yet Lucy caught them together,' I said. 'She'd just flown home, after a week in New York, let herself in to his flat and found a woman wearing nothing but wet hair in the bedroom. The shower was running, Craig was delivering his usual off-key rendition of *Rolling in the Deep*, and there were two sets of everything—coffee cups, wine glasses, underwear—scattered around.'

'Then that's it.' Angie looked pole-axed. 'He really *was* cheating.'

'Nicole's not what I expected,' I admitted. 'Don't get me wrong, she's a good-looking girl behind those glasses—' Nowhere near as classy as Angie, or as outgoing as Lucy Fuller. '—but let's say, more mouse than cat.'

This is my fault. Nicole hugged her arms to her bony, flat chest and stared at a point on the carpet. *If Craig and I hadn't met in that coffee shop—* Her eyes screwed shut in unquestionable grief. *The stupid thing was, I knew it was a mistake, hooking up with him again.*

Because you can't relive the past?

Because he'd changed, Mr. O'Donnell. Hot one minute, ice cold the next, so much so, I wondered if he wasn't on drugs. But the police didn't find anything in his apartment.

Doesn't mean he wasn't using.

She bit her lip. *I'll be honest with you, Mr. O'Donnell, I don't really know about things like that. Only that Craig wasn't the man I remembered, and I felt so bad for his girlfriend, walking in on us like that. What a shock—*

'She said that?' Angie downed the contents of her glass in one shot. 'Hot one minute, ice cold the next?'

You didn't need to be a mind-reader to know what she was thinking. *Just like when Lucy was stabbed…*

'Jesus Christ, are all men liars and bastards? Get out. Get out of my house!'

'Angie—'

'Don't you "Angie" me. You lied to me, Frank.' She slumped down, with her head in her hands. 'You told me Craig was innocent.'

I leaned with my back to the worktop, watching the way her long, blonde hair tumbled round her sculpted collarbones. Remembering the vanilla scent of her shampoo, as she'd sobbed on my shoulder. *You have a tight grip, Mr. O'Donnell…*

'I won't apologize for my methods. Raking up the past, making people hurt, that's my job. It's how I get results. How I find the truth.' I pulled out a stool and sat opposite her. 'But I didn't lie to you, Angie. Your son didn't kill Lucy Fuller.'

* * *

The theory that began to take shape in St. Peter's office had crystallized with every step I'd taken. Because if neither the victim nor the accused are lying, you have to ask, who else had a motive?

Her head shot up. *'Nicole?'*

'Nicole.' What, for Craig Langstone, was a couple of dates and casual sex, turned into an obsession for her.

'She loved him that much, she'd kill to have him?'

'Love had sod all to do with it, Angie.'

With stalkers, it's about control. They don't take kindly to being dumped, much less supplanted, and maybe Craig gave her a key to his flat, maybe she copied it. Either way, she bugged the place and planted cameras, recording every move he made, every word he uttered. I know, because when I called on Nicole, I used that old trick of asking to use the bathroom to have a good old snoop around.

'How long she'd waited for the right circumstances to come together is anyone's guess,' I said.

Weeks? Months? before Craig and Lucy's schedules dovetailed and she could put her plan into action. Starting with that so-called random meet in the coffee shop.

'Knowing Craig had left early for work and that Lucy was on her way round, Nicole let herself in with a key. She swirled wine in the glasses, coffee in the cups, placed them on the bedside table. Then she rumpled the sheets, scattered clothing around, ran the shower and played a recording of Craig's god-awful singing. After that, it was only a question of stripping off and waiting for Lucy.'

No doubt her original intention was to drive her away. Craig could deny the affair until he was blue in the face, but Lucy had seen the evidence with her own eyes, and men who cheat lie all the time.

'Nicole would be there to pick up the pieces. Hers would be the shoulder he'd cry on.'

Only stalkers don't have normal emotions, so turning up on his doorstep, bursting with plans for their future, wasn't the smartest of moves.

'That's when he most likely told her he didn't love her, how could he, hell, he hardly *knew* her. It was Lucy he loved, and whatever it took—and however long—he'd never stop trying to win her back.'

God knows how Nicole responded to that. Did she threaten him? Beg? Plug away with her crazy plans for their future? Whatever, it was enough to make him lose his temper. *There is no "us",* he shouted at her. *I want you out of my life—*

'Which is when she realized that staging a tryst wasn't enough. Would *never* be enough.' Her only chance of having Craig was to get rid of Lucy once and for all. 'Except killing her wasn't enough, either. She needed to rub her nose in it.' Make her suffer mentally, as well as physically, so that the last words she'd hear were Craig, telling her that he didn't want her. 'Seventeen stab wounds is a lot,' I said, more to myself than to Angie. 'Suggesting a crime of overkill and rage, regardless of how carefully it might have been planned.'

Lucy thought she'd tripped, but at five feet five to Craig's six foot three, he'd have had no trouble overpowering her. Nicole, on the other hand, was petite, and one look at the crime scene showed me why she chose that particular spot. Two silver birches, one either side of the footpath. Where better to stretch a piece of string?

As plans went, Nicole must have thought hers was pitch perfect. Until Craig ruined everything by killing himself. No wonder the poor girl was gutted.

'There's a problem, though.' I took both Angie's hands in my own. 'To prove it, and put this bitch in jail for the rest of her life, I need help. Your help, to be precise.'

I could run, I could jump, I could smile, I could cry, and prick me, like Shylock, then I bleed. But Frank O'Donnell was buried in North London four years earlier. He can't suddenly stand up in court.

* * *

In the meantime, the sun was setting and, as every good general knows, an army marches on its stomach. I could, I said, rustle something up here. Spaghetti, chilli, chicken in white wine, because if there was something I *was* good at round the house, then it was cooking.

'I do a mean paella,' I said. No idle boast. 'Or, if you prefer, we could go down the pub?'

I'd spotted a pretty thatched inn, just a stone's throw away. All oak beams, horse brasses, and roaring log fires.

'Uh-uh.' Angie pointed to her streaky, panda eyes. 'I look a fright.'

She looked beautiful.

'You look fine.'

'Really?' She reached for her jacket. 'Then what are we waiting for? It's been ages since I've eaten out.'

'Me, too.'

With a table right next to that roaring log fire, we ate and we laughed and we drank and we talked. We talked about the trials of being a teenage mum, the tribulations of being a teenage orphan, and the problems we'd faced in our marriages. But mostly it was about music and movies, trivia and travel, the best advice our mothers ever gave us and who we'd hate to be stuck in a lift with. Did I mention that we laughed a lot, too? A real lot?

Quite how our lips touched, I'm not sure. One minute I was saying goodnight on her doorstep, the next we were in each other's arms like a couple of lovestruck teenagers. I tried to pull away, telling her this was wrong, she was vulnerable, it would be taking advantage. She said shut up, Frank, at fifty-three she knew her own mind, and she'd decide what was taking advantage and what was not, thank you. Maybe so, but I explained that I was just passing through. So help me, I'd never be able to see her again. Not once this case was over. She didn't ask why. Just kissed the tears from my big, ugly eyes, and led me into the bedroom.

Later—much later—she rolled on her stomach and said, 'Do you believe in the afterlife, Frank?'

'If you're asking, do I think Heaven's made out of clouds, that angels have wings, and St. Peter sports a long, straggly beard, I'd have to say no.'

She laughed. 'Next you'll be telling me they don't strum harps all day, either, and the Pearly Gates aren't made out of mother-of-pearl.'

'Who'd go to Heaven, if eternity meant buffing those to a shine?' I kissed her forehead. 'Why do you ask?'

'Craig. He said, *Be happy for me, Mum.*'

'He meant well.'

'I know. And for seven years, I've put on this brave front, thinking, Christ, if he *is* up there looking down, the last thing I want is him feeling bad about killing himself. He needs to know that I fully accept he was a grown man at the time, capable of making his own decisions. Even if I didn't agree with them! And that he's my son and that I'll always love him, just as I will always be proud of him.' She twisted round and cupped my face between her hands. 'But until today, that's all it's been, Frank. An act. Then you came along, and I can honestly say, you've made me happier than I've felt in a very long time.'

For the second time that night, I heard myself saying, 'Me, too.'

While wondering, who'd have thought happiness could hurt so bloody much?

* * *

I didn't report back to the Boss in person. Just submitted a brief statement of facts, exonerating Craig, endorsing Lucy's testimony and confirming that justice was done. No lengthy explanations about how, between us, Angie and I pulled the same "bumping into" trick that Nicole pulled on Craig. Or how, while the women chatted, I played the Artful Dodger, easing Nicole's purse out of her handbag, thereby giving Angie the perfect excuse to call and return the wallet that had somehow fallen on the floor.

In any case, St. Peter wouldn't be interested in how, once inside Nicole's starter home on the south side of the city, Angie asked to use the bathroom. Then snooped around, just like I'd primed her, capturing, on her cell phone, walls covered with pictures of Craig, of hundreds of DVDs, CDs and scrapbooks through which Nicole relived her obsession, as well as a variety of cameras, audio devices and computer hardware. All the paraphernalia, in fact, that every self-respecting stalker needs.

I did, however, mention that the police, with a bit of pushing admittedly, reopened the case, and that their search warrant provided them with all the evidence they needed. Adding, at the end, how Nicole, far from repentant, remained arrogant in her belief that Lucy wasn't good enough for Craig. Killing her was like squashing a spider, good riddance to bad rubbish, she said. The bitch was only holding him back. Her only regret seemed to be that Craig committed suicide before he understood who he was meant to be with.

I stayed with Angie in Winchester for as long as I could, toasting Nicole's arrest with champagne, making love in the moonlight, listening to Pink Floyd at full pelt with our eyes closed. And when it came time to leave, you can forget that *parting is such sweet sorrow* crap. Sorrow is sorrow, full stop. I simply threw myself into reuniting lost loved ones like there was no tomorrow, and, given all those astral planes I had to contend with, never gave it a thought when St. Peter summoned me to his office.

'Do you remember what I asked you, Frank, last time you were here?'

'Did I want coffee, tea or a glass of cold beer?'

'I asked, you dolt, if you were happy!' Grinning like a loon, he motioned me to sit. 'After that lorry ploughed into you, we asked if you wanted to be young again. To go back to the time before your parents were killed, because nearly everyone wants to relive the days when they were happiest. But not you, Frank. You didn't change one damn thing.'

'Yeah, well. I'm comfortable inside this plug ugly hide. Kinda grown used to it over the years.'

'You're also one of the few, who didn't want your bad memories erased, either.'

'Good times, bad times.' I shrugged. 'They made me who I am, and if there's one thing I learned on that little planet called life, it was that the moment you move one piece of the puzzle, another slips out of sync. All I wanted was to keep on doing what I'm good at. Finding answers.'

'That's what we're here for. Giving people what they want. But the thing is, Frank. Sometimes they don't see the full picture.'

'Meaning?'

'You believed you were that plug ugly flatfoot who never got the girl, so that's what you became. And to compensate for the loneliness, you immersed yourself in helping people. Trying to give everyone a happy ending. Didn't always happen. Obviously. But it never stopped you trying.' He gave a couple of clicks on the celestial mouse. 'Not once, Frank. Not once.'

I can't remember what I was about to reply, because I was distracted by the music that suddenly filled the office—*Hey, teacher, leave those kids alone*—and the scent of…the scent of…

Vanilla shampoo?

I twisted round in my chair. On the left, cherubs were weighing the feather of truth. On the right, angels read the newcomers' auras. Then, while I watched, the elegant, grey-haired old lady who'd shuffled over the Threshold just as I arrived emerged from the Tunnel of Light in a tight top, skinny jeans, with her long blonde hair tumbling over her shoulders.

'*Angie?*'

'Like I said. People go back to the times they were happiest.' St. Peter stroked his neat little Van Dyke beard with satisfaction. 'Now go take that woman's hand, and the next time I ask you, are you happy, I want to hear you say, yes you bloody are. Oh, and Frank.'

'Boss?'

'Do everyone a favour, watch a Humphrey Bogart movie, will you? Ugly guys *do* get the girl.'

Bad Taste

When a senator throws a banquet, you know it's going to be good.
When that senator happens to be a second cousin to the Emperor, even
if it is three times removed and through a second marriage, you know
it's going to be memorable. And when he's Horatius Clemens Stolus,
Clem to his friends, you know it's going to be something really special.

Forget the river running with red wine, and the rose petals that fell
like fragrant snowflakes from a contraption rigged to the ceiling. Clem
had brought in Sicilian jugglers, Corsican conjurers, acrobats all the
way from Dalmatia. He'd arranged for dancers to be dressed up like the
gods—blue-skinned Neptune wielding his trident, Apollo in gold,
Hades in black, Jupiter flashing his dark, goatskin thundercloak. And
that was only the start. To the gentle strains of lyres and harps, he had
satyrs chasing wood nymphs with balletic precision. Clowns and
buffoons telling jokes, making riddles. He had slaves reciting poetry.
Boxers and wrestlers. An Egyptian who could mimic anything from
voices to birdsong.

'Claudia! My dear Claudia, there you are! Sorry I didn't get a chance
to welcome you personally. Got nabbed by some bore of a general just
back from the Rhine, who insisted on giving me every detail of how he
quashed the latest uprising.'

There's something about powerful men, isn't there? Clem was
beyond the first flush of youth, he was losing his hair, cultivating a
paunch, and an overlong nose prevented him from being handsome. So
why this magnetic pull?

'And here's me, thinking you'd run me to ground in a dark corner for an ulterior motive,' she purred.

'Don't think I'm not tempted,' he laughed. 'But mind telling me what you're doing behind a bust of my great-grandfather? Don't say you're not enjoying yourself.'

On the contrary. For a girl who'd screwed and schemed her way out of the gutter, hobnobbing with the Empire's elite was as good as it gets. But when she'd also spotted the marble merchant she'd swindled out of eight thousand sesterces, a quiet corner seemed the perfect retreat.

'It's hot.' Claudia wafted her fan. 'I was taking a breather.'

'Exactly why I opted for an informal gathering. Can you imagine if we'd had everyone squashed together on couches in this heat? We'd have poached to death in our own perspiration.'

'Only the men, Clem. Ladies don't perspire, it's beneath us. We'd have elegantly glowed to death.'

'Talking of death.' The smile dropped from his face. 'I can't thank you enough for—'

'I didn't do anything.'

'You saved my life, Claudia. Those men would have beaten me to a pulp, if you hadn't come along.'

'Nonsense.' She dismissed any heroism with a wave of her hand. 'Thieves are rarely that industrious. How *are* the ribs, by the way?'

'Sore. But not half as sore as my pride. It's we men who are supposed to rescue maidens in peril, not the other way round. As for getting beaten and robbed, I'm ashamed to say, I followed through with my threat and told everyone I was knocked down by a wagon. Seems more…manly, somehow.'

'Run over, rolled over, it doesn't matter to me. I'd still have put you in my litter, patched you up, and brought you home.'

'Which is why I am indebted to you, Claudia Seferius. And as a reflection of my gratitude, there are several wealthy merchants here today that I'd like you to meet.'

'In which case, senator, you are looking at a hero. Lead the way.'

'Seriously, my dear, it's the very least I can do, but a word of advice?

Give it an hour.' He lowered his voice to a conspiratorial whisper. 'Once they've been caught canoodling with someone else's wife behind the laurels, or the wine's made them disclose confidences that should have stayed secret, you'll find they're infinitely more amenable to signing contracts.' He chinked his goblet against hers. 'Trust me.'

No one trusts a politician. Although it went a long way to explaining how certain votes got passed.

'So while I butter up the foreign dignitaries and get my ear chewed by some wearisome judge, you go enjoy the rope-walkers, the fire-eaters and the quick-change artists,' he murmured. 'Then I'll come back, make some introductions, and we'll see just how much my miserable life is worth! Oh, and Claudia? Don't forget this is supposed to be a banquet. Can't have you going home half-starved, can we?'

Fat chance of that, because if the entertainment was spectacular, the food—dear me, the food was to die for!

Gazelle marinated in honey. Fig-peckers in pastry. Peppered dormice that had been fattened for weeks. In fact, every imaginable delicacy was laid out on display. Lobsters, suckling pig, hazel hens and quail. Truffles, smoked duck, veal. Just looking at it made Claudia's mouth water. It made her mouth water, her tongue tingle, her mouth burn. Now her face was on fire. She was shaking and sweating. Her breath was coming shallow and fast.

But the funny thing was, as hard as she tried, as hard as she gulped, she couldn't—she just couldn't breathe…

* * *

'Drink this,' said the doctor.

'Suck this,' said the herbalist.

'Don't put anything in your mouth,' a rich baritone ordered. 'Not one damn thing, do you hear?'

Through the convulsions, the pain, the numbness and blurred vision, she made out a mop of dark, wavy hair. It seemed to be attached to a horribly familiar face. 'Orbilio?'

'Marcus Cornelius Orbilio at your service, ma'am!' He pressed his fist to his breast in mock salute. 'Although after you threw up over my toga, my tunic and a brand new pair of boots, the least you can do is call me Marcus.'

'For heaven's sake, Orbilio, what do you expect, when you ram your fingers down somebody's throat?'

'Seriously?' A jerk of his thumb cleared the room of doctors, herbalists and slaves. 'You're busting my balls because you're not dead?'

'No one dies from one bad oyster.'

'Nausea plus numbness plus dizziness plus burning equals classic aconite poisoning.'

'Roast goose plus pheasant plus pomegranate plus wine equals classic overindulgence. You're making mountains out of molehills, I'm fine.'

He shot her a wink, which was his way of saying *you look it*, then made her swallow a pile of black, crispy crumbs.

'Fine. I threw up over your boots. That doesn't give you the right to choke me with volcanic dust.'

'I'm choking you with charcoal, actually. Old family recipe, simple, but effective. Absorbs the poison like a sponge.' He sat down on the bed, folding his arms to make himself comfy. 'And while it works its gentle magic, perhaps you'd care to tell me who, at this splendiferous banquet, wants Claudia Seferius dead.'

She tried to roll her eyes, but the painted cherubs on the ceiling were spinning like tops.

'Honestly! Who'd want to kill a poor, defenceless, grieving, young widow—and while we're at it, what are the Security Police doing at said splendiferous banquet, anyway? Other than waiting to stick their fingers down some unsuspecting female's throat?'

'You're not poor, you're not grieving, and the last I heard, rabid tigers backed off fighting you.' He shovelled another handful of dust in her mouth. 'Now then, why am I here? Let me think. Was it to shadow the prime suspect in a nasty case of fraud? The same person, incidentally, who's not paying her taxes? Is also selling her blended wines as vintage? Has run up astronomical gambling debts, even though betting's against the law? Has helped slaves escape, by forging their master's signature? Is up to her big, brown eyes in—'

'I'm sure, if you put more than a token effort into your investigations, you'd find those slaves were owned by some smarmy marble merchant, who treated them so cruelly, it's impossible to believe anyone could be that sadistic. Just as I'm sure you'll find that the eight thousand sesterces your suspect swindled him out of is chicken feed to him; whereas, it goes a long way between ex-slaves.'

Less thirty percent commission, but who's counting?

'Thank you, Claudia. Hardly a deathbed confession, but close enough. Mind you.' He cracked his knuckles. 'Had you let me finish, you'd have heard me tell you I was invited for the simple reason that Clem's my mother's cousin.'

Bugger. Thanks to stomach cramps and this terrifying numbness in her limbs, she'd forgotten Orbilio was the only patrician member of the Security Police. Now she'd given him enough ammunition to trace the victim (victim, there's a joke!) and quite possibly the runaways, as well.

'If this *is* aconite poisoning—and that's a very big "if", Orbilio— there are a hundred people milling around downstairs. It has to be random.'

'I tend to think of it as a hundred suspects,' he said cheerfully. 'Random only works when other people are affected, whereas this. This is designed to look like food poisoning.'

Didn't it just. And if Marcus Cornelius Orbilio hadn't been snooping around, she'd have called a litter to take her home, where, by the time anyone realized the situation was serious, it would have been too late. Not so much on the scene, she thought, as on the ball. Goddammit, the lengths some people go to, to have their suspects fit and healthy enough to stand trial!

'Check, and I'm sure you'll find loads of other guests that have mistaken the symptoms and taken themselves home.'

'The Phoenician ambassador passed out from the heat, two

magistrates and a consul threw up from drinking too much, the tribune's wife broke a tooth biting into an almond, and my Uncle Petronius's ulcer is giving him hell. Other than that, Claudia, everyone's fine.'

As prisons went, she couldn't complain about this one. Swansdown mattress, gilded mirrors, scented damascened sheets, and if nothing else, Clem showed excellent taste in the fresco department. But for all the marble, bronze and porphyry, that's exactly what it was. A prison, where her next move would be to a dank, dark, communal cell underneath the Capitol. If she had any chance of avoiding ten years exiled on some godforsaken island, with just her cat and the clothes she stood up in, Claudia needed something to trade.

But for once, there were no loaded dice up her sleeve.

'I wouldn't say you were lucky, but you certainly got off lightly.' Orbilio pulled her eyelid down, checked the temperature of her forehead, and generally inspected her as if she was a horse. 'You ingested a very mild dose and, all things being equal, you should make a quick recovery. But since no self-respecting poisoner slips their victim a mild dose of aconite, can you think of anything you spat out, because you didn't like it?'

'Nope.'

'Something that tasted odd, that you pushed to one side of your plate?'

'No, and before you ask, I selected every one of those delicacies myself.' No question of any tainted food being passed by a third party. 'Nor did I sneak titbits off anyone else's plate.'

'And you have absolutely no idea why you were targeted?'

'For once in your life, Marcus, you'll have to accept that I'm telling the truth.'

She must have slipped into unconsciousness at that point, because the next thing she knew, the sun was sinking over the Palatine, an oil lamp flickered in the corner, and someone was lying on the counterpane next to her, his head propped up on a mountain of pillows.

That someone appeared to be reading a book of poetry, Catallus unless she missed her guess, just as that someone smelled of basil, instead of his customary sandalwood unguent. Without the usual hint of the rosemary, in which his posh clothes were rinsed. Claudia wondered what kind of household kept an entire wardrobe of clothes on hand, for their guests to change into. The sort of household, obviously, where female guests regularly throw up over male guests.

'Why aren't you downstairs, clapping poisoners in irons?'

'You're awake, then.' Orbilio tossed the poems aside. 'Feeling better?'

Much. The room had stopped spinning, the cramps had turned to dull aches, and Claudia could feel both her legs, her left arm and two, possibly three, of her toes. But if a girl's going to be in prison, it might as well be a comfy one. 'Terrible. In fact…if anything, Marcus, it's getting worse.'

'Hmm.' His grunt had the word *Capitol* written all over it, you could practically hear jail keys clunking. 'In that case.' He stood up and stretched. 'Before you have another relapse and take that final ferry ride over the Styx, why don't you walk me through the sequence of events? Every last detail, every conversation you took, from why Clem extended the invitation until the moment you wrote off my boots.'

'He owed me a favour.' No good deed goes unpunished. 'At least, he thought he did.'

Pure chance made her peer between the curtains of her litter the other day, and instead of the usual yellow-wigged street walkers or dirty children begging for scraps, she saw a man being set upon in an alley between two tenement blocks. Both attackers were armed with cudgels, and while one beat the shit out of their victim, the other was cutting his purse.

Orbilio had reached for a quill and was dipping it in the inkwell. 'Where was this?' he asked without looking up.

'Just off the Forum.'

'Can you be a little more precise?'

'The Subura.'

'Precise means specific, Claudia. I need to know *exactly* where this took place.'

What hadn't improved was the crushing fatigue. She was just too bone weary to lie. 'The Street of the Wig-Makers.'

Orbilio leaned back in his chair and let his breath out in a slow whistle. 'Now what would a senator devoted to moral reform be doing in an area renowned for prostitutes, gamblers and hemp-dens?'

'He said he was lost.'

'Not impossible for the average merchant, perhaps. The slums being worse than a warren.' Marcus was grinning from ear to ear. 'But my mother's fine, upstanding cousin?'

'Mock all you want, but I believe him. Nobody chooses to wander down alleyways running with sewage, cabbage water and despair.'

'You did.' If possible, the grin had become even wider.

'I had an appointment,' she sniffed. With her bookie, but that was none of his business. 'Besides. I had four sturdy litter bearers along for protection.'

'My point exactly. Men at Clem's level don't set foot outside without a small army of minders, much less into the tenements. Yet not only were there no bodyguards to protect him, he was attacked in broad daylight, where even the most dim-witted felon knows that assaulting senators is a serious offence.'

The tingling in her neck was fading rapidly, and the feeling had returned to nine of her toes. 'Why should they think he was a senator?'

'You don't think the purple stripe on his tunic and high, black boots with a silver C on the ankle might have been a clue?'

'If you weren't such a stuffed shirt, you'd know that men who have shameful vices tend not to advertise their status.'

Senator, orator, father of four? Small wonder he told everyone he'd been knocked down, and dear god, how her stomach lurched when she saw him curled up on the cobbles, trying to make himself small. And if the crunch of wood against ribs wasn't sickening enough, it was the hatred on the thieves' faces. The loathing of rich men, who had it made—

Not just the mansion, the money, the slaves and the comfort. We're talking men who have everything from fresh water to their own teeth, and doctors who ensured they stayed in good health. Men who wouldn't be dead before their fortieth birthday. Whose diet was more than just porridge and beans. Who had grave markers set up when they died, so they would not be forgotten…

Seeing him—seeing *them*—the years fell away, pitching Claudia back to the yelling, the touting, the shouting, the sobs. To sores that refused to heal. To babies crying from hunger, and dying of it, too. To the stench of urine, house fires, oppression and eggs. That was why she'd ordered her litter bearers to stop. The reason she'd rushed to Clem's aid. To rescue him, not so much from the attack, but from the grip of the slums.

To rewind the past, and make everything right—

'Orbilio?' She looked round. 'Marcus?'

Surely she hadn't passed out again, but suddenly the room was empty. Just a swish of a drape to show the speed of his leaving.

And there you go! One minute you're in prison, facing a horrible, lonely, penniless exile. Next thing, those loaded dice are back up your sleeve. Who says the gods don't smile on the righteous?

Claudia massaged her legs, rubbed at her arms, flexed as much life as she could back into her fingers and toes. She felt like shit, no question of that. But Clem's slaves had replaced her soiled gown with a magnificent creation of soft peach shot with gold, and her tiara would hide any sweat-streaked strands of hair. Step by step, no matter how long it took, she would inch her way round to the back of the house, call for her litter and take off to the country until the dust had died down—

'Sorry, ma'am.' An oak of a guard was blocking her exit, and by blocking, she meant he filled the whole bloody doorway. He also had the sort of face that looked like it had fallen out of a tree and hit every branch on the way down. 'The boss said not to let anyone in before he's apprehended his suspect. Or, for that matter, miss, let anyone out.'

Sod the sweaty ringlets. 'Orders are orders, I appreciate that,' she said sweetly. 'But it's urgent I go home.' While she rattled off her address, she stabbed herself with a hairpin hard enough to make her eyes water. 'I've just received news that my daughter is dying…'

'Very sorry to hear that, ma'am.'

Not sorry enough to move out of the way, though. 'I need to be with her at the end, I'm sure you—no doubt a father yourself—understand?'

'Well—'

'Oh, thank you. Thank you so much, you're a good man. Maybe your wife would like this? I'd intended to pass it on to my daughter, only—'

'That's right kind of you, ma'am.' The tiara disappeared inside his tunic with the speed of greased lightning. 'Only Master Orbilio said you'd try these sorts of tricks. You don't got no kids, miss. And trying to bribe an officer is against the law.'

'Really? Well, unless you hand that tiara back, I'll report you for accepting backhanders.'

Ideally, she'd have glared him to death, then slammed the door in his face. In her current state, it was more a gentle waft.

'And in future, you mind your manners,' she called over her shoulder. 'When you address me, it's "you don't got no kids, *my lady*".'

* * *

How long Marcus Cornelius had been gone, Claudia had no way of telling. When you're aching from head to foot, feel like you've been kicked by a mule, and your mouth tastes—and probably smells—like rancid goats' cheese, time loses all meaning. Darkness fell. Through the thick, stone walls of Clem's magnificent mansion, she could hear muffled laughter and clapping, cheering and gasps, as the entertainment played through the evening and into the night. Occasionally, she heard the crash of dropped china, the clang of a gong, even, once, the slap of a face, when a kiss went too far. Music ebbed and flowed in time with the revels, varying from strings to pan-pipes, and at one point the harsh blare of trumpets, suggesting speeches or some kind of announcement.

Why it was taking so long to arrest the marble merchant, though, was beyond her. Perhaps he'd got wind of Orbilio's intent and made his escape? Perhaps he'd resisted arrest and needed further restraining? Or maybe he'd simply come clean and was making a detailed and lengthy confession? No matter, the sadistic little prick was in irons, that was the main thing, though with hindsight, it was obvious who'd slipped Claudia the poison. Who else had she defrauded out of eight thousand sesterces?

Apart from that Syrian merchant, but then he was just passing through.

Oh, and that one-eyed Macedonian, though that was purely to recoup the money he'd taken from her by cheating at dice.

If you can call it cheating, when he'd swapped her own loaded dice for a new set, but that was beside the point.

The point was, she hadn't just defrauded the marble merchant out of eight thousand sesterces, she'd robbed him of seven house slaves, each worth around the same sum. Making sixty-four thousand reasons for wanting revenge. Because, for a man for whom money means nothing, humiliation is beyond price—

And how naïve to imagine he hadn't seen her at the banquet. Worse, the bastard had come prepared. Which was some consolation, she supposed. When it came to trial and she was called to give witness, she'd have the satisfaction of knowing he'd be paying twenty times over. Of course, since she hadn't actually died, he'd probably argue that he simply intended to teach her a lesson, meaning he'd escape with exile rather than be forced to take his own life.

What irony, if they ended up on the same bloody island.

Because if Orbilio was here on a family invite, Claudia was the Queen of bloody Sheba. He'd been trailing her like a bloodhound from day one.

And talk of the devil—

'That went well.' He looked like the cat that had got the cream, the duck and the family parrot, as he breezed back into the room. 'Even his wife hasn't twigged that he's missing.'

The old medical emergency ruse to draw him outside, he explained, where two burly guards had been waiting to bundle him into a litter, with two more inside to restrain him with shackles.

'Not because I didn't want to put a dampener on the party. I just don't want his accomplices getting wise to what went down.'

Accomplices? Plural? She knew she'd pissed him off, but just how many marble merchants does it take to slip poison into— 'How *did* he manage to dose me with aconite?'

'When you chinked goblets, he dropped it in your wine, no doubt expecting you to drink it quickly in this heat. Silly man still had the phial on him when we arrested him, and that alone's a capital offence. Did you know it's illegal to even grow the plant in your own garden?'

Stuff landscape gardening. 'You're not talking about the marble merchant, are you?'

'Hardly, although now you mention it, he had a nasty accident earlier. As I passed him at the top of the stairs, poor chap took a terrible tumble over the rail. Broke his shoulderblade on the marble, apparently. As well as a sprained ankle, broken jaw and three crushed fingers.'

Orbilio did all that? Well, well, well.

'Accidents will happen,' Claudia said solemnly. Try taking a whip to your slaves now, you sadistic bastard. 'So given that Clem was the only person with whom I chinked goblets, I assume it's our illustrious senator you took into custody?'

The Security Police perched itself on the edge of a table. 'First, I take a job my father feels taints our fine aristocratic heritage. Then my wife divorces me for a common sea captain and I refuse to enter into another political marriage. Now I arrest my mother's favourite cousin.' Orbilio rubbed his hands with glee. 'The old man will be climbing the walls for months, when he hears about this.'

'It's called job satisfaction, Marcus. But back to Clem a minute, I'm guessing he didn't try to kill me, just to hush up some tawdry commerce in a house of ill-repute?'

Any moral crusader worth his salt would maintain he was conducting research incognito. Murder took it to a different plane. Especially premeditated.

'Rumours have been circulating for some time about plans to assassinate the Emperor—'

'Why would anyone do that?'

Augustus had stabilized an unstable Empire after years of civil war, he'd made Rome a force to be reckoned with, and brought prosperity to every single one of its citizens.

'Power.' Orbilio picked up a silver elephant paperweight and tossed it from hand to hand. 'Power was the one thing Clem didn't have, and the one thing he wanted more than all the rubies in the desert and all the gold in Egypt.'

For months, he'd been gathering a band of co-conspirators, plotting how, and indeed when, to take over from the current administration. What the authorities lacked was hard evidence. What the traitors lacked was a professional assassin, since, like Caesar's wife, they needed to appear above suspicion when this monstrous crime went down.

'As soon as you mentioned the Street of the Wig-Makers, I knew we had him,' Marcus said. 'It's the haunt of a well-known hit-man, where, again, we've never had enough proof to pin him to any of his fine achievements. Witnesses either disappearing, too scared to testify, or floating in the Tiber.'

So far, so good, Claudia thought. Dressed in ordinary clothes, and without his bodyguard to verify his whereabouts, Clem obviously paid a visit to the assassin. No doubt cut a deal. Then had the misfortune to be set upon by thieves.

'Why me? All I did was save him from a bigger kicking than he'd already had.'

'You're the only person who could tie him to the assassin, and how better to eliminate you, than by staging a simple bout of food poisoning in full sight of a hundred of our city's finest?'

Crafty bugger made sure no one saw them together. Didn't even come forward to welcome her when she arrived, biding his time until she took refuge behind his great-grandfather's bust. 'You really weren't shadowing me, then?'

'I work for the Security Police, Claudia. Our role is to keep the Empire safe, not worry about who's fiddling her taxes or fleecing Syrian merchants and one-eyed Macedonians.'

Janus, Croesus, he knew about *them*? Was nothing in her life secret anymore?

'So why the Cyclops outside the door?'

'To stop Clem—or one of his associates—coming in and finishing the job. And, of course, to stop you sneaking out and preventing Clem—or one of his associates—from waylaying you and finishing the job.' He replaced the silver elephant on the writing desk. 'Can't have our star witness giving evidence from Hades. Oh and congratulations on that miraculous recovery, by the way.'

The only thing to do with sarcasm is ignore it. 'In other words, I'm free to go.'

'As a bird.'

No charges, no probes, no stains on her character. Free as a bird—to fleece another poor sucker.

'And I really did ruin your tunic, your toga—and did you say *brand new* boots?'

'The softest kid leather, with the most elegant tooling.' Orbilio clucked his tongue in regret. 'Best boots I ever had, those. '

'Beyond fixing?'

'Way past.'

Claudia tucked her hair behind her tiara, slipped into her sandals and pocketed the silver elephant for a souvenir. 'Quite honestly, Marcus.' She shot him a smile as she swept past. 'Today just gets better and better.'

Stakes & Adders

'You've got to help me.'

I put down my pen. The voice was so soft, so sibilant, at first I thought it was the wind in the leaves, but no. There it was again.

'Please. You're the only person who can.'

Pushing my glasses to the end of my nose, I had to admit that, even by snake standards, he looked pretty miserable.

'Go away.' I tugged at the hem of my mini-skirt, because who knows how far those slitty eyes reach. 'I'm marking examination papers and you're in flagrant breach of the rules.'

And dear me, will that Jenkins girl ever learn? It's eye of newt, not wing of bat. *C minus.*

Undeterred, he slithered onto the page.

'Fine for you to say "go away". No one turned you into a reptile, did they, and in any case it's not fair. In the books it's always handsome princes, and then they get turned into frogs.' His little scaly mouth turned down in a pout. 'Hell, I wasn't even a courtier.'

'Hell, you weren't even handsome.'

'Very funny.'

'I thought so.'

How many times do I have to tell these stupid children you use brimstone, not soapstone. Was it any wonder the dragon didn't retreat back in its lair? *D, I scribbled, and consider yourself lucky to get that.*

'No, really. You *are* the only one who can help me,' You had to hand it to him. He was a persistent little adder. 'After all, it was your great-grandmother who did this to me.'

'For a very good reason I'm sure.'

'Good? Good?' He writhed round the desk like a scaly green dervish. 'I'd worked in that woman's tavern from the age of sixteen, humping beer kegs, pulling pints, tossing out drunks from midday until midnight, seven days a week, fifty-two weeks of the year, until one day I have the temerity to ask for a rise. You call *that* a good reason to turn me into a snake?'

'I've heard better,' I admitted, 'but right now I'm busy.'

These were merely the Spell Tests I was marking. I still had Stage 3 Wizardry and Advanced Werewolfing to wade through, and midnight oil was in short supply in those days.

'Anyway,' I told him, 'it's got to be a cushy life, being a snake.'

'Oh? Then what do you call being unable to bask on the river bank for fear of being eaten by herons?'

'Once bittern, twice shy?' (And who'd have thought something so thin and so slimy could snort.)

'Mock all you want,' he hissed, 'but it's no joke minding your own business on a drystone wall, when suddenly you're scooped up by some greasy garage mechanic, marched into the repair shop over the way and forced to dangle there utterly helpless while he yells "Who's was the BMW that needed new vindshield vipers?" To them, it's a hoot. To me, it's simply more humiliation.'

'Pity, because if it was for real, you'd get a drive in the country out of the deal.'

'Don't talk to me about driving. Not after that scoundrel St. Patrick drove all my cousins out of Ireland.'

'Only because he couldn't afford the air fare,' I quipped, reaching for the next paper.

'Sun in Venus, moon in P—'

Ugh. How vulgar. *It might rhyme*, I scrawled, *but that is NOT how you spell Pisces. F minus minus, and you'll hang upside down for an hour after school for that, and no cheating with Blu-tack like last time.*

'I'm not going away,' my visitor said, entwining himself round my coffee mug. 'However long it takes, I shall—'

'OK.' I slammed the book. 'OK, I'll help you, but only because it was my great-grandmother, right?'

'You're an angel.'

Oh come on. Even *my* shapeshifting powers aren't that good. 'What do you want?'

'It's Crowberry Heath.' He slithered down the handle and I really didn't like the way he eyed up my computer mouse. 'Do you know it?'

Know it? Who could fail to be enchanted by its riots of yellow gorse and purple bell-heather that sparkled with butterflies and hummed with bees, where warblers sang and kestrels hovered, and nightjars nested in summer.

'Yes, I know it.'

'Well, that's where I live, only now a group of developers want to cover the heathland with houses—'

'And you want me to look into the future and see whether Skimpey Homes get their way?'

'That wasn't exactly what I was after, but…hey, it's a start.'

I was beginning to understand what prompted my great-grandmother all those years ago. Not so much snake in the grass as a pain in it.

'Fine. You want the future, I'll give you the future.'

I pulled the crystal ball out of the drawer, gave it a rub with my hankie (last time I forecast snow when in reality it was nothing more than a layer of dust on the glass and I won't make that mistake again in a hurry. Until you've had snowmen prodding you in the breadbasket with an angry carrot, you haven't lived.)

'Here we go.' I peered into the ball and waited. 'I see…oh, I see a young woman.'

'Yeah?' His scales perked up at that. 'What's she like?'

'Blonde. Very pretty—'

'Prettier than you?'

'Oh, she's gorgeous.' I shook my head in wonder. 'I have to hand it to you, you tempter of Eve, this is one girl who won't *stop* until she's found out everything there is to know about you.'

'Everything?'

'Everything!'

'Wow.' He covered the desk in one slither. 'Don't suppose that crystal tells you when I'm going to meet up with this lovely lady?'

'What about the crisis at Crowberry Heath?'

'First things first.' He ran his forked tongue round his lips. 'Can you, er…can you look in there and see if she's kissing me? It's what pretty girls do to frogs, and you know reptiles and amphibians aren't that far apart on the evolutionary scale.'

'Sorry, chum, this crystal is rated strictly PG, but if it helps, the answer is soon. You will meet the girl who wants to know you inside and out very soon.' I gave the ball another rub. 'Within minutes, in fact.'

He preened himself in the glass. 'Is it too much to ask where?'

'Hmm, let me see. Ah yes.' I lifted my head and looked him square in the eyes. 'The school biology lab.'

Trust me, you've never seen a snake move that fast. With a grin, I picked up the Werewolfing papers and worked right through until the midnight oil finally ran out.

* * *

St. Sylvester's is precisely the sort of building that Charles Dickens loved to spend seventeen pages describing. I could have saved him a whole lot of ink, because you can sum up the school in one word. Ugly.

Actually, that's not true. St. Sylvester's really needs two words to do it justice. Very ugly.

Of course by now you're thinking Gothic. Cracked stonework, grimacing gargoyles, a world of windowless turrets and creaking staircases, where the wind howls down long, lonely corridors and phantoms moan in the night. You'd be wrong. St. Sylvester's is a monstrosity of sixties design, all square blocks and concrete, built in a style that would give even the most hardened Eastern Bloc architect the shivers. Trust me, no self-respecting ghost would set plasma inside these walls. Until political correctness invaded our society, it used to be an upmarket ghouls' school. Nowadays, though, they let in every Tom, Dick and Harry Potter. No wonder educational standards are falling.

'Pay attention, class.'

I folded my wings and rapped on the blackboard.

'If you're going to take up a career in politics, you will need top grades in shapeshifting, so repeat after me. *Abracadabra, abracazoo, I want to turn, into a bat just like you.* No, no, no. Isabelle, dear, that's bat with a *b*, not cat with a *c*. Now drink your cream and try again. That's better. Right, class. Who knows how we turn ourselves back again?'

I can't quite remember who answered, that squeaky little pipistrelle or one of the mouse-eared variety, because at that moment, out of the corner of my eye, I noticed something long and green slinking out from behind the waste paper basket. I muttered the incantation for human reversal very quietly under my breath, so the class couldn't cheat. They'll get enough practice with that as politicians.

'That was a mean trick you pulled yesterday.'

'Hiss off. Can't you see I'm taking a class?'

'You should be ashamed of yourself.'

'Take your sticky scales off me.'

'I don't know how you can sleep at night, I really don't.'

'Very well, I apologise from the bottom of my heart. I. Am. Sorry. Now will you kindly twist off? There are twenty impressionable young students flitting around under this ceiling, all of whom seem to have forgotten the incantation for reverting to human shape. One wrong phrase, my serpentine friend, and these kids are vampires, and how on earth does one explain to their parents that sorry, your Kylie's turned into a bloodsucking monster.'

'So they become lawyers instead of politicians.' He shrugged his lithe little shoulders. 'Who cares? At least you'll be able to turn them back again, which is more than I'll get. This spell's irreversible. Well.' He rolled his eyes. 'Apart from one week where I'm able to adopt human form again, on account of your great-grandma missing a word out of the curse.'

'Be grateful. On my father's side they're dsylexic.'

I've lost track of the numbers of messes I've had to clear up there. Cows going "oom". Grammy's neighbour who was turned into toast instead of a stoat. Not to mention Grammy herself yelling "Are you a man or a moose?" at poor Gramps. (Oh, and don't even *ask* about whether that woman believed in Dog or the Devil.).

The viper wound his way up the desk leg and tilted his head on one side. 'You're the only one left who has the power to turn me back into a man,' he said. 'It's all I'm asking. My one chance to save Crowberry Heath from total destruction and my fellow adders from ending up as footwear—'

'Excuse me?'

'That was the other thing,' he said miserably. 'Skimpey Homes intend to round us up and open a snake farm on the side, to breed a steady supply of handbags and boots.'

'Very well.' We witches don't really like undoing someone else's spell, but as he said, this one was irreversible. Might as well grant the poor chap his wish. 'Seeing as it's Crowberry Heath.'

'Whoopee!' If he had them, he'd be kicking his little green heels in the air. 'When can we start? Now?'

'Now? Um, well, I—er, don't see why not.'

No time like the present, I supposed, to reverse the past and rewrite the future. I scooped him up and ran my hands lightly over the length of his body.

'Ooh, that's nice.' He rippled with pleasure under my fingertips. 'Better than nice, actually. Part of the reversal process, is it? Analysis of the subject?'

'Absolutely,' I assured him.

Not strictly true, but since one never knows how things might turn out in the future, it didn't hurt to check this guy out. I could really use a smart pair of shoes.

* * *

Everyone knows Skimpey Homes, of course, if only for that TV advert four or five years ago. You remember? The one in which Prince Charming kisses the Sleeping Beauty awake with those immortal words *'Your dream is our reality,'* and hey presto! she's no longer inside some draughty, thorn-encrusted castle, but a luxuriously decorated modern home, *come and visit our showhouse today.*

Naturally, the media had a field day, especially since Prince Charming was played by Skimpey's rather portly Chairman, who'd clearly taken drama lessons from the Forestry School of Acting he was that damned wooden. But mostly the press attached themselves to it, because the advert could have been invented for cartoonists and impressionists to poke fun at. *Your realty is our dream* was my personal favourite, but its sheer naffness lent itself to all manner of take-offs, which is exactly what Skimpey Homes wanted. With one ghastly advert, they became a household name, synonymous with—irony of ironies— quality, would you believe? Now they could dub themselves "Britain's No. 1 Builder" without fear of contradiction and, portly or otherwise, the Chairman was *this close* to a knighthood in the next New Year's Honours List.

As you'd expect, then, their headquarters was as prestigious as any of their exclusive developments. Smack bang on the River Thames, its glitzy design of marble and glass knocked the MI5 building into a cocked hat and, standing next door, it made sure it also dwarfed it. The message was clear. Skimpey Homes made Big Business look small.

'I really appreciate your help on thisss, Sssusssanah.'

Hmm. I suppose I ought to tell you about that, but it was the dust, you see. All my great-grandmother's stuff was in boxes right at the bottom of the cupboard in the back of the classroom. Recipes, spell books, broomstick (just kidding), they were all there, and it took a fair bit of searching through, even allowing for Sebastian—that's his name, by the way—slithering in through the smallest of gaps to search for the right tome that would change him back to human form. OK, OK, it didn't take that long, since she wasn't much of a hoarder my great-grandmother. But she's been a Guardian Angel for over fifty years now, and fifty years does leave a fair old layer of dust.

So it was inevitable, I suppose, that I would sneeze at some point during the recitation but, as I pointed out to Sebastian, you can't have everything and it could have been a lot worse. Far better he was left with a hissss than a forked tongue, I suggested, though he was far from convinced by the argument and, to be honest, I'm not entirely sure he believes it was an accident, even now.

'It's just a little lisp,' I pointed out. 'Hardly noticeable unless you—'

'Unlesss I what? Ssstop usssing pluralsss or wordsss with an *sss* sssound?' I didn't like the way his eyes narrowed when he leaned down to glare at me, which was a pity, because they were a really attractive shade of green. 'Like Sssebassstian, for inssstanccce?'

'No, more like dusky jade or wood sorrel, or even the colour of new ferns in the spring.'

'*Huh?*'

'With teensy weensy little red flecks in them, if you peer closely.'

'Did you by any chance take a pinch from that box marked "Do Not Take a Pinch From Thisss Box"?'

'What? Oh, sorry, I'd kind of lost track.'

Easy to do when you're strolling along the River Thames with a man whose hair has the colour and sheen of ripe horse chestnuts and whose smile is as wide as the ocean.

'We were talking about the hisss you've left me with. Sssomething, I might add, that I didn't have before.'

'And won't have once you're a snake again,' I assured him, giving his arm a comforting squeeze and finding it pleasantly muscular. 'After all, it's only for a week—'

How could I have been so tactless? Sebastian was overjoyed to be back as a man, and funnily enough so was I. OK, you wouldn't put him up there with George Clooney or Brad Pitt, but he was far from ugly; years of sliding round drystone walls had left him lean and supple, and the basking had given him an good all-over tan—and I do mean all over. Talk about embarrassing! I blame the fact that he was in such a hurry, and what with rummaging round the cupboard to find my great-grandmother's Book of Irreversible Spells (right under The Foresight Saga as it happens, and underneath a file marked Trivial Pursuits), we just hadn't stopped to think about clothes. Like I said, one can't have everything, so I stopped blushing and turned my thoughts to the issue in hand. Saving Crowberry Heath.

'It'sss ssstill good of you to help me, Sssusssannah.'

'Not at all.'

After all, it wasn't as though I had anything better to do. Oh, didn't I say? Yes, that was another thing. I'd been sacked, and there's an odd thing. In all my ten years of teaching at St. Sylvester's, I've never once seen the headmaster cross.

'Nothing that's wrong can't be put right with a kind word, a nod or a smile, that's my motto, Miss Hardcastle.'

And for ten years, yes indeed, the headmaster nodded, smiled and kindly worded his way through every awkward situation you could imagine. For instance, when those boys from Form B were caught smoking heroines (*Lorna Doone*, *Camille*, dear me no book was sacred), did the headmaster get out his cane? He did not. He merely teased the little ankle-biters about the error of their ways, got them to replace the smoke alarm and sentenced them to two *Moby Dick*s for detention. So for a man who was Father Christmas incarnate, you think he might have saved just a little ho-ho-ho for me, wouldn't you?

'You're not seriously giving me the bullet, headmaster?'

'Discharged, dismissed, fired, and sacked. Given the boot, the elbow, your cards and your marching orders, and if you so much as set foot within the grounds of my school, I will personally evict you myself.'

'You mean eject, expel, remove and turf out—?'

Not so much as a twinkle.

'Miss Hardcastle.' He rose out of his chair, placed his hands on the desk and leaned forward. 'Miss Hardcastle, this is no laughing matter.

You walk out leaving Class C flitting about the ceiling—'

Ouch.

'I apologised for that.'

'*APOLOGISE?* Good god, woman, have you any idea of the psychological damage you've inflicted on those children? Fatima will only eat fruit upside down now. Raymond, dammit, still refuses to come down from the ceiling, and little Edna can't sleep at night unless the blanket's tucked in tight, like it's her own wings folded round her. Miss Hardcastle, in all its illustrious history, St. Sylvester's has never even seen a single lawsuit—until now!'

'Suppose I turn Form D into sharks, so we can breed our own lawyers to fight back?'

But I already knew that comedy wasn't going to help me this time around. The headmaster turned red five minutes earlier. Now his colour deepened to purple.

'One more shapeshifting joke, Miss Hardcastle, and I am *this* far from violence.' He drew a deep, shuddering breath and sat down. Rather foolishly, I took that as a good sign. 'The bat problem we can get round. My brother-in-law happens to be a very good child psychiatrist and I am hoping the settlements from those claims can be negotiated into something approaching reasonable figures. However.' I really didn't like the way that muscle started to twitch in his cheek. 'Nudity in a school is another matter entirely, and for you to be flaunting your lover—'

'Begging your pardon, headmaster, that's far too strong a description for someone I'd only met the night before.'

'Smut!' the headmaster exploded.

At least I sincerely hope it was an *m* and not an *l* that I'd heard.

'I will not tolerate smut in my school, Miss Hardcastle, and I will certainly not tolerate grown men running round naked. You can consider yourself lucky that you've escaped with dismissal, now that eight-hundred and fifty litigious parents have decided to sue St. Sylvester's for encouraging paedophiles. OUT!'

'I don't suppose there's any chance of a reference—?'

Ooh, that gesture was no nod, that was no benevolent smile. And that word wasn't what I'd call kindly, either.

'No, ssseriousssly.' With no job and no prospects, I'd almost forgotten Sebastian standing beside me. 'It wasss good of you to take a week off from SSSt. Sssylvesss—ssschool—dammit, *college!* to help me organize my protessst rally.'

'My pleasure,' I said weakly.

Though you had to hand it to him. The instant he was back in human form (and fully clothed, I hasten to add) he was lobbying Downing Street, blitzing environmental pressure groups and enlisting the support of the Countryside Rescue Society in aid of the wildlife and beauty of Crowberry Heath before you could whistle Dixie. In three days, he'd produced posters depicting the orchids, the lily ponds, the butterflies, the birds, to show what would be lost forever, once Skimpey Homes covered the heath with their invidious concrete. His campaign was slick, it was impressive—and it wasn't enough. One week wasn't anywhere near enough to organize a blaze of marches, rallies, protests, sit-ins on the scale that would stop a multi-million pound corporation from bulldozing Utopia before the media got hold of the story. And one week was all my great-grandmother had allowed for Sebastian to revert to his original form. One measly week!

Please, he had said. *You've got to help me. You're the only person who can...*

'What we need is to put a bug inside the Boardroom of Skimpey Homes,' I told him, choosing a seat on the embankment facing their Headquarters.

'Great!' he exclaimed. 'Is it anyone we know?'

'Electronic bug, you doughnut.'

I opened my briefcase and showed him the wingdings and widgets that Henry in the Cloning Department had lent me. To be honest, I'm not quite sure why the Cloning Department needs to use such high-tech surveillance equipment, but even more worrying was that, when I asked Henry, he just tapped the side of his nose and said knowingly, 'Two heads are better than one.'

And to think I actually dated that guy! Anyway, the upshot was, Henry lent me this case full of stuff, and bless him, he even showed me how to use it, as well. Basically, all you have to do is this: place something that looks like a Victorian gentleman's collar stud in the room you want monitoring, direct some pointy black thing at it, then put on a pair of earphones and listen. (Excuse the science, but I'm only quoting Henry who in turn read it aloud from the NASA Handbook on Satellite Surveillance, page 337 if you must know.)

'How did you plant the bug?' Sebastian asked, melting me with those big, green fern-in-the-springtime eyes of his.

'Flowers.' I was proud of that. 'I sent a huge basket of roses to the Board of Skimpey Homes and signed it "A Satisfied Shareholder".'

I thought he would laugh at my silly ASS pun. Instead, his face crumpled. 'Is it true their shares rose ten percent as a result of this proposal?'

'Executive homes have a massive profit margin,' I told him, 'and because of their exquisite location, we're talking *footballers' houses* here!'

'Terrific. I get kicked off, ssso they can kick on.'

'Oh, stop sulking and pick up your earphones. The Board Meeting's about to start.'

Actually, although I liked his smile, I quite liked that mean, manly, moody look of his, too. I liked the brush of his skin against mine, as he leaned to pick up the headset, and I liked his faint citrussy scent.

Trust me, I thought, to fall for a guy who's only got four days left before he turns back into a snake.

Usually, it's much later that I find out the men I am dating are snakes.

* * *

AS HEARD THROUGH TWO PAIRS OF EARPHONES VIA SOME POINTY BLACK THING:

Clip clop of male feet inside Boardroom.

'I say, old chap, what wonderful roses! A—what does it say? oh, satisfied shareholder, eh? Ha, ha, wasn't you, was it, Chairman?'

'What? Waste money on flowers? Certainly not, Clive, but I'm betting that whoever sent them is going to be a lot more satisfied after we've announced the end-of-year profits, and so will we, dear boy, so will we. Crowberry Heath is going to make us very rich men, Clive.'

Short snort of laughter. 'We're rich now, Chairman.'

'Yes, and that's entirely due to Skimpey Homes' continued commitment to the redistribution of individual wealth.' *Pause.* 'And the suckers purchasing the Crowberry Heath homes will be very wealthy indeed!' *Rustle of papers.* 'Have you seen the designer's plans for the interior?'

'Have I! Wouldn't mind some of that marble in my own place.'

'Me, neither, but between you and me, dear boy, and before the others get here, there's a couple of things that are troubling me.' *Voice lowers to whisper.* 'One of which is mahogany.'

'Take it from me, old man, once the wife threatens to leave and take all your assets with her, you'll adapt fast enough.'

'Not monogamy, you clot. I'm talking about endangered hardwoods.'

'You against stripping the rain forests bare, then?'

'Don't be an ass, man. What I'm trying to tell you is that I can't decide between ebony and mahogany—ah, ladies, gentlemen.'

Murmur—babble—in fact, the classic rhubarb-rhubarb of St. Sylvester's drama department extras.

During the bout of back-slapping and handshaking, a pleasure boat carrying a coachload of camera-clicking Japanese waving wildly went past. Sebastian and I waved wildly back, while from the boardroom we listened to endless champagne corks popping, lots of chinking and glugging sounds, then finally, oh finally, a scraping of chairs.

'Very good.' *Chairman cleared throat.* 'Welcome to the hundred and forty-fifth meeting of the board of Skimpey Homes. I'll run through the

Minutes of the last meeting later, and I'm sure we can skip the Any Other Business stuff, because we all know the reason we're here.'

Murmurs of agreement, backed, I swear, by a licking of collective lips.

'There was a time, ladies and gentlemen, when I was a young man, that I truly believed that wealth and power would bring me happiness. Well, as Chairman and Chief Executive of this prestigious company, I'm delighted to say I was right—'

Roar of laughter.

'—and since Skimpey Homes is dedicated to social ideals, it's only fair that we continue to expand on that theme—and make ourselves even more powerful and wealthy!'

Hear, hear.

'At our last meeting, you were shown the video of the proposals for Crowberry Heath. Just to recap, this is to be a select development of high specification build projects in one of the loveliest corners of England.'

Irony seriously noticeable by its absence.

'We're talking luxury at the highest level for the highest possible returns, but since Skimpey Homes is also a modern, forward-thinking corporation, the Marketing Department, under the direction of the ever-reliable Rupert here, have identified opportunities to diversify and expand. The reptile population, for example—'

Click-click of slide show, followed by gasps of revulsion.

'Ugh!'

'Eugh.'

'Is that *slime*?'

'Yes, indeed, Letitia, and for that reason it is not in our interest to have our precious clientele repulsed by these creatures, unless...' *tantalising hint entered voice* '...unless, ladies and gentlemen—'

Click-click of slide show, followed by gasps of delight.

'Ooh.'

'Aah.'

'I *do* like those.'

'Boots, shoes, bags, purses. Ladies and gentlemen, snakeskin is making a serious comeback and Skimpey Footwear intends to be at the very forefront of this fashion movement, and let's not forget the moles, either. Marketing are confident several top designers can be drafted in to promote moleskin for next season, and you've all seen the plans for the factory?'

Affirmative rumbles.

'The idea is that we collect all the moles and adders on Crowberry Heath to use as breeding stock.'

(Beside me, Sebastian groaned and buried his head in his hands.)

'Not always easy, getting wild creatures to reproduce in captivity, Chairman. Think about the trouble zoos have had in the past with giant pandas and the like.'

'Good point, Clive, but we at Skimpey Footwear have a plan to ensure a plentiful supply of snakeskin.' *Chairman gives little snigger.* 'Using the timber we fell from Crowberry Heath, we split the trees into logs, chop the logs into tables and put them in the cages with the snakes.' *Snigger louder.* 'Everyone knows that for adders to multiply one needs log tables!'

'Haw-haw-haw.'

'Very witty, Chairman.'

'Did you think that joke up yourself?'

'As a matter of fact, Letitia, I did. Anyway, moving on to the lily ponds.'

Another click of slide show/gasps of delight.

'Ooh.'

'Ah.'

'Lovely.'

'Yes, indeed, ladies and gentlemen, but once again frogs and designer shoes are incompatible.' *Hum of agreement.* 'Whereas frogs and designer kitchens, on the other hand, are not!'

More clicks.

'Ooh!'

'Yum.'

'Scrummy!'

'Exactly! In addition to diversifying into footwear, designerwear and luggage, I am proud to announce that Skimpey Auberges will be opening an exclusive French restaurant close to the development, serving frogs' legs, snails in garlic—'

I never got to hear the rest of the menu. Beside me Sebastian had turned pale and was shaking.

'Cannibalsss,' he whispered. 'Those bassstardsss are going to eat my friendsss!'

I put my arm round him, intending to comfort him, and felt only his pain and fear.

To the Board Members of Skimpey Homes, the destruction of Crowberry Heath was just another money-spinning, get-rich-quick scheme which, with the callousness of property developers everywhere, was also one huge joke.

For Sebastian, the survival of Crowberry Heath in its natural state wasn't a matter of life and death any more, or even an issue of freedom and slavery. It was Man's capacity to ride roughshod over what it considered lesser creatures—and with it the obliteration of morals and decency. In his view, this fight was quite simply Good versus Evil.

Please, you've got to help me. You're the only person who can.

As the earphones emitted noises of chairs scraping, of goodbyes and thank-yous and see-you-again-soons, I stared across the cold, grey waters of the Thames and wished with every ounce of my body that I'd refused to undo my great-grandmother's spell.

Please.

He wouldn't have known. He wouldn't have known what fate awaited the inhabitants of Crowberry Heath, not until it was too late. Now he'd have this on his conscience, and although his human form had allowed him to do everything in his power to prevent it, he'd be living for the eternity my great-grandmother had consigned him to, tormented by the knowledge that he could see into the future and was unable to change it.

You're the only person who can.

As his shoulders slumped with hopelessness and despair, I reflected that Sebastian had put a heck of a lot of faith in a failed schoolteacher whose great-grandmother had turned him from a good-looking young man into a stone-basking reptile, and whose own reversal spell had left him with a lisp for the one week he was allowed to revert.

But that was the point. Faith moves mountains, not multi-million pound corporations.

Crowberry Heath and its beauty were doomed.

* * *

I couldn't sleep. Every time I dropped off, I'd dream I was stuffing frogs' legs into my mouth four at a time as I winkled snails out of their garlicky shells, then I'd wake up in a cold sweat with images of sweet-and-sour butterflies, crispy Peking warblers and coot à l'orange going round in my head as concrete mixers covered Paradise with cement.

I tossed, I turned, the dreams changed.

Now, I was walking along streets thronged with beautiful people dressed in snakeskin shoes and moleskin jackets, but as they passed, their clothes mouthed the word *traitor* and bats shrieked *I hate you, I hate you* into my ear, and *Raymond won't come down from the ceiling.*

I got up, I made coffee, I went back to bed.

This wasn't my fault. Crowberry Heath was lovely, but it was hardly the Garden of Eden. Sebastian wasn't Adam, I wasn't Eve, it was just the serpent in paradise bit that was making my head whirl, only everything was back to front with that scenario. This time the snake was the good guy, and he had eyes like spring ferns, smelled faintly of citrus and had a smile as wide as the ocean.

I blame too much caffeine at three in the morning for making me weepy. I'm not normally given to blubbing.

'You're the only one who can help me,' he'd said. 'After all, it was your great-grandmother who did this to me.'

'For a very good reason I'm sure.'

'Good? Good?' I remember how he'd writhed round the desk like a scaly green dervish. 'I'd worked in that woman's tavern from the age of sixteen, humping beer kegs, pulling pints, tossing out drunks from midday until midnight, seven days a week, fifty-two weeks of the year, until one day I have the temerity to ask for a rise. You call *that* a good reason to turn me into a snake?'

Just what kind of people was I descended from, I wondered miserably, that inspired them to turn honest, hardworking, loyal folk into snakes for such trivial matters? Wait a minute… I put down the coffee mug. What was the name of that weighty tome underneath the Book of Irreversible Spells? The Foresight Saga, right? And on top of the Book of Irreversible Spells? A file marked Trivial Pursuits! Suddenly, I remembered shoving it aside and the spring-clip flying open, with several pages rearranging themselves on the floor of the classroom. Without thinking, I'd scooped them up and stuffed them back in the file, but a few lines in my great-grandmother's writing had registered in the back of my brain.

The first rule of spellcasting—she'd always had a neat hand, my great-gran—is that one never enchants without the most powerful of reasons.

To turn a man into a snake for eternity for little more than saying boo to a goose is hardly a powerful reason, unless… I jumped out of bed and ran straight for the Hardcastle family tree (it's an oak) to see exactly when my great-grandmother became a Guardian Angel. Well, well, well. It was exactly two days after she'd turned Sebastian into a snake.

And underneath the Book of Irreversible Spells she'd left the Foresight Saga.

Coincidence? I don't think so.

I showered, I dressed, I bought some more roses. This time, though, I bought two large bouquets.

* * *

'Susannah.'

The change had already started. The lisp was gone, and he seemed taller, somehow, and slimmer.

'Susannah, you really don't have to be here.'

There were tears in his eyes. The last tears he would ever shed, I thought. And he was trembling as he hugged me goodbye. Inside I felt strange, while all around us, frogs croaked, warblers sang and butterflies explored the blossoms for nectar.

'I, er, have some good news,' I told him shakily. 'Crowberry Heath is safe. It can never be built on. Not ever.'

'Really?' I thought it would perk him up. Instead, he crushed me to his chest even tighter. 'Oh, Susi, my Susi, how I shall miss you!'

'You will?' Well, at least one of us was able to perk. 'Honestly?'

'The minute I saw you, tugging at your mini-skirt as you marked those exam papers, I fell in love with you, Susi. That silly curl that falls over your left eye. The way you toss your head when you're cross. I adore them, and although I'm grateful for what you've done—not to mention surprised, I might add!—it's my love for you that will keep me going for the whole of etern…'

I think he was going to say eternity, but there wasn't much time left for human kissing. I wanted to snatch what I could.

'Wow.' Sebastian seemed to be reeling. (Or maybe that was just me.) 'How did you *do* that?'

'Oh, it was so easy when you stop to think about it,' I said.

March into Chairman's office bypassing all secretarial dragons since I am clutching a bouquet of roses, being the Satisfied Customer of before, etc, etc, etc. Chairman charmed by young girl in short skirt (and maybe a touch of fairy dust, too). We talk. Or rather, I coerce aided and abetted by much crossing of legs, fluttering of eyelashes…and maybe just a touch more of Mum's fairy dusty. Its effects are very short-lived.

Finally, though, I lay it on the line for the Chairman. I want Crowberry Heath saved for posterity, and I want it in writing, while you want to be richer than Croesus and get a knighthood into the bargain.

He nods. I nod. We knuckle down to business. Drop the Crowberry Heath development, I tell him, and I'll show you where you can find oil. Now obviously I have to show him my credentials at this juncture, which is rather unfortunate for the hapless Clive who just happens to pop his head round the door at that time. But most people like parrots, and I really needed to prove my point.

'Go on,' the Chairman of Skimpey Homes said, feeding Clive a peanut on his perch, so I did. I turned his secretary into a ginger tomcat, Rupert of Marketing into a tortoiseshell and the teaboy into a tabby.

'I meant go on with the oil thing,' the Chairman said, 'but no matter. Always had a soft spot for cats. Never had 'em at home, see. They give the wife asthma.'

I wasn't interested in his wife's health and I doubted the Chairman had ever had a soft spot in his life. But having proved my abilities, and with him admitting to having taped every episode of *Dallas*, we moved on.

'Crowberry Heath is to be left untouched forever,' I said.

'Agreed.' With the New Year's Honours Lists being drawn up, he signed without even looking. 'And the oil?'

I handed him a map with detailed and accurate directions, left the roses on his desk to remind him what I'd come up smelling of, then left the second bouquet on my great-grandmother's memory stone.

'No, I meant how did you come to *kiss* me like that,' Sebastian said. 'It's…it's as though…'

'As though I love you, too?' Men! 'Well, of course I love you, you doughnut.'

Already his eyes had turned into slits, though, and scales now covered the whole of his skin.

'I shall always love you, Sebastian.' In fact, the thought of French kissing with those long white fangs made me tingle to the tips of my toes. 'Now where did you say you go for the winter?'

What was left of his hand pointed to a distant drystone wall.

'Ooh, goody, we can coil round each other for months on end, just me and you,' I giggled.

And you should have seen his face when my tongue forked.

'You're coming, too?'

'Try and stop me,' I hissed, writhing alongside him through the undergrowth.

Because that's the thing, see. We shapeshifters never die. When our human lifespan is over, we invariably turn into Guardian Angels, and since my great-grandmother had the Book of Foresight in her keep, she'd have known the end of her lifespan to the hour.

I'd worked in that woman's tavern from the age of sixteen, humping beer kegs, pulling pints, tossing out drunks from midday until midnight, seven days a week, fifty-two weeks of the year, until one day I have the temerity to ask for a rise. You call that a good reason to turn me into a snake?

One never enchants without the most powerful of reasons.

My great-grandmother had known Sebastian from when he was sixteen, and in those twelve years he'd never so much as taken a day off. Now if he'd been that devoted to the old woman, she must have adored him in return, so with just two days before the thread of her human lifespan was cut, she gave him the finest gift in her power.

Eternal youth.

All good things come to those who wait, Susannah.

In his case, it was fifty years slithering round Crowberry Heath's worth of waiting, but as I said, my great-grandmother had had the Book. She knew exactly what Sebastian was waiting for.

Me.

Did you really think I would miss a word out of a curse? Me? A *Hardcastle?*

Perhaps she'd foreseen my cackhanded efforts in the Book, too. Knew I'd let the side down eventually with my dreadful mistakes. (Poor Raymond, poor Fatima, oh poor little Edna.) And I suppose she'd known from the outset that I wasn't cut out for teaching, much less casting spells, but believe me, this was one irreversible spell I didn't mess up. Eternal youth, eternal happiness and eternal love are well worth the additional effort, though you have to hand it to great-gran. That woman certainly understood why the Garden of Eden is ablaze with serpents—not to mention the reason we hibernate through the winter! (And personally, I think temptation's a jolly good thing, don't you?)

What? The oil? Oh, didn't I say? Even as I was lodging the Chairman's agreement with solicitors that would finally secure my future home from the developers' greed, he was following my extremely detailed and accurate directions.

Right to the oil tank in the basement of St. Sylvester's.

About the Author

Marilyn Todd was born in Harrow, Middlesex, but now lives with her husband on a French hilltop, surrounded by woodlands and vines.

Award winning author of 19 historical thrillers, she is also a prolific writer of short stories, most of which are crime, but which range from commercial women's fiction to comic fantasy and all points in between.

For more information and news, go to www.marilyntodd.com